MW01097382

black box

black box

a novel by

LARRY JONES

WHITAKER
HOUSE

BLACK BOX

ISBN: 0-88368-872-7
Printed in the United States of America

Feed The Children
P. O. Box 36
Oklahoma City, OK 73101
800.627.4556
www.feedthechildren.org

Whitaker House
30 Hunt Valley Circle
New Kensington, PA 15068
www.whitakerhouse.com

Library of Congress Cataloging-in-Publication Data

Jones, Larry.
Black box / Larry Jones.
p. cm.
ISBN 0-88368-872-7 (Hardcover : alk. paper)
1. Survival after airplane accidents, shipwrecks, etc.—Fiction.
2. Wilderness survival—Fiction. 3. Asia, Central—Fiction. I. Title.
PS3560.O498B58 2004
813'.54—dc22
2004017749

1 2 3 4 5 6 7 8 9 10 **w** 10 09 08 07 06 05 04

1

The constant flow of passengers bustling through Hong Kong's International Airport kept the modern terminal looking like rush hour in any metropolitan subway. People bumped into each other, pushed to the side, and hurried on without a word of apology. Intermingled with the sophisticated travelers were locals, clothed in the traditional native dress, gushing over their visiting children and grandchildren. The travelers chattered in a thousand dialects, causing the corridors to sound like a meeting of the United Nations. Monitors flashed departure and arrival schedules to passengers as they paused to squint at the blinking screens. People of countless nationalities converged before flying away to a million different destinations.

Dorothy Chandler stood to the side, holding her stomach. The thirty-two-year-old flight attendant's normally lovely face looked ashen as she leaned against the wall for support. No one noticed as she bolted into the women's restroom. She hurried to the sink and hovered over the bowl, reaching a trembling hand up to pull her auburn hair off her face. After a few minutes, the nausea subsided and color returned to her cheeks. She dashed cold water on her face, rubbed her eyes, took a deep breath, and straightened up.

Dorothy patted her hair back into its usual smooth style and studied her reflection in the large mirror. Her mother had always said she had the type of face to make a man look twice, though she didn't think she was particularly beautiful. She did the best with what God had given her, although she did like her Irish green eyes and was proud of her porcelain white skin.

A petite woman in a business suit entered the restroom and glanced curiously at Dorothy. Flight attendants weren't supposed to get airsick. Dorothy adjusted her Global Airlines flight uniform, thinking it didn't do much for her figure. Almost immediately, she realized the pettiness of such a worry and laughed inwardly. At this point, she didn't know how she would make it through the long flight to New Delhi and then on to Frankfurt, Germany.

After reapplying her raspberry ice lipstick, Dorothy walked slowly out of the restroom into the maddening rush of people. Her flight didn't leave for hours, but she had to board soon to set up for passengers. She dreaded getting on the plane. Besides her queasiness, Dorothy didn't want to have to talk to the pilot.

Jack.

Each time he crossed her mind, Dorothy felt the same love-hate tug-of-war that always turned her emotions inside out.

■ ■ ■

As Global Airways Flight 027 climbed to its cruising altitude, Captain Jack Harris was cursing under his breath. A three-hour delay at the gate in Hong Kong had put them off schedule, and the one hundred forty-six passengers on the 757 had given the crew plenty of grief over it, as if complaining would get them there faster.

Flight 027 was a regular run, scheduled to leave Hong Kong around dinnertime, cross several time zones, and get passengers into Germany early in the morning, Frankfurt time. A number of ticket holders had canceled or rescheduled, and those who remained on board made it clear to attendants and flight crew alike that Global Airways had messed up their plans.

Captain Harris had plans of his own for the layover in New Delhi, and the delay meant there might not be enough time for what he had in mind, unless he could figure out a way to cut some flight time.

Jack had over twenty years experience flying for Global—enough to know it was dangerous to think of any flight as routine. Their route took them over rugged mountains, and the weather was always a concern this time of year. Additionally, they would be flying close enough to the Chinese border that politics were a factor. But he knew the route, had taken all the variables into account. He wasn't concerned. The big airplane settled into level flight, and onboard computers took over the controls. Jack crunched the numbers, trying to find an alternate route. The layover in New Delhi was important to him. Very important.

Jack had too much on his mind to worry about his crew. Matt Simpson was a good navigator and Jack didn't have to give him a thought. But copilot Dave Beckman was a problem—a drinker—and it showed if you looked close. Dave was carrying some extra weight, the slack, bloated kind that comes from hitting the bottle too often. His face was pudgy and flushed under a crewcut, a carryover from his military days.

Beckman had been missing for an hour during the delay in Hong Kong, and Jack suspected he had used the downtime to fortify himself with a few preflight cocktails. Beckman favored vodka because he thought others couldn't smell it on him. He used breath mints, eye drops, and cologne liberally to mask the telltale signs, but Jack wasn't fooled.

Beckman's fitness reports were coming up in a few weeks, and his annual physical soon after. Jack had confronted him about his drinking and had threatened to write him up numerous times if he didn't shape up. But Jack had held off because Beckman was a good copilot in spite of himself, and he had never failed Jack in the cockpit. Still, Jack wouldn't give him the kind of fitness report that would put him in line for captain's wings. He would rather keep Beckman on his crew where he could watch him, keep him out of trouble.

Jack glanced over at his copilot, who was studying the Hong Kong weather reports and the radar screen. Beckman was frowning.

"How's it look?" Jack asked.

"Not good. Check out that front."

"Rather rough."

The color-coded radar display showed a broken line of heavy weather cells running north and south, snowstorms blowing in from the north. More storms were building along the mountains ahead of them. Jack had seen worse, and ordinarily he would allow for it by adjusting altitude, climbing above the upper-air disturbances if he had to. But fighting the storm would make the flight longer—he could forget New Delhi altogether.

Jack didn't look at the copilot as he asked, "You clear today?"

"What do you mean?"

"Are you drunk or hungover?"

"I'm fine."

"Hungover, then."

"Come on." Jack turned and studied Beckman. His eyes were watery, his cheeks flushed and sweaty. Jack felt a tug of concern.

"I'm really fine."

"You'd better be clear," Jack said. "Because we're going to make adjustments."

"What?"

"A shortcut to make up time and skirt the bad weather. We're going to amend our flight plan."

"The weather's bad all over, Jack. I've got the reports right here, snowstorms spreading all over the mountains. Two fronts—one up ahead and another off to the north."

Their standard route would take them point-to-point through carefully negotiated international airlines across Vietnam, Laos, and Thailand, then south over the Andaman Sea before turning back north by northwest across much of India to Delhi. But Jack had a more direct northerly route in mind, over Myanmar—much closer to the Chinese border, but still well south of it, skirting Bhutan and Nepal and staying well out of the mountains.

"Is it doable?" Jack asked navigator Matt Simpson.

"Sure, but I wouldn't advise it," Matt answered with a shake of his head. The tension between Harris and Beckman was getting to him. He rubbed the tension in his neck as he double-checked the numbers.

The front due west of them was still collecting, and the one coming down from the north over the mountains wouldn't drift far enough south to give them any serious problems.

Simpson handed the new flight plan to the pilot.

"Here you go. I did the best with what we have, but I'm not responsible when the big bosses complain about the risk we're taking," Simpson said.

"There's nothing to worry about. We'll make good time, with no problems," Jack answered. He turned to Beckman.

"Punch in the new coordinates. We're going to cut straight across to India."

"Are you kidding? We already fly closer to the Chinese border than I'd like," Beckman protested.

"The weather looks better that way," Jack insisted. "And we won't bother the Chinese unless you screw up. You can file the amended flight plan en route. Tell them we're working around the weather, making up for the late start."

"It's kind of risky, Jack."

"Not if we do it right." Jack gave him a look, and Beckman caved under the pressure. He knew Jack could have his wings revoked with one phone call. That meant he would do whatever Jack said. After all, it was his career on the line.

"I hope she's worth it," Beckman muttered.

"Who?"

"Your hot date in Delhi."

"You're not making sense, Dave. Are you sure you're sober?"

"If you worry about my drinking, I get to worry about your love life."

"Stop stewing and do your job. Hear?" Jack gestured impatiently to the map and then the navigational computer in front of Beckman.

Beckman swiped a beefy hand across his forehead and tried to focus his eyes on the map. His head ached and his stomach was rolling, even in the relatively smooth air, which would soon give way to more palpable turbulence over the mountains. He wasn't totally sober, but knew he was within limits—his own personal limits anyway. He had done his job this way before.

Jack monitored the instrument panel and the radar, watching his copilot work over the map, making calculations and adjustments. Beckman fed the new latitude and longitude coordinates into the Inertial Navigation System and the computer did the rest. It had long since replaced human navigators and raised the odds against human error. The system never screwed up.

"Remember, GIGO," Jack said.

"Huh?"

"Garbage In, Garbage Out." Jack smiled tightly at his co-pilot. "Just make sure you get it right."

■ ■ ■

In the passenger cabin, flight attendants were hustling to serve a late meal to their hungry passengers. The passenger load was light this time out. The plane hadn't been full even before several passengers canceled or rerouted because of the delay. The flight still had its VIPs in first class, however. Senator H. George Meyer was probably the most well-known among them. A fit and impeccably groomed man in his late fifties, the senator enjoyed seniority and influential committee assignments. He enjoyed the kind of recognition that came with frequent guest appearances on Sunday morning network television programs. The Washington rumor mill touted him as a possible running mate in the next presidential election. He had worked hard to build his image as a champion of the workingman and family farmers, not only in his Midwestern home state but also at the national level in trade negotiations.

Meyer assumed he was recognized by the crew and his fellow passengers, while pretending to be engrossed in the official-looking papers he had spread across the tray table in front of him. Anyone who knew him would have known he was posing because he hadn't bothered to put on his reading glasses, a concession to his vanity. Senator Meyer was actually focused on the woman in the seat across the aisle from him, sneaking occasional sideways glances in her direction. He had noticed her when they boarded and was glad to see she was traveling alone.

Meyer had been married for almost thirty years. His wife was an effective politician's wife, running their homes in Georgetown and back in their home state of Iowa while skillfully filling the roles of hostess and campaigner as well. They had two daughters, one away at college, the other already practicing law in Iowa and thinking about going into politics herself.

Unfortunately, Senator Meyer was not thinking about his wife now. During his first years in the senate, George had kept himself out of trouble, but there had been no shortage of temptations in Washington. As the months turned into years, the constant lure and the loneliness had weakened his opinion of fidelity. Seductive women were always around—smiling, nodding, winking. Attractive women young enough to be his daughters were drawn to him by his reputation or his mature good looks. Eventually, Meyer slipped. A few one-night stands here and there eventually led to a mistress, young and attractive enough to appeal to his vanity but mature enough to appreciate the need for discretion.

Senator Meyer had always been discreet. His life was complicated enough as it was. He was a long way from home and glad to be leaving China after a tough couple of weeks, with more work awaiting him on the European leg of his trip. So far from his wife and mistress, he couldn't help thinking a little female companionship would be welcome.

What could be the harm?

The woman across the aisle was an American. Meyer had heard her talking to one of the flight attendants. He wondered what she was doing here, flying alone halfway around the world.

As he looked up from his papers, he caught her looking across at him. He smiled and she blushed, a charmingly vulnerable thing for her to do.

"Excuse me," she said. "I didn't mean to stare."

"That's quite all right."

"But aren't you...famous?"

"I wouldn't say that, *exactly*."

"I'm sure that I've seen you somewhere. On television, maybe?"

"You might have."

She was lean and tall, with brown hair to her shoulders and dark eyes that crinkled when she smiled, as she did now. Meyer guessed she was in her late thirties.

"We both seem to be traveling alone," she offered. "Would you think me forward if I invited myself to join you?"

"Not at all." He smiled, collecting his papers and reaching for his attaché case under his seat. "Please do."

He admired her legs as she stepped across the aisle and settled into the seat beside him, a drink in her hand. Her white silk blouse settled gently over a tailored taupe skirt hemmed well above the knees, and she wore shoes with low heels. *Sensitive about her height*, Meyer thought.

"I'm Helen Bridwell," she said, offering her hand.

"George Meyer."

"Meyer? Oh my goodness. Of course, Senator Meyer."

"It's always nice to bump into an American abroad."

"I can't believe I didn't recognize you right off the bat. You're practically a household name."

"You flatter me. Where are you from, Helen?"

"Kansas originally, but I've lived in Hong Kong for ages."

"Then it's a wonder you've even heard of me. I'm flattered."

"Oh, please. You've been on TV in Hong Kong as much as in the States lately, with the trade talks and everything. Stupid of me not to make the connection."

"I probably look different in person."

"Yes. Taller."

"I should hope so," he said, with a chuckle.

"I mean..." Helen looked down at the drink in her hands. "You're a very handsome man, Senator. I haven't been very smooth up to this point, so I guess I might as well just blurt that out, too."

"And you're a very attractive woman, Helen."

"Well, I'm glad we've got that out of the way," she laughed.

"A toast," Meyer offered. "To two very attractive Americans a long way from home."

"I'll drink to that." Helen raised her glass. Her eyes sparkled as she sipped her wine.

"Care for another glass?" a flight attendant asked the senator and the woman. She filled their glasses and added, "If you need anything, let me know. Just ask for Dorothy."

2

Wearing a blue smock over her uniform, Dorothy made her way from passenger to passenger in first class, delivering dinners, checking drinks, and more often than not, answering the question, "Exactly how far behind schedule are we?" Most of the passengers chatted pleasantly, though with the late start, some had fallen asleep.

The Right Reverend Anthony Coleridge Forbes looked up at Dorothy from his window seat directly in front of Senator Meyer with pursed lips and a furrowed brow, as if choosing a dinner entree merited his full attention. His portly girth and double chin gave him the look of a man given to solemn deliberation, especially where food was concerned. Wearing a purple clerical shirt and gold pectoral cross under a handsome suit hand-tailored in Hong Kong, Bishop Forbes looked like what he was, a man of high office in the Church of England. His graying hair raggedly curled a bit in the back, suggesting he was burdened with weightier concerns than grooming.

"Steak, lamb, or chicken?" Dorothy repeated, in case he hadn't heard her the first time.

"The lamb, I think," Forbes answered finally. "No wine with the entree, and a green salad. Light on the dressing."

"I'll have the steak, please," the man in the seat next to Forbes told the attendant. "Same as His Holiness here on the salad, but I'd like to try the wine. There's nothing like a nice red wine with steak."

Bishop Forbes turned to eye his fellow passenger, prepared to be offended, but the man smiled good-naturedly to imply he meant no harm, and Forbes had to smile back.

"Albert Reese," the man introduced himself. Reese was a lean and wiry man, with a dark tan and neatly trimmed brown hair. He looked out of place in his Armani suit, a hard little man dressed for success.

"Anthony Forbes," the bishop said. "Tony." They shook hands.

"It's bishop, isn't it?" the man asked, still smiling. "Or cardinal, or something?"

"Bishop. Anglican."

"Nice to meet you. You're English?"

With that brash attitude, he's obviously American, Forbes thought. *Maybe a salesman.*

"Yes. Your accent is Southern, isn't it?"

"South Carolina. Heart of Dixie."

"Bully." Forbes' mouth lifted in the slightest of smiles.

Reese chuckled. His companion obviously wasn't one to waste words. Reese turned to watch the attendant as she worked her way down the aisle. Reese studied her casually as she leaned over to speak to the two passengers in front of them.

"You're traveling on business?" Bishop Forbes asked, making conversation as he finished his salad.

"Yes, business," Reese snorted. "You wouldn't catch me in these boondocks on vacation. You?"

"Likewise."

"I guess business is going well for you," Reese offered, turning back from his inspection of the attendant. "No bear markets in sin, huh?"

"Regrettably, no. What market are you in, Mr. Reese?"

"Tobacco."

"Speaking of sin," the bishop said, raising one eyebrow.

"Aw now, Your Grace. People want to light up. Somebody's gotta roll the smokes."

"And what brings you to the Far East, then? Looking into cheap labor?"

Reese cut the bishop a sharp look. "Nah, not me. I'm in smokes, not sneakers."

"Hmm," was all the comment Bishop Forbes mustered, finding himself losing interest in his fellow passenger and thinking he should have brought something to read on the flight. He turned his attention back to his dinner.

"As a matter of fact," Reese went on, leaning toward Forbes and lowering his voice as though he were going to share a secret, "I've been over here checking up on some of our orphanages."

"Orphanages?" Forbes asked, suddenly more interested. "What a coincidence."

"Yeah. What the media won't tell you is that we're the most charitable business going. Millions in philanthropies."

"Tobacco?"

"Absolutely. We subsidize orphanages all over the place. Hospitals, too. Relief operations. You name it."

"That is a coincidence, I must say," Forbes said, shifting in his seat. "I happen to be returning from an inspection tour myself. I've been out to our missions, many of whom operate orphanages."

"Really?"

"Yes. Where are yours? What are their names?"

"Well..." Reese blinked a couple of times and reached up with one hand to smooth his collar as he cleared his throat. "The thing is, Your Holiness, we never divulge any details like that about our charities. Story might leak, make it look like a public relations scam or something."

"I see."

"It's like you guys say, do good deeds in secret. Right?"

"Absolutely," Bishop Forbes smiled benignly. "The Good Book says, Do not let your left hand know what your right hand is doing." The bishop poked Reese with his elbow. "But I bet at the appropriate time you'll let the left hand know." Forbes winked. "How very Christian of you."

■ ■ ■

Behind Reese and the bishop, Helen Bridwell and Senator Meyer chatted over their dinners. She had succumbed to his insistence that he wanted to hear all about her life and was in the process of describing the Hong Kong social scene and explaining why she was flying to India. She was flattered that he wanted to know more about her, and he seemed genuinely interested. She found herself going into much more detail than she had intended. But even with his desire to hear absolutely everything about her, Helen didn't feel it was necessary to mention her husband.

Behind them, the aisle seat was empty and Mary Lee McMurray slouched in the window seat, pretending to read the latest Grisham paperback while listening to music in her earphones. She was a diminutive black woman with hair pulled back in a ponytail. Dressed in a baggy sweater and jeans, people often mistook her for a kid at first glance. But she was no youth, and she wasn't reading or listening to music.

Pen in hand, Mary Lee was making occasional notes in the margins of her paperback, and her earphones were playing the conversation of the two passengers in the seats in front of her. Every word they said was being picked up by a small and sophisticated pin microphone Mary Lee had managed to embed in the senator's seat back, strategically positioned to pick up anything said in either of the two seats and to transmit it to the recorder clipped to Mary Lee's belt as she listened over her earphones. The receiving equipment was designed to look like a personal tape player.

■ ■ ■

Dorothy and her fellow flight attendants were relieved to wrap up meal service in first class. Soon they would be able to turn out the lights, and most of the passengers would sleep for the rest of the flight. Dorothy moved back to coach to help the other attendants with their passengers. She started with a young mother who was traveling with two young children. Dorothy had spent some time with them before takeoff, and she had given them souvenir wings, peanuts, and a quick tour of the cockpit.

"Thanks for helping with the kids," the young woman said. "It's not easy to keep them entertained."

As soon as Dorothy put their meal trays in front of them, the two youngsters pounced on the food, both of them going straight to the dessert.

Dorothy lingered for a moment, watching the children. Their mother looked frazzled, but not cross. She was used to her kids' behavior and chided them gently to eat their dinners first, then the desserts. They settled down for a moment and then the boy, who was probably five, threw his roll at his younger sister. Dorothy sighed.

Kids are little monsters, she told herself, rolling her cart to the next passenger.

The last dinner to be served was a vegetarian meal for a Chinese woman in a long blue dress with the traditional high-collared jacket. Dorothy smiled as she set the tray on the table in front of the woman, who thanked her with a nod, like a half-bow.

It hadn't been easy, handing out trays when the last thing she wanted to think of was food. Dorothy was relieved that she had managed to finish without being sick. Then the smell of stewed carrots wafted up from the Chinese woman's meal. The odor assaulted Dorothy's nostrils, immediately making her stomach churn. She excused herself and dashed to the nearest restroom.

She gagged over the toilet, but there was nothing left in her stomach to throw up. She stood up and ran water from the tap over a paper towel. She worked the damp towel over her temples and her throat.

"You look terrible," she told her reflection, although she looked perfectly normal except for the anxious expression on her face.

She forced herself to smile.

There.

Now that she had recovered, her secret was safe. It would stay hidden until New Delhi when she could take care of one little problem. She tossed the towel, squared her apron, then stepped out of the restroom and pushed her serving cart into the aft galley.

The crew intercom pinged and she answered.

"Yes?"

"How are you doing back there?" Captain Harris asked.

"We're just finishing up meal service."

"Good. It looks like we'll be picking up some turbulence in a few minutes. You'd better make sure everybody's buckled in."

"Great," Dorothy moaned. "That's all I need."

"We're working our way around the worst of it," he assured her.

"Good idea."

"We're making up some time. We should be nearly back on schedule getting into New Delhi," Jack offered.

"Okay."

"I wanted us to have as much time as you need. I...just wanted to let you know."

"Jack..." Dorothy heard something and looked over her shoulder. One of the other attendants was pushing her service cart into the galley from the other side. The tone of Dorothy's voice changed subtly as she said, "Just keep the turbulence to a minimum, Captain. That's the sentiment back here."

"I'll see what I can do," Harris signed off.

She could hear the smile in his voice. He certainly knew how to push her buttons. She would do what she had to do.

3

The Wan Chow radar station was a backwater dump by anybody's standards, even the People's Army of China. It was a huddle of shacks with leaky mud walls and salvaged sheet-iron roofs on a windswept hill overlooking the Wan Chow airbase. The base was little better, a weather-beaten collection of hangars that housed an understrength flight of MiG-15s from the Korean War.

Except for the radar array on a mast above the shacks and a landline that connected the station intermittently with the tower down at the airbase, the hilltop radar station might have been a farmer's hovel anywhere in the Chinese interior.

Radar operator Yong Ling had escaped from such a hovel by volunteering for military service at the age of seventeen. Now, at twenty-five, he considered himself better off than his kinfolk and neighbors, though not by much. His family had a farm in an isolated district on the Mongolian border where he had grown up. He was not as far removed from those days as he had hoped.

Life at the radar station was little better than his childhood, sleeping on a pallet and cooking his own meals of rice and cabbage in the same small room, with nowhere to go when he was relieved from duty every couple of weeks except down the hill to the airstrip where the only improvement was bunk beds and army chow. His only company on the lonely post was his superior officer, Lieutenant Zhou Du, who seemed to spend all of his days at the tiny desk on the other side of the partition, in what he called his *office*.

A good soldier keeps his mouth shut and follows orders. Yong knew that as well as anybody. Still, there were too many soldiers in China, and so little action these days. How was a young man supposed to advance himself? With a posting down by the Taiwanese Straits—or on the border with India, even—he might have a chance to make something of himself. Unfortunately Wan Chow was near Tibet, where nothing ever happened. They'd be lucky to get a rogue mountain goat.

As he sat hunched over his radar screen, Yong watched the mesmerizing sweep of the arm as it rounded the screen. He registered the blip on the screen the first time the arm swept past it but didn't react. Hundreds—thousands—of hours he had sat staring at the screen and seen nothing. On the rare occasion when there was what the lieutenant called "an anomaly," it always turned out to be weather or an unannounced friendly on approach to the field down the hill. Sometimes the blips were a malfunction in the ancient radar equipment itself, a lashed together Soviet job at least as old as Yong himself.

At the second pass of the arm, Yong stirred himself. The blip was still there. An actual aircraft, where it had no business being. He had heard of airliners straggling down from the north in bad weather, but this was coming up from the south.

Erect in his chair now, sitting at attention with his mouth open, Yong watched the blip work its way up the screen on a steady course that would take it deep into the Wan Chow control zone.

"No," he muttered. "Worse than *that*." The object was on course to fly directly over Wan Chow airbase itself.

The lieutenant was at his desk on the other side of the partition, no more than twenty feet away, but Yong knew the man insisted on the silly business with the phone. "We will not shout back and forth," the lieutenant had scolded him countless times. "It's not military."

Yong picked up the phone and pushed the button on the left. The one on the right connected with the airbase down the hill. The one in the middle was for the command center at district headquarters.

"Yes?"

"Lieutenant, I have an intruder."

"What?"

"An intruder. On the radar. Approaching from the south."

"Are you sure?"

"Absolutely, Lieutenant."

Yong wanted to tell him to get off his rear and come see for himself, but he knew better than that.

Yong heard his lieutenant hang up the phone on the other side of the partition and looked up as he stomped into the room. Yong said nothing. He just pointed to the blip on the screen. The two men watched as the arm made another circle. Then Lieutenant Zhou picked up the phone beside the radar display and punched the button in the middle.

Yong had never seen anyone at the radar station call district headquarters. When a call came in on the line in the middle, everyone at the little radar station stood at attention to answer it.

"Command Center," Yong could hear the voice answer, sounding distant and tinny.

"I must speak to Colonel Qong at once," Lieutenant Zhou snapped, trying to sound urgent and in control.

"He is not here," the operator informed him.

"Where is he?"

"You are a bold one to ask, Lieutenant."

"I ask only because we have an emergency situation," Lieutenant Zhou hastened to explain. "Immediate guidance from the colonel is required."

"Your request will be relayed."

The line went dead.

Lieutenant Zhou cursed under his breath. "He's with a woman again," he mumbled to himself. "We've had this problem before." Zhou turned to look at the radar screen again, ignoring Yong.

"We have no means of identifying the craft by radar," the lieutenant mumbled, thinking aloud.

"No, sir," Yong said, thinking his lieutenant expected an answer.

You know that as well as I do, Yong thought. There were newer radars, of course, equipped to decode and display IFF signals—identify Friend or Foe squawks—which distinguished between ally and enemy aircraft, but not this old Soviet model. They were lucky it still worked at all.

Lieutenant Zhou picked up the phone again. This time he punched the button on the right for the airbase down the hill. He asked for the flight leader and explained the situation quickly.

"No," the flight commander confirmed. "There were no friendly aircraft in that area that we know of."

"Can you reach the intruder by radio?" Lieutenant Zhou asked. The flight commander wasn't sure. "Give it a try and keep me advised."

While they waited, the lieutenant and his radar operator watched the ominous blip on the screen work its way north, heading straight toward them.

"We must identify the craft as soon as possible," the lieutenant mumbled. "Nobody would accidentally come so far inside our border. But for what purpose?" Lieutenant Zhou shook his head, baffled.

"Surely they are not American warmongers. A spy plane?" Yong suggested.

"Or provocateurs."

"Not an attack though," Yong looked up at his lieutenant. "Who knows, with a single plane. Maybe they thought it could slip through our defenses undetected."

Yong mulled that idea over. He wanted to see some action, but he thought about how isolated and exposed the little radar station was on its hilltop.

"How is your English?" Lieutenant Zhou asked.

"Fluent," Yong lied.

"Good. If we can make radio contact, you will interrogate the pilot."

"Yes, sir."

Yong was thrilled at the possibility. Finally, a chance to make a name for himself. He could see a medal in it, maybe a new posting at a better place, with modern equipment and the opportunity to work his way up.

The phone rang, the button on the right flashing—the flight leader at the airbase.

"We are unable to contact the intruder," the flight leader reported. "You must authorize me to launch my fighters."

"I have tried to reach the colonel at district headquarters, but..." Lieutenant Zhou attempted to explained, but the officer at the airbase cut him off.

"There's no time. As senior officer, you must give the order."

Lieutenant Zhou knew the flight leader was right. Without orders from headquarters, the senior officer on the scene was responsible. Zhou had the bad luck to be senior to the lieutenant in charge of the fighters at the base. Besides, air defense doctrine called for Radar Command to direct air operations in such a situation. Of course, the doctrine anticipated that decisions would be made by district headquarters at the very least, if not division headquarters—or even higher up the chain of command—not some lowly lieutenant on a hilltop out in the wastelands. But rules were rules. There was no getting around it.

"Very well," Lieutenant Zhou said, an ominous weight settling in his stomach. "Launch interceptors. Identify intruder aircraft and stand by for further instructions."

"Yes, sir!" the flight leader barked and clicked off.

He sounds enthusiastic, Lieutenant Zhou thought. *He can afford to be. Flyers live for this kind of nonsense. It's my neck on the chopping block, after all.*

As the two men in the radar shack heard the roar of jet engines at the airbase down below, Lieutenant Zhou called the command center at district headquarters again. He looked out the one small window on the side of the radar shack facing the airbase and watched three MiGs scream past, their noses almost vertical as they took off in search of the intruder.

"What a sight, huh, Lieutenant?" Yong asked, a proud smile on his face as he stepped away from his radar screen and craned his neck to look out the little window at the jets disappearing into the clouds.

"Impressive," Lieutenant Zhou offered for Yong's benefit. He knew there should have been four fighters assembled, but it was no surprise that only three were airworthy. *What do they expect of us,* he thought, *with such ancient machines?*

Zhou was no pilot, but he knew their maintenance crews had to cannibalize some of their planes to keep the others flying. Spare parts were unheard of, much less replacements. He sighed as he listened to the voice on the other end of the line explain that the colonel was still not available.

Once again, the voice assured him that his message would be relayed.

■ ■ ■

A battered old fishing trawler bobbed up and down in the swells of the China Sea. The aged paint peeling off her rusty hull gave her the look of a tub well past her prime, a scrap yard candidate—if the next storm didn't scuttle her outright.

Below decks, she was something else altogether.

In the data reception room, the vessel looked like what she was, a floating surveillance and intelligence center, code-named the Shark and jointly operated by the U.S. Navy and the CIA. She was on post, electronically monitoring Division Four in the Chinese interior.

Banks of radio transmission intercept receivers, computers, and electronic surveillance machines were packed with space-saving precision along every bulkhead and in clusters on the deck, leaving barely enough room for the sailors who monitored and maintained all the technical hardware.

At one console, a sailor fluent in Mandarin Chinese listened in on radio traffic between Wan Chow airbase and what sounded like a pilot or squadron leader reporting in. Directly behind him, another radio operator was searching the commercial air traffic band.

An officer stood behind Petty Officer Gates, the non-com operating the centerpiece of the high-tech snooping operation, an over-the-horizon radar system that was feeding them images from the Chinese interior.

"That's just freakin' weird," Lieutenant Alvin Stiles announced to the room. He pointed at a blip on the screen. "That bird right there squawks Global 027. A 757 out of Hong Kong to Delhi. But they've swung back over the border into China in a big loop. How can they be that lost?"

"Beats me, sir," Gates said, shaking his head. "But they're on course for Wan Chow airbase. We have to warn them, don't we, sir?"

"Oh, no," Lieutenant Stiles groaned. "Look at this. Division Four fighters coming up from Wan Chow. What's the radio traffic?"

"Base to the MiGs," the sailor working the radio intercept console called back. "Vectoring them to intercept the intruder."

"Intruder? That's bandit to you and me!" Lieutenant Stiles muttered.

"We have to do something, Lieutenant," Gates insisted. "They're gonna pop a planeload of civilians."

"I know, Gates." Lieutenant Stiles answered. "Heaven knows that I know."

"They're way off the flight plan they filed in Hong Kong," a sailor reported from across the room. "Maybe they're trying to fly around the storm front over the mountains."

"They should've taken their chances with the weather," Lieutenant Stiles said dryly. "Maybe they've been hijacked. That's the only thing makes sense to me."

"Can't we just call them, let them know what's coming?" Gates asked, watching the blips close on his radar screen.

"Negative, and you know better. It'd blow our cover. The Chinese would be on us in a heartbeat if we transmitted direct."

"Sir?" the operator asked.

"Stand by to go code to the Front Office, priority relay." Lieutenant Stiles put his hand on Gates' shoulder. "We'll get somebody to go through the Global Positioning Satellite system. They can give him a wake-up call."

"Hope it's in time," Gates said.

"Me, too."

"You know how many people they can put on a 757, sir?"

"I know, Gates. It's practically half the state of Vermont."

4

Bishop Forbes sipped his cup of hot tea and glanced at the second glass of wine that the man sitting next to him was drinking. Decades had passed since Forbes had touched a drop of alcohol but a longing for just a small glass lingered. Every time he looked at the glass, the clergyman could see himself, his eyes, his face, reflected in the crimson nectar. The sight stirred his memory.

Tony Forbes knew he wouldn't succumb to the temptation. He wasn't about to jeopardize his entire life. He knew that he would always be a recovering alcoholic...even though the incident had occurred when he was barely old enough to be called a man.

The incident? Forbes sighed and settled back in his seat. *Why do I always call that tragedy an "incident"? What a terrible, terrible moment in my life...and for that poor young man.*

Images flew through his mind. Tony could once again see himself driving down the narrow English lane out of Woking, ambling the old family car down the dark country road that led toward Salisbury. He hadn't felt drunk, just a bit tipsy. Suddenly a young man on a bicycle came out of nowhere. One moment the road was empty, the next a figure was in front of him.

Where did he come from? Tony wondered. *I still have no idea. The boy appeared as if out of a dream.*

Even after all these years, Tony could still hear the crunching sound as the car's fender clipped the boy, sending him flying off into the grass. The bicycle hurled through the air and crashed into the ditch with an awful, empty thud.

In that moment Forbes made the decision that forever changed his life. He hit the accelerator and didn't stop. Panic wrapped around his throat like a noose and he sped away into the night. He knew the alcohol in his system was far too strong. He made a fatal decision that plunged him into a year of legal problems and jail time, ruining everything he'd planned.

When the authorities found the boy, he was dead. The guilt had flung Tony into a new world of religious fervor. After time in jail, he entered an alcohol rehabilitation program, and a local church took him in. The days went by slowly, but out of the furnace of his affliction, a new person slowly emerged. The young man who loved hitting the bottle turned into a devout believer, called to the priesthood.

One of the church members who worked with Tony had insisted he memorize Bible verses. Over time the experience grew in meaning and importance. The first Scripture he memorized was from Philippians 4:13: "I can do all things through Christ who strengthens me." Soon the passage was engraved on the tablets of his heart as the words and the promise gave him a new and revitalized sense of courage beyond anything Forbes had ever known.

Still, the frightening isolation Anthony Forbes had felt in prison never left him. Every time he looked at a glass of wine, he remembered the coldness of that small stone cell with nothing but a thin cot. The memory always gave him the strength to refuse to drink, no matter how powerful the urge.

The bishop forced himself to stop staring at the wine glass on the tray next to him. He looked out into the sky, watching the clouds hurl past as he reordered his wandering thoughts.

■ ■ ■

Albert Reese paid no attention to the flight attendant when she took away his dinner tray. The steak hadn't been bad, and he had eaten most of it. What he wanted now was a cigarette. Of course, they had rules against smoking on airplanes and pretty much everywhere else these days. Not an ideal thing for a tobacco man.

To his right, Bishop Forbes seemed content after his lamb dinner. Reese could tell the bishop was way more into food than he was, and they hadn't exchanged more than some chatty small talk since their trays were placed in front of them.

"How was the lamb, Your Holiness?" Reese asked with a smile.

"Not bad at all, actually."

"You look like you could ask for seconds." Reese winked. "Maybe they can fix you up with a doggy bag." Reese laughed then reached down to unbuckle his seat belt.

"I think I'll stretch my legs," he said. "Maybe go back in coach and mingle with the riffraff."

As Reese stepped into the aisle, Senator Meyer was edging past Helen Bridwell, and the two men almost bumped into each other.

"Excuse me," the senator smiled.

"After you," Reese said, stepping back out of the aisle.

"Thank you."

From her window seat behind the senator and Helen, Mary Lee McMurray watched the brief exchange. As the senator went forward toward the first-class restroom and Reese stood aside to let him pass, she scrawled "no sign of mutual recognition" in the margin of her paperback.

When the senator had passed, Reese stepped into the aisle and struck out toward the rear of the cabin.

Reese planned to sneak a smoke if possible, maybe in one of the restrooms back in coach. The preflight briefing had included an admonition that smoking anywhere on the plane was against regulations, but a smoke after dinner was a tough habit to break, and Reese was hardly a stickler for regulations.

As Reese drew the accordion partition aside and stepped through into coach, he found himself face to face with the attractive attendant he had noticed earlier. He couldn't decide if her striking green eyes or her figure were more alluring.

"Can I help you, sir?" Dorothy asked with a smile.

"No, I'm fine," Reese said. "Just stretching my legs."

A young woman with two small kids beckoned to the flight attendant, leaving Reese alone in the aisle.

The wiry man rolled his shoulders and neck to loosen up. Reese was energetic by nature. Sitting still for any length of time was hard on him, especially if he couldn't smoke. At least he wasn't crammed into the small seats back here in coach.

Reese eyed the many empty seats in coach, and he wondered what the break-even point was on a plane this size. He made his way to the rear of the passenger cabin almost able to taste his next cigarette, but he would have to wait. Both restrooms were occupied.

While he waited, Reese stepped out of the aisle into an empty row and looked out the window. The sky was cloudy and dark, with dusk coming on and a storm brewing. Nothing much to see out there. Then he looked down, idly wondering if he could see through the cloud cover and spot any landmarks. He liked the way everything looked so small from this altitude. When flying over farmlands, he often tried to picture the little scrap of land he had grown up on. Reese remembered how tiny, hopeless, and unimportant the place was where he and his brothers and sisters had wasted so much of their youth raising tobacco.

Below them, the clouds were less solid, and Reese thought he could see a bit of land down there, mountains or rolling hills, when something else caught his eye. Far below and rising from behind them, he saw three small figures in a V. He watched them for a moment in idle curiosity. "What's that?" he muttered. Suddenly it registered.

"What is it?" a voice said behind him.

Reese turned to see the attendant with the green eyes standing in the aisle behind him.

"Is there a problem?" Dorothy asked.

"Down there. Look."

He lowered himself into the window seat as she leaned across him to look out the window.

"I see," she said.

"What do you make of them?"

"I'm not sure. It looks like..."

"I'll tell you what they are," Reese cut her off. "Those are jets—fighters."

"Are you sure?"

"Yeah, I'm certain. And they're coming right for us."

■ ■ ■

In the cockpit, an unfamiliar voice broke in on the regular frequency.

"Global Flight 027, this is GPS requesting clarification."

Jack Harris glanced at Matt Simpson as he keyed his mike.

"Global 027, GPS. Go ahead."

"We're reading an extreme irregularity in your flight pattern."

Jack looked at Beckman.

"You filed the variation, didn't you, Dave?"

Beckman looked at him, and Jack could see the panicked look in his face. The copilot put his hands to his temples and cursed softly.

"I forgot. I'll do it right now."

"Beckman, you..." Jack caught himself. There was no use tearing into him now. He would have plenty of time for that later. He keyed his microphone again. "Global 027, GPS. Report our intention to deviate from our original course to avoid developing storm patterns. We're in the process of sending the meter to Chicago at this time."

"Global 027, state your current course and position."

What is this all about? Jack wondered. *I have the prerogative to change course for weather.* He quickly gave them his coordinates and heading. They were flying parallel to the Chinese border, at a safe distance, on a heading for Delhi.

"Negative, Global 027. Repeat, negative. You have circled back to the northeast. You are in Chinese airspace. Repeat, you are in the People's Republic of China!"

"What?" Jack blurted, gulping hard. "That's impossible! Global 027, GPS. Confirm ID."

Jack scanned his instrument panel, the radar screen, the navigational system readouts. "What's going on here?" he mouthed to Beckman and Simpson.

"ID confirmed, Global 027. You're on a heading to overfly Wan Chow airbase in the People's Republic. Recommend course correction urgent. Repeat, urgent!"

Jack looked at Beckman, but all he saw was confusion and panic in the man's face. Beckman and Simpson grabbed for their maps and charts.

"I don't understand," Beckman stammered. "What the..."

"Global 027, GPS." Jack kept his voice calm in spite of the pang in his chest. "Request you recommend new heading, best correction."

The voice crackled with urgency as it read off the new heading, and Jack threw the 757 into a hard banking turn to the left. There was no time to warn the attendants. He had told them to expect turbulence, and he had to hope everybody was buckled up back there. He'd give them a story when there was time. Jack brought the nose of the big plane hard around to the new heading, almost due south. His cockpit radar was forward-looking, designed to give him a picture of weather and air traffic along his projected route, but it told him nothing about what lay behind his aircraft.

"What was that?" Jack spat, catching sight of the three hot exhausts of the MiGs in the darkening sky as they darted by outside his cockpit window. As he brought the 757 around to the new heading and leveled out the wings, he craned to look out to his left, but saw nothing.

"I don't know." Beckman mumbled without looking up, still scrambling desperately through his charts and notes.

"I think we've got company," Jack said. "It looks like trouble."

■ ■ ■

Senator Meyer had just returned from the restroom and was moving to his seat when the plane suddenly lurched sharply to the left, seeming almost to stand on its wing. Meyer was thrown into Helen. He grabbed the arm of her seat and she threw her arms around him, stifling a scream.

Pillows, magazines, blankets, and small bags flew across the cabin. In a matter of seconds, the plane lurched back to the right and rocked as it settled back into level flight.

Meyer found himself practically sitting in Helen's lap, her arms clasped desperately around him. After waiting a moment to be sure they were flying straight and level again, he looked up at her and grinned sheepishly.

"Thanks," he said. "I think you saved my life."

■ ■ ■

In the cockpit, Jack Harris was as mad as he was scared. He hadn't been scared at the controls of an airplane in a long time, but this was as bad as it gets.

"Where are we, Matt?" he spat at his navigator. "Tell me something!"

"Oh, no," Beckman wheezed.

"What? What is it?" Jack cried in alarm, turning to his copilot.

"I screwed up, Jack."

"What?" Jack barely managed to control his fury.

"When I put in the new coordinates, I forgot to use east readings."

"You can't be serious!" he yelled.

"I punched in west longitudes by mistake, Jack."

"So where are we?"

"We've been flying in a giant circle, working our way back toward Hong Kong."

"I don't believe this."

"GPS is right," Beckman groaned. "We're in Chinese airspace. Way inside their border."

■ ■ ■

The MiG flight leader brought his nose around, still climbing as he rolled his head hard left to maintain a visual on the big intruder. He was sure of what he had seen, a big airliner, probably a 757, but that didn't mean it wasn't American military or CIA. Everybody knew they used civilian planes for covert missions. As he and his flight squad came around and leveled off above and well behind the intruder, the flight leader reported what he saw to his base.

"Please be aware," the flight leader barked into his microphone, "the intruder appears to be breaking for the border. We must act quickly or they will soon be beyond our range."

Nothing came back. He heard only a crackle of static and the rushing wind outside the airplane.

The flight leader again reported his position. "I repeat. We must act quickly or the intruder will slip away."

No response.

At the radar station on the hilltop above the base, Lieutenant Zhou listened to the squawk box on the wall. He could monitor radio traffic between the tower and the MiGs, but he couldn't transmit directly. He had to relay his directions to the flight leader over the landline and through the tower down below.

"Evasive action," Zhou said, nodding. "A sign of guilt. What is their heading now?"

The air controller in the tower relayed Zhou's question to the flight leader and passed back the answer.

Yong confirmed it on the radar.

"Ah," Zhou nodded again. "He's making a run for the border. But that path will still bring him dangerously close to us here."

Zhou cursed as he listened to the transmission. One of the three MiGs had developed a fuel leak and was dropping out, returning to base. That left only two, and no time to request backup aircraft from district in time to overtake the intruder before he reached the border, if that was his intention. But what if he had something else in mind? Something such as an attack on Wan Chow.

No word had come from the colonel or the command center at district headquarters. *I'd call division if I could,* Lieutenant Zhou thought. *But that's out of the question.* It was district's job to keep division informed. A phone call could mean a firing squad if he went over their heads.

Division is monitoring our radio traffic, and they know about the situation, he thought. *Surely they know. Don't they?*

Jack Harris pegged the throttles wide open and double-checked to confirm his new heading. He could lose some altitude, he thought, and try to get below the Chinese radar, but this wasn't good country for skimming the deck. The terrain was mountainous, and they were flying into even rougher territory ahead, the Himalayan foothills along the border. He had his position and course from GPS, but he couldn't trust his copilot for details about what lay ahead of them. He cursed silently, *I should have written him up. Stupid drunk!*

The intercom pinged and Jack answered.

"What was that sudden lunge all about?" Dorothy demanded. "We've got a mess back here."

"It couldn't be helped," Jack said, still trying to sound calm, reassuring. "Where are you?"

"In first class. One of the other attendants went down pretty hard. What's going on?"

"We've got a problem, but we're working on it. Keep everybody calm back there."

"What am I supposed to tell them, Jack?"

"Tell them..."

Out of the corner of his eye, Jack caught a glimmer of motion out the cockpit window to his left. He turned and saw a MiG off his left wing. It was one of the old models, with a skinny silver fuselage, a tall, canted tail, and swept wings. He saw the gun slots in the ugly rounded snout, and the red star on the tail. As the smaller fighter bounced up and down in the turbulence off his wing, Jack thought he saw a missile riding underneath its near wing.

"Jack!" Dorothy Chandler almost screamed over the intercom. "There's a..."

"I know," Jack cut her off. "I see him. Just tell the folks we've got some company. It's all a misunderstanding, and we're working it out. Tell them not to panic."

"Easier said than done," she told him, and clicked off.

"Dave," Jack turned back toward his copilot. "Do you know where we are right now?"

"Uh...yeah, yeah, I've got it now."

"Swell. How far to the border?"

"We'll never make it, Jack."

Jack looked past Dave Beckman out the window on the right side of the cockpit. There was a second MiG off their right wing.

Simpson gaped, dropping the map he was holding. Beckman followed his stare and saw the MiG.

"Geez," he muttered. "That's an old one. Korean War model. Must be fifty years old."

"It'll still do the job," Jack said flatly.

"We'll never make it," Beckman said again.

"Well, Dave, we're sure gonna try."

■ ■ ■

The Chinese flight leader was worried. He was down to two aircraft and knew reinforcements were unlikely. There were a couple more airworthy planes back at Wan Chow, but standing orders were to keep them in reserve. Only the district command center could authorize sending them up.

They wouldn't have far to go, he knew. On its new course, the intruder was no longer flying directly toward the base, but he would still pass within a few miles of it. Certainly close enough to launch an attack, if that was the plan. If what they had been told about American air-to-ground missiles was true, the intruder was a threat to military targets all over the district, even the division.

For that matter, the flight leader mused, *he could launch from well beyond our borders. Why is he here, where he must know we will intercept him?* The flight leader was glad he was only a pilot. *Let the others worry about the intruder's intentions. All I have to do is keep him in sight and follow my orders.*

That could be difficult enough, he knew. They had burned a lot of fuel on the fast climb to altitude, and they couldn't tag along with the big jet forever. Fuel would be getting critical soon, and he could only hope the bosses on the ground would make a decision before he had to.

He had already made up his mind that he would send the remaining pilot in his flight squad back to base when their fuel ran low. For himself, he would stay with the intruder as long as he could, then he would have to take his chances. Better the mountains below than to return to base without accomplishing his mission. He just wished the brass on the ground would tell him what that mission was.

■ ■ ■

In first class, Senator Meyer was now buckled securely in his window seat, his arm around Helen's shoulders. She was crying softly, her head on his shoulder. Meyer rang for a flight attendant.

"Good heavens!" Bishop Forbes murmured from the seat in front of Meyer, his face pressed against the glass of the window. "Is that what I think it is?"

Meyer pushed up the shade on his window and looked out.

"It's a MiG," he said softly, recognizing it from his time in the armed forces. "A Chinese MiG."

"There's a plane over here!" a voice cried out from the left side of the cabin.

"What on earth is going on?" Bishop Forbes demanded of no one in particular.

"I don't know," Meyer said. "But I'm going to find out." He looked up as Dorothy appeared in the aisle.

The attendant looked past Helen and the senator, out the window at the MiG. Along with the other flight attendants, she had been busy clearing the cabin of debris from the captain's abrupt maneuver, and she was holding a folded blanket and a plastic bag full of garbage.

"I've spoken with the captain," she said. "There's been some kind of misunderstanding, but he's working..."

"I want a word with your captain," Senator Meyer interrupted.

"No, please," Helen whispered. "Don't leave me."

"I'm sorry, but that's not possible," Dorothy said, shaking her head. "As you can imagine, the flight crew is busy at the moment."

"I am a U.S. Senator," Meyer informed her.

"Yes, I know," she said.

"No, I don't mean to be intrusive," he assured her, using all of his political charm, which usually guaranteed people would do what he wanted. "I'm not just being difficult. There are national security implications. Have them patch through to Washington if they can. The State Department, the White House if they have to. Get somebody on the horn to the Chinese embassy and have them call off these MiGs."

"I'll see what I can do," Dorothy promised and disappeared up the aisle.

"Do they know you're on this flight?" Helen asked, looking up at the senator. "Is that why..."

"No, absolutely not," he said, shaking his head as he reached for the in-flight phone and fumbled his credit card out of his pocket. Any other time, he would have an aide to punch in the numbers for him, but he had sent his staffers on to Frankfurt a day ahead of him because he'd wanted another day for especially sensitive negotiations. "Quite the opposite. I've just been in Hong Kong meeting with some of their top people. If they knew I was onboard, they'd never..."

Meyer caught himself before he finished his thought. He had been about to say the Chinese would never shoot them down, but there was no point scaring Helen any more than she was already.

Meyer punched in the numbers and waited, but nothing happened. He cleared the digital keypad and tried again. Still nothing.

"Is it working?" Bishop Forbes asked, turning in his chair and leaning over the seat back.

"No," Meyer said, shaking his head in disgust. "I don't know where we are, but it's not anywhere the telecom satellite can pick us up."

"Most unfortunate," the bishop shrugged.

"Did you see those things?" Reese came loping down the aisle from coach. "They're MiGs!"

"Yes, we all see them," Bishop Forbes assured him. "They're hard to miss."

Reese took his seat and leaned over the bishop's shoulder to look out the window.

"What do they want?" Reese asked. "What are they doing here?"

"Ask the senator," Bishop Forbes suggested, pointing over his seat back at Meyer.

"You?" Reese asked, looking at Meyer. "You're a senator?"

"George Meyer. How do you do?"

"Albert Reese. What's up with the phone?"

"Nothing, as it turns out." Meyer slapped the phone back into its slot. "I can't get the satellite from here."

"Yeah? Who were you going to call?"

"State Department, White House, anybody to call these guys off."

"You could do that?"

"Maybe. If the phone worked."

In the seat directly behind the senator, Mary Lee slipped the earphones off and let them dangle around her neck. The recorder on her belt was taping everything, but the senator and his fellow passengers were talking loudly enough for her to hear them without the electronics.

Like everyone around her, Mary Lee was looking out at the MiG bobbing along off the right wing of the 757.

"Stay right there, you naughty boy," Mary Lee muttered under her breath as she fumbled in her carry-on bag for her camera.

Mary Lee pulled the camera out and clicked the lens open. *I hope taking pictures with this thing is as foolproof as they say,* she thought, lifting the tiny automatic to her eye. When she looked through the viewfinder, the MiG looked tiny and far away. She switched to telephoto and tried again. *Better.* She snapped away, getting half a dozen shots just in case. *Nice touch,* she thought. *Bonus points.*

■ ■ ■

Dorothy picked up the receiver on the intercom and dialed the captain.

"What is it?" Jack barked.

"I thought you should know that Senator George Meyer is trying to call Washington, D.C. He's trying to get a connection right now."

Harris grunted. "The screwball! There's no way in the world it's going to work out here."

"He's trying to call the White House, the Chinese Embassy, anyone that might get us some help."

"Listen, Dorothy, let him call whoever he wants. I don't care what he does." Jack's voice turned hard. "We're dealing with a problem that could explode any second. If Senator fat mouth wants to do something helpful, he can pray. This confrontation is going to be over in a matter of minutes...one way or another."

Dorothy choked. "You think they'll shoot?"

"They could. We're over their airspace."

"What do I tell the Senator?"

Harris sighed. "Tell him to try Hong Kong if he gets a signal."

"Okay." Dorothy started to hang up the phone but stopped. "Jack, are we going to make it?"

"I don't know, baby. This is a tough one."

■ ■ ■

At the Wan Chow radar station, Lieutenant Zhou stood with his hands clasped behind his back and stared out the little window as if he could see the drama unfolding far above him in the darkening sky.

Zhou had made a full report to the command center at district headquarters, but there was still no word from the colonel. He knew that District knew what was going on here. They had his report, and they had their own radar, newer and better than his. They could monitor radio traffic between Wan Chow air control and the pilots, too, just as he could. Where was the colonel? They were running out of time.

"Yong."

Yong looked up from his radarscope as the lieutenant turned from the window and fixed him with a searching gaze.

"Lieutenant?"

"Our tower is again trying to raise the intruder by radio. If we make contact, it will be your task to communicate with them. I doubt that they speak Mandarin, and you are the only one here who speaks English."

"Yes, Lieutenant."

"Your English is fluent, you say?"

"Yes, Lieutenant."

More or less, Yong thought.

Yong had leapt at the chance to go for language training at his last post because he thought it would improve his chances of advancement. It hadn't dawned on him until later that most of the senior officers scrupulously avoided English language training and everything else that had to do with the West. It might make him a better soldier, but he had realized too late that it might also mark him as a man with too much curiosity about foreign ways.

The language school had been less than thorough, taught by loyal party members whose exposure to English had been minimal at best. He had memorized vocabularies and been shown snippets of old Hollywood movies, and that was about all. Yong was by no means confident he was fluent enough for the challenge that faced him, but he knew he had little choice.

Be optimistic, he told himself. *This is the big chance you have been waiting for.*

Yong watched the three blips on his radar screen, the two MiGS and the intruder. They were merged into one fuzzy bright ball now, his equipment incapable of discriminating among aircraft flying in such tight formation. He had already reported the intruder's sharp turn and increased speed. There was nothing to do now but watch and wait for his big chance.

Behind him, he heard Lieutenant Zhou on the phone, calling the command center at district headquarters again.

"I must speak to Colonel Qong immediately," Zhou yelled into the phone, his temper rising. "It is extremely urgent."

"Your request has been noted," the flat, emotionless voice on the other end informed him.

"Listen," Zhou growled. "We are dealing with an international incident here. Our pilots have the intruder in sight, but they will soon run out of fuel. They are waiting for orders."

"Your request has been noted."

"I want it on the record that I have done my duty. You are warned, and the responsibility is on your head," Zhou said. Lowering his voice, he added, "You know I am recording this conversation."

Zhou was bluffing—there was recording equipment, but it was not working properly and the lieutenant had no tapes in any case.

"Noted."

The line went dead.

6

Aboard the Shark, Lieutenant Stiles was huddled in one corner of the data reception center with the ship's commander, Captain Maxwell. An old hand, the captain had spent most of his thirty years in the Navy in Asia, stepping out of intelligence jobs now and then just long enough to get his ticket punched for promotion.

"The good news is they've corrected course and are heading for the border," Lieutenant Stiles explained, tracing the route of Global 027 on a map of China with his finger.

"The bad news is they're too far in and too close to Wan Chow. The MiGs are on them?"

"Gates," Stiles called across the tiny, crowded compartment. "What's going on with the MiGs out of Wan Chow?"

"One returned to base, but the other two are flying tight formation with the 757," Gates called back.

"It could be worse," Maxwell said, rubbing his chin. "They could've opened up on them right off the bat. Are we monitoring all radio traffic, Wan Chow and the 757?"

"Monitoring and taping," Stiles assured him. "Captain, do you have any idea what they're doing that far off course?"

"What do you mean?"

"It's hard to believe they could screw up that bad."

"You're thinking CIA, something suspicious?"

"I can't help wondering. What do you think?"

"I wouldn't put anything past them, but I don't think so. I haven't heard anything."

Lieutenant Stiles didn't want to press his commander for more information. If anyone knew, Maxwell would. But if he knew, maybe he wasn't supposed to tell. "Think they'll try to force him down somewhere?" Lieutenant Stiles asked, changing the subject.

"Where? There's not a strip in range that's long enough. Not with him coming out of Hong Kong and flying that circle route he was on."

"He's really hauling, sir," Gates volunteered. "He's got the pedal to the metal."

"And burning fuel like crazy," Captain Maxwell said. He scanned the map of the Chinese Fourth Division again. "There's no place for him to set her down, not that I can see. Even in a 757, you run out of gas eventually."

"They might take him to Wan Chow," Lieutenant Stiles offered.

"The runway there isn't long enough. Nowhere close."

A sailor popped in through the hatch behind him and handed Captain Maxwell a decoded message.

"Good news?" Lieutenant Stiles asked hopefully, as Maxwell read the message.

"Response from the Front Office. 'Maintain cover. Let Dragon make the mistakes. Keep us advised.'"

"That's what I figured," Lieutenant Stiles said glumly.

"What did you expect, Stiles? We can't invade Chinese airspace to chase those MiGs off his tail. It would be a heck of a dogfight before it was over, and the 757 would be the first to go down. Not to mention lighting the fuse on a war."

"I know, Captain, but there's gotta be something we can do."

"We're doing it. We've got a carrier group heading that way now."

"To do what? Search for survivors?"

"If it comes to that," Maxwell answered.

■ ■ ■

Jack was worried about the MiG off their left wing. It had started pulling some scary maneuvers. First he would bank away, then he'd come sliding back in toward the 757, pulling up just short of hitting the wingtip. Then he'd look across at Jack and make motions with his hands, pointing at Jack and then down toward the ground.

The two pilots were separated only by the length of the 757's wing, close enough to see each other's faces.

"I get the message," Jack muttered under his breath, cursing the Chinese pilot. *He's gonna cut it too close one of these times,* Jack was thinking. *He'll clip my wing and spin himself right into me.*

"What?" Beckman asked, looking up from his charts.

"I'm telling him I understand," Jack answered, nodding his head with exaggerated motions through the cockpit window at the MiG pilot. "He wants us to land."

"Where?" Beckman snorted.

"That's a good question, Dave. How far to the border?"

"We'll never make it."

"Stop saying that."

"Hey, look at this," Beckman said, adjusting his radio earphones.

"What?"

"Somebody's trying to raise us on a higher frequency. Maybe it's them, the Chinese. Maybe they want to talk."

"Dial them in, let's hear what they have to say."

■ ■ ■

At the Wan Chow radar station, Yong held the telephone tight to his right ear and plugged his left with his finger. The line was noisy, the relay from the air control tower none too clear. Lieutenant Zhou nodded, signaling him to speak in English.

"Hello...intruder," he began. "You hear me?"

■ ■ ■

Helen rested her head on Senator Meyer's shoulder and thought about saying a little prayer, but she shook her head at the thought. *It's a little late for praying,* Helen told herself.

Meyer felt her move and looked down at her.

"Are you all right?" he asked.

She nodded. "Is it still out there?"

"Yes. I don't think he's going away."

"It seems like hours."

"It's been a couple of minutes, actually." Meyer checked his watch.

"Time's the strangest thing, isn't it?"

"It's going to be all right," he told her. He hugged her to him and put his hand on hers. "You'll see."

In front of them, Reese was offering to swap seats with the bishop.

"Pardon me?" the bishop asked, opening his eyes.

"Swap seats," Reese repeated himself. "You sit here on the aisle and do whatever it is you want to do. I'll take the window seat and keep an eye on our friend out there."

"I think not."

"Why? You were going to close the window shade, for Pete's sake."

"I'd rather not switch," the bishop insisted. "I prefer not to tempt fate."

"What? Oh, I get you. Like if we switch and the plane goes down, maybe I'll make it and you won't. The joke's on you then, huh?"

"Something like that."

"It could work the other way too, though."

"I suppose."

"Look, Your Holiness, if you want to do something in the fate department how about saying a prayer? That's your thing, isn't it?"

"Mr. Reese, I've been praying since the pilot stood this cursed airplane on its ear."

The bishop looked out the window at the MiG again, flying so close to their airplane. The Chinese craft looked small, innocuous, and yet the bishop knew that the airplane could literally blow them out of the sky.

For a few moments, Tony Forbes thought about the times in his life that he had survived brushes with danger. He had never been in the military, had never felt the threat of battle. Yet he was a veteran of other dangerous situations and had many life-threatening experiences under his belt.

I probably would have always stayed in the parish setting if it hadn't been for that one time that caused the officials of the church to notice my potential, the bishop mused. *I could have simply stayed hidden in some remote little congregation.*

The incident came back to his mind. Five men from the IRA had come down from Ireland and infiltrated an ammunition dump not far from his village church. The terrorists had been exposed. Suddenly, the entire countryside was filled with soldiers and police. The locals were evacuated. The orders were to apprehend the terrorists at all costs. If a gunfight erupted, an explosion at the dump could have turned the town into rubble.

"We don't see much choice. There's a risk of blowing up the village," Constable Larkin had said to Reverend Forbes. "But we can't let these chaps threaten us. We have to make an example of them."

Forbes studied what he saw in front of him. Heavily armed police were everywhere. They didn't care if terrorists lived or died, as long as the national security was protected.

"No one wants to go in there and talk to these thugs," the constable continued. "Too dangerous."

"Why?" Forbes asked.

"Why!" The constable shook his head. "It could be death!"

The word *death* rang through Anthony Forbes, touching all the sensitive issues in his past. If there was anything that he needed to do, it was repay the life he had taken. The possibility of death galvanized Forbes into action.

"I suppose they might listen to a priest," the clergyman said simply. "In my calling, we've been taught not to be afraid. Many years ago I memorized a passage from the Bible that changed me. Have you ever heard the words, 'I can do all things through Christ who strengthens me'?"

"You're joking!" The constable's mouth dropped open.

Forbes smiled. "Not at all. Constable, you don't understand me. I said *all things.* If I'm not mistaken, this situation falls under all things. I might find these Irish lads to be reasonable fellows. It's worth a try, isn't it?"

Larkin took a step backward and stared at the priest.

It took the constable some fast-talking, but in the end, the army officials in charge decided that if Forbes would go, they'd allow an exchange. The priest buttoned his coat over the bulletproof vest they forced him to wear and walked across the no-man's-land toward the barricades.

Tony could still see the looks on the men's faces when he walked into their shelter. The five terrorists turned out to be young—children, really—probably sent down to England with no idea what they were getting into. As he had hoped, the IRA intruders were terrified. None of them wanted to die.

After two hours of hard discussion, Tony convinced the boys that blowing up the village would get them nowhere. In the end, the lads marched out with him and went off to jail with a minimum of fuss.

Forbes thought of the picture of him printed on *The London Times* front page. The public relations had certainly proved to be good for his career. He'd even received a congratulatory note for exemplary performance from the Archbishop of Canterbury. When the interest of the press died out, he had time to think about the step he'd taken. Tony didn't remember being afraid of dying. His life for the life he had taken. It was a fair exchange.

Strange, he thought to himself. *After all these years, I still feel that same burning need to make amends. I wonder if it will ever end? Nevertheless, whatever is required of me...I know where my strength comes from.*

■ ■ ■

"Global 027, China. Please identify. Who are we talking to?"

Yong was taken aback. The pilot sounded American, and his English was not like the vocabularies at language school, more like the Hollywood movies. He hadn't truly believed the aircraft was American until this minute.

"Wan Chow Radar Command to Intruder. Identify please."

"This is Global Airlines Flight 027, en route from Hong Kong to Delhi, India. I'm afraid we've had a computer malfunction in our navigational system. We have corrected it now, and we're outbound your airspace. Repeat, we are outbound. Do you copy?"

"Wan Chow Radar Command to Intruder. You in Chinese airspace. Over."

Yong hadn't been able to catch everything the pilot said. He understood Global Airlines and the flight number, but most of the rest was gibberish. He'd heard Hong Kong, but wasn't clear if that was the intruder's origin or destination. From the direction he was flying, Yong concluded they must be heading for Hong Kong. He tried to remember his language training.

Yong's English was heavily accented, and it was obvious to the pilots that he wasn't able to understand them.

"Global 027, Wan Chow Radar Command. Affirmative, we acknowledge we are in your airspace. We made a mistake. You copy mistake?"

"Wan Chow Radar Command, Global 027. Affirmative."

That part had come back to Yong, affirmative and negative. He thought he had that straight.

"We are correcting now, proceeding to leave your airspace. Acknowledge."

"Global 027, identify you aircraft."

Harris thought he got what the Chinese was saying, although it didn't really matter what he said if the guy couldn't understand his English. "We are a civilian airliner. Repeat, civilian airliner. Carrying passengers only. Civilian passengers. Acknowledge."

"Why you spying on People's Republic of China?"

"No, no. We're not spying. It's a mistake. A computer malfunction. We're a civilian airliner. No spying," Harris said as slowly as he could. He was sure they would be fired on at any moment.

"Stand by, Global 027."

Yong had remembered that, too. Stand by. He turned to his lieutenant.

"They claim to be an airliner, a civilian air transport. They identify as Global Airlines 027, Lieutenant."

"Then what are they doing here?"

"Global 027, what you doing here?" Yong passed the question along. *They may have already explained that,* he thought. *But I'm not sure what they said, how they phrased it.*

"Wan Chow, I say again, we had a problem with the computer in our navigational system. But we have fixed it now, and we are leaving your airspace. Copy?"

"Lieutenant, they claim a malfunction of some kind. I believe they are saying it was an accident."

"That is nonsense," Lieutenant Zhou said, shaking his head. "They have computers that can fly in any weather. How could they come so far off course by accident? It is a lie."

Both of them watched the radarscope, the fuzzy bright glob that was the 757 and the two remaining MiGs working their way south toward the border. The flight leader had long since radioed his concerns about fuel. They were running out of time.

■ ■ ■

"Good Lord," Jack muttered, watching the MiG out his copilot's window. "Now what?"

Beckman looked up from his charts and cursed.

The second MiG overtook the 757 and dropped into a leading position. The orange glow of its exhaust looked like a flickering tiger's eye in the gathering darkness.

Dusk was coming fast, and Jack could see storm clouds rolling in low ahead of them, as well as ominous images on his radar screen. The colors he was seeing represented the worst level of storm.

"What's he doing?" Beckman wondered aloud, his voice cracking.

Jack looked at his copilot. Beckman was a wreck, bug-eyed and sweating through his uniform shirt, his face flushed a bright red.

"It doesn't matter," Jack told him. "We're toast if they decide to shoot us down."

"They won't do that!" Beckman blurted and then stopped. "Will they?"

"How should I know?" Harris growled.

"But they can see us. They know we're civilian."

"Maybe they think it's some kind of imperialist trick," Simpson offered. He was pale, but holding up well under the pressure.

Jack watched the MiG ahead of them seem to grow larger as he reduced his speed and the 757 gained on the fighter plane.

"What's he doing now?" Beckman asked.

"Trying to slow us down," Jack said. "And our friend on my side over here's trying to get us to turn right. They want us to land."

"Where?" Beckman scoured his charts.

"That's a good question."

Their charts were blank as far as Chinese airstrips were concerned—that was top-secret stuff. Jack knew it was a long shot that the Chinese had anything within range that would accommodate a 757. Even if they had a strip he could set down on without risking a crash, there was no way it would be long enough to take off again. He figured the best strip nearby was Wan Chow, where these MiGs came from. Although logically, Wan Chow landing strip's was probably no longer than it had to be to accommodate the MiGs. They were awfully small old fighters. Their home base would offer little more than a crash landing for a 757.

Jack thought about the passengers. None of them had bargained on being taken prisoners by the Chinese when they bought their tickets. Still, he would opt for that possibility rather than making a run for the border and taking the risk of being shot down, if the Chinese had any place for him to land safely. Unfortunately, they didn't, and Jack knew that narrowed his list of options dramatically.

"Get on the horn," Jack told Beckman. "Put out our position and heading. Make sure we don't surprise anybody. I don't want to pop up on somebody else's radar unannounced and start a panic."

"Right."

"Raise Calcutta and tell them we're going to try to land there."

"Calcutta?"

"We've been out a long time, Dave, and at this speed we're burning fuel fast."

"Yeah."

"And while you're at it," Jack added, "bury your nose in those charts and help Simpson find a backup, an alternate strip somewhere, just in case."

"I'm on it, Jack."

Maybe there's something just across the border, Jack thought. *It's less than ideal, but at least we won't be in China...if we can just make it to the border.*

The Chinese flight leader couldn't afford to wait any longer. His fuel was running low, and the other pilot had reported he was losing oil pressure. They couldn't keep up the chase much longer. Their ancient aircraft could not hold up against the 757.

The leader called Wan Chow for instructions and made the situation clear to Lieutenant Zhou. It was time for a decision. They had to do something quickly.

At the Wan Chow radar station, Lieutenant Zhou tried once more to reach Colonel Qong at the district command center. Still no luck. The matter was up to him.

The intruder was moving away from the base now and seemed to pose less of a threat to launch an attack but, perhaps, that had not been his intention in the first place! Possibly, he was on a spying mission, or merely testing their defenses. Zhou could not allow the American to escape after violating their airspace so blatantly and menacing the airbase. And yet, to order the fighters to shoot down the plane might have consequences far beyond his imagining. He desperately wanted Colonel Qong to make that decision. Failing that option, Zhou was desperately trying to think of some middle course.

When the MiG flight leader reported the 757 had ignored their attempts to turn him from his course for the border, Zhou knew his hope that they could force him to attempt a landing at Wan Chow was not to be. He had no choice but to order the MiGs to take the next step.

■ ■ ■

Reese felt the turbulence rock the plane and saw Bishop Forbes open his eyes and look out the window.

"Nothing to worry about, Your Holiness. You just keep praying. Put in a word for me while you're at it."

"You could talk to Him yourself," the bishop suggested.

"I don't credit God when things are going good," he shrugged. "It wouldn't seem right to go running to Him when I'm in a jam."

"It's never too late to turn to God, Mr. Reese. Nor does it matter what the reason."

"That would make me a hypocrite, wouldn't it? I could promise Him I'll do anything if He'll get me out of this, knowing I wouldn't."

"Just put it in His hands, Mr. Reese. That's all."

"You do the praying for both of us. If He saves you, hey, I'm right here with you. Odds are, I'll do all right, too."

"I'm not praying to be saved."

"You're not?" Reese raised his eyebrows. His mouth dropped slightly. "Really?"

"No," Bishop Forbes smiled indulgently at him. "It doesn't work that way, actually."

"I thought it did." Reese frowned. "I don't understand."

"There's a passage in the Bible that you ought to read sometime," the bishop offered. "It's in the book of Romans."

"Yeah?" Reese raised an eyebrow. "What does it say?"

Forbes smiled. "'We know that all things work together for good to those who love God, to those who are the called according to His purpose.'" The bishop shrugged. "The issue isn't my survival at all. I'm praying that His will be done."

"That's pretty much a given, isn't it?"

Forbes shook his head. "You think if I pray, maybe God will save us, let us cheat death. But God looks at a much bigger picture—eternity. He knows every action has affects we can't see. Even if we die, life won't be over—just life as we know it. I suggest you try to redefine your perception. Our time on this earth is over in the blink of an eye." Forbes patted Reese on the shoulder. "But God focuses His mind on *forever.*" The bishop winked. "Emperor Nero buried the Christians in his gardens as human torches. One hundred years later, Tertullian wrote that the blood of the martyrs was the seed of the church. Get my point?"

Reese frowned.

"The point is, those men suffered, but more good came of their sacrificial deaths than if they had lived long, easy lives...."

Bishop Forbes was cut short by the ominous rattling sound he heard out the window. He and Reese both turned to look. They both saw the bright white balls of fire arcing over the right wing and disappearing beyond.

"Tracers," the bishop mumbled.

"They're shooting at us!" Reese said. "The commies are shooting at us!"

■ ■ ■

Jack was relieved when the MiG flying in front of the 757 banked away and disappeared under his wing. *Maybe they're just escorting us to the border,* he told himself, *to make sure we get out.* But he knew that wasn't what they had in mind when he saw the MiG on his left drop back into position above the left wing. When he saw the flashes rimming the MiG's snout and heard the rattling of its cannon, he knew what it meant. He watched the arc of the tracers.

"Hey, we're being shot at!" Beckman reported nervously, craning his neck to see out his side of the cockpit.

"On this side, too," Jack said. "Warning shots, over the wings."

"Now what do we do?"

"Put out the Mayday. I don't think we're going to talk our way out of this."

"That might spook them even more," Beckman said.

"Put out the Mayday, Dave. Broadcast it. Let everybody know. If anybody in the Chinese army speaks English, maybe they'll get the picture we're just civilians with a screwup copilot."

"Don't blame me!"

"Who forgot what side of the world we're on?"

"I wouldn't have had to put in new coordinates if you weren't so eager to make your hot date in Delhi!"

"Shut up!" Jack snapped at his bleary copilot. He took a deep breath. *We don't have time for this,* he told himself.

"I made an honest mistake, Jack. I..."

"Okay, okay. We'll hash it all out later. Right now, just put out the Mayday, and let everybody know we've got a problem."

■ ■ ■

Aboard the Shark, Lieutenant Stiles scanned the latest radio intercept printouts and briefed Captain Maxwell.

"Wan Chow ordered the MiGs to fire warning shots. The 757 captain is broadcasting a Mayday, but he's still on course for the border at top speed. Here's something." Stiles listened more closely. "One of the MiGs just dropped out, turned back to Wan Chow. Reports he's losing oil pressure."

"That still leaves one."

"Yes, sir. The 757 repeated its earlier message about Senator Meyer being on board and requested it be relayed to the State Department. Is that credible?"

"Maybe," Captain Maxwell shrugged. "According to our manifest, Meyer was in Hong Kong for trade talks. He was due to leave yesterday, but I guess he could have stayed over an extra day."

"Are the Chinese monitoring this traffic, too, sir?"

Maxwell scratched his head.

"Out in the boonies? Who knows? Send it to the Front Office again, Stiles, priority relay. Maybe they can ring up the Chinese embassy and do some good before it's too late."

■ ■ ■

In the first-class passenger cabin, Bishop Forbes was praying again, and Reese rose in his seat, looking back at Senator Meyer.

"What's up with your Chinese pals?" Reese demanded. "We're in international airspace. How can they come across the border like this? Isn't that illegal?"

Meyer had his hands full with Helen. The sound of the MiGs firing and the sight of the tracers had unnerved her, and she was sobbing in his arms. The senator looked up at Reese. "I have no idea what's behind this. The Chinese were upset about the military exercises in Taiwan, but.... Maybe it's just a little saber rattling. I don't know."

"They wouldn't actually shoot us down, would they?" Reese insisted. "I mean, this isn't like that Korean airliner that drifted off course over a Russian base or something. We're in international air, for heaven's sake."

"I'm sure you're right," the senator agreed and held Helen close, trying to sound calm for her benefit. He was genuinely at a loss to explain China's actions. Unless, of course, they weren't in international airspace. Maybe the captain had made a mistake. A serious mistake.

Reese slid back down in his seat.

"I never trusted those stinkin' commies," he muttered. "I do business with them, but I never trusted them."

Reese reached inside his Armani jacket and pulled out a gold plated cigarette case.

"Hang regulations," he said. "I'm going to have a smoke."

He flipped open the case and offered it to the bishop.

"Care for one, Your Holiness?"

Bishop Forbes looked up from his praying. He blinked.

"No, thank you. I watched my mum die of lung cancer, smoking too much." He shook his head. "I saw a biopsy of a piece of her lung." The bishop pursed his lips. "It looked like a black piece of shoe leather."

Reese slipped the cigarette between his lips. "Sin will do that to ya." He smiled and flicked the lighter.

■ ■ ■

At the Wan Chow radar station, Lieutenant Zhou heard the flight leader's report on the squawk box. "Warning shots fired, with negative results." The intruder was maintaining heading and speed. Only the flight leader was left, and his fuel was running low. What were his instructions?

Lieutenant Zhou passed the word through the Wan Chow tower for the flight leader to maintain his position and stand by. He rang up the command center at district headquarters one last time.

"Urgent directive is sought from Colonel Qong," he told the voice on the other end. "Intruder is on a course to the border at high speed. Our interceptor is low on fuel. We must take action immediately or the intruder will escape."

"The request has been noted."

"Listen! This is urgent. Urgent!" Lieutenant Zhou took a moment to collect himself. He glanced at the image on the radar screen. "If I do not receive orders in two minutes, I will assume the colonel endorses my decision, and I will order our interceptors to fire on the intruder. Do you understand?"

"The colonel is expected here at any moment."

"Two minutes," Zhou warned.

That was all the time he had.

■ ■ ■

In the first-class cabin of the 757, Dorothy had her hands full. The other attendant in first class had been thrown by the hard banking turn and appeared to have suffered a concussion. She was woozy and complaining of neck pains. Dorothy had buckled her into an empty seat and put an orthopedic collar from the first-aid cabinet around her neck.

Dorothy stepped out of the first-class cooking area and gritted her teeth as a wave of nausea swept over her. The smell of cigarettes had hit her like a brick in the face. She looked around the cabin. Curls of smoke wound their way up from a seat on the right side.

"What are you doing?" Dorothy barked at the man peering out the window with a cigarette in his hands.

Reese turned around. "Looking at the MiG out there."

"You're smoking!" Dorothy yelled at him.

"Yeah? Well, we're afraid this whole plane may end up in a smoking ruin. I don't think my cigarette is a real problem."

Dorothy's eyes narrowed, and she felt her stomach turn again. "You know the regulations. Put that cigarette out this minute!"

"Hey, I'm not trying to cause any trouble." Reese took a last puff off the cigarette and ground it out on his tray table.

"I won't warn you again." Dorothy fanned the smoke away from her face. "You understand?"

"Whatever." Reese looked back out the window.

Dorothy sighed.

Back in coach, the attendants struggled to keep the passengers from panicking. They worked their way down the aisles from one passenger to the next, trying to reassure them. "There's been a misunderstanding," they told them. "The captain is working it out."

With everything so out of control, Dorothy shrugged and went back to coach to check on the mom and her two preschoolers. The children were terrified, watching the MiG out their window. Their mother looked up at Dorothy with worry in her eyes. Dorothy assured her everything would be all right. "Just a misunderstanding," she said. "We'll be landing soon." Dorothy knew the woman didn't believe her, but she nodded, attempted to smile, and turned to comfort her kids.

■ ■ ■

"Here's something!" Beckman abruptly shouted, stabbing the chart on his lap with a thick finger.

"What?"

"Military airbase, just over the border."

"Where?"

"Right there." Beckman showed Jack the chart.

"Whose is it?" Jack asked.

"I don't know," Beckman scratched his head and looked again.

The base didn't look like much on the chart, and Beckman didn't like the looks of it. Eyeballing the scale of the runway, he figured it couldn't be much more than 5,000 feet long. Long enough to land on—maybe—but they wouldn't be able to take off again and it was situated in a small mountain valley surrounded by peaks and ridges. At a glance, it looked like a worse option than Wan Chow.

"What do you think, Simpson?" Beckman asked.

"It's in Bhutan, I think," Matt answered, checking the chart reference. "It's hard to tell. According to this, it's in a disputed area. Whatever that means."

"It means keep looking, guys," Jack sighed.

■ ■ ■

Lieutenant Zhou's two minutes ran out without a word from the command center at district headquarters. He paced the short hallway that ran the length of the shack, his hands clasped behind his back. The boards of the floor, worn smooth with years of footsteps, creaked beneath his feet. A faded portrait of Chairman Mao hung on the wall at the end of the hallway. Lieutenant Zhou could feel the eyes following him as he turned toward the front of the little building.

When he stopped at the window, he could see nothing. Darkness was falling, and the threat of bad weather was closing in on the base as storms rumbled down out of the mountains.

Zhou imagined the scene far above him with the remaining MiG flying alongside the big intruder. His fuel was now too low to risk any signaling or menacing maneuvers. It was all he could do to maintain contact, and he wouldn't be able to do even that much longer. The flight leader had already warned him that he was only minutes away from the point of no return—and he wasn't even sure if the second MiG would make it back to Wan Chow.

The flight leader would stay with the intruder as long as he could, even if it meant running out of fuel and crashing in the mountains. Lieutenant Zhou knew the capabilities of their search and rescue crews almost as well as the flight leader. They both understood that to crash in the mountains, even without the storm front rolling in from the north, would mean certain death—that is, *if* the flight leader was able to bail out in time and survive a parachute landing in that terrain.

Time had run out for all of them.

Lieutenant Zhou picked up the phone and punched the line for the air control tower at the base down the hill.

Inside the 757's cockpit, Jack double-checked his fuel gauges and navigational system readouts. If Beckman had gotten his act together and plugged in the right data from GPS, they should be closing on the border fast. Fuel was a concern. Jack wanted options, something better than the abandoned military strip in the mountains, in case they couldn't make it to Calcutta.

"Simpson, have you got anything yet?" he asked.

"No, just that..."

"Hey," Beckman interrupted.

"What?"

"My MiG just left."

"Mine's still with us," Jack noted dryly. "Maybe yours is repositioning."

"No, he pulled out. I saw him. He's going back the way we came."

Jack looked out the cockpit window along the length of his left wing at the remaining MiG.

"I wonder how long this one can stay with us," he worried.

■ ■ ■

"Now it's just you and me," the flight leader muttered into his oxygen mask as he eyed the cockpit window of the 757, the pilot's face visible in the ghostly greenish glow of his instrument panel.

The flight leader knew that by staying with the intruder, he was dooming himself. His chances of surviving a bailout in the mountains, with night coming quickly and the weather deteriorating, were negligible. He had always known it might come to this moment. His young wife would receive a widow's pension. He was prepared to die for the People's Republic, but he would have preferred that it not be in vain, flying into the ground while waiting for orders from Wan Chow that never came.

He began to think about what he would do if he didn't receive any instructions before his fuel ran out and he lost power. Even as he began his glide to earth, he would still be able to lock on to the big target and launch one of his missiles, perhaps both of them. The heat-seekers were not likely to miss. At least the trip wouldn't be for nothing. He would not be the only one lost in the oncoming mountain blizzards.

Suddenly, his radio crackled with orders from Wan Chow.

■ ■ ■

A cheer went up in the 757's first-class passenger cabin. A man in a window seat announced to his fellow passengers that the last MiG had pulled out.

"They're gone!" the man shouted again. "They've both left!"

"I told you," Senator Meyer reassured Helen Bridwell, patting her hand. "Just a little saber rattling."

"Maybe they got the message you were on board," she smiled up at him, though she continued to grip his arm. "They figured they'd better leave us alone."

"It was His Holiness that drove them away," Reese proclaimed, slapping Bishop Forbes heartily on the back. "Good job there, Bishop! Your prayers pulled us out."

"Earnest prayer is never wasted." Bishop Forbes looked out his window to reassure himself the crisis was over. "I'm not sure I can take credit."

"Praying is like chicken soup, I figure," Reese said. "It might not help, but it can't hurt."

"When I walk through the valley of the shadow of death, and that's where we are right now," Bishop Forbes paused and took a deep breath, "all I know is that I don't walk alone."

■ ■ ■

In the window seat behind the senator, Mary Lee leaned back from her window and scrunched low in her seat. With no noticeable sign of relief or rejoicing, she opened her Grisham paperback to a new page and began scribbling notes. Mary Lee checked her watch to verify the time that she wrote in the margin.

In front of her, Senator Meyer checked his watch, too, and looked over the back of his seat for a flight attendant.

"I wonder how long until we get into Delhi," he mused.

■ ■ ■

Jack saw the last of the MiGs pull his nose up and disappear off his left wing. He shifted in his seat to see as far back toward the rear as he could, but he saw nothing.

"Mine's gone," he said softly.

"What?" Beckman asked.

"My MiG's gone, too," Jack said a little louder this time. "As far as I can tell, we're clear."

"Thank God," Simpson sighed. "I thought we were done for."

"They must have turned back," Jack thought aloud. "They didn't want to risk a shoot-out, I guess. Or maybe we got through to the White House, and they knew we had a senator on board."

"I don't care why they left," Beckman said. He brushed his hand over his crew cut and took a deep breath. "As long as they're gone."

"I'm going to maintain speed until we cross the border," Jack said. "Then I'll cut back to conserve fuel. We're going to cut it close to make Calcutta. Stay on those charts, Matt. We may still need an alternative landing site."

Jack punched in the intercom to first class. Dorothy answered.

"How's everybody doing back there?" he asked.

"Better now. Did you hear the sigh of relief when that last MiG pulled out?"

"Yeah, and you should have heard us up here. Okay, it looks like the worst is over. Keep everybody buckled in, though. We've got rough weather ahead, and it's going to be bumpy going over these mountains."

"How long to landing?" she asked.

"Not long now. Just relax, baby. The worst is over."

"Right."

Dorothy hung up the intercom and braced herself as the floor lurched beneath her. *He shouldn't call me baby,* she thought. *That's the one thing he shouldn't call me.*

■ ■ ■

The MiG settled into position off the right stern of the 757. The flight leader prepared to execute his orders from Lieutenant Zhou at Wan Chow. He was relieved orders had finally come, but he was curious about command's decision.

He regretted that he would never have the opportunity to ask Lieutenant Zhou about that.

"Do not fire missiles," the radio cracked in his ear. "Use cannons to knock out starboard engine and disable control systems. Repeat, do not fire missiles."

He felt a sense of relief as he centered the 757's outboard engine on the right side in his gun sight. He wasn't going to die for nothing after all.

■ ■ ■

Jack computed the distance to the border in his head and scanned Simpson's charts in search of an alternate landing site when he heard a series of clattering thumps like hail on a tin roof.

"What's that?" Beckman turned in his seat to look out the right window, in the direction of the noise.

Jack saw tracers in the dark sky again, arcing over his right wing like the first blasts had, but these weren't warning shots. His stomach knotted as he realized that this time the shooting was in dead earnest. As he looked past Beckman out the window, he felt the 757 shudder and yaw.

"They're shooting us, Jack!" Beckman stuttered, incredulous. "The reds are shooting us!"

■ ■ ■

Aboard the Shark, the sailor monitoring radio intercepts called out the news to Captain Maxwell and Lieutenant Stiles as a play-by-play, dispensing with written transcripts.

"MiG pilot reports target engaged."

"No!" Lieutenant Stiles grimaced. "Just like that Korean airliner. Target engaged."

"Pilot reports hits, heavy damage."

"Send a message to the Front Office, priority relay," Captain Maxwell ordered the sailor on the communications console. "MiG reports firing on Global 027, heavy damage. Gates, what's their position?"

CPO Gates, monitoring the over-the-horizon radar display, read off the longitude and latitude printed out on his screen.

"Include coordinates," Captain Maxwell instructed the communications tech. "Copy to carrier group. Advise them stand by for Front Office approval to launch search and rescue operations."

"In China?" the communications tech asked, looking up at the captain.

"They're close to the border. Let's see where they go in."

"MiG pilot reports target is going down, right wing on fire," the sailor working the radio intercepts called out. "He's following her down to confirm impact."

"Yeah," Captain Maxwell said, shaking his head in disgust. "A real pro."

Jack cursed as the 757 shuddered with the roar of an explosion somewhere behind him on the right side of his airplane. He felt her slew to the right, then bank sharply in that direction, almost pivoting around the mangled wing.

"We're hit. Jack, we're hit!" Beckman screamed.

"God help us," Jack muttered under his breath. "Grab the yoke, Dave. Reduce power to engine number three. Cut power to number four."

"We're on fire, Jack. Number four is burning. The wing's on fire."

"Cut number four! Reduce power to number three. And get hold of this yoke with me. We've got to level her out, get her nose up."

They were skidding into a steep downward spiral, the crippled right wing with its burning engine dragging them down toward the dark earth below. Seconds felt like hours as Jack and Beckman struggled to regain control. Finally, they were able to get her nose up and flatten out the spiral, but they were still in danger of losing her to a spin.

"Feels like we're losing hydraulics," Beckman reported. "Controls are mushy."

"Throttle up number three. See if she'll take a little more power without blowing. We have to play with the balance, left and right, see if we can use alternation to get some control, see if we can steer this thing that way."

The two men struggled the mortally wounded ship into an ugly parody of level, controlled flight. They had lost a lot of altitude, and Jack knew the mountains loomed around them. Steering her wouldn't be easy, but at least they had averted disaster...for the moment.

■ ■ ■

The interior walls of the passenger cabin shimmied and screeched while the 757 careened like a carnival ride gone mad. The plane rolled steeply to its right, causing the overhead bins on the left side of the cabin to fly open, releasing a blizzard of bags, blankets, and jackets. Seconds later, the bins slammed shut as the plane rolled back to her left just as steeply, and the overhead bins on the right side added their contents to the confusion in the cabin.

The passengers and flight attendants could all see the fireworks through the windows on the right. Sparks sizzled and popped along the trailing edge of the right wing as spewing fuel and hydraulic fluid swept over hot electrical junctions and wiring yokes severed by the MiG's cannon shells. Flames engulfed the outboard engine, fed by ruptured fuel cells and lines in the viscera of the shot-up wing.

The cabin rolled and dipped until the passengers were fighting just to stay in their seats. The oxygen masks dropped down but some of the passengers still found it hard to breathe in their panic. Many people were reaching for the airsickness bags, and many more didn't bother. All they could do was hang on for the ride. Couples like Senator Meyer and Helen clutched each other and held on. In coach, the young mother clutched her children tightly, repeating, "Shh, it's okay. We'll be all right." Most of the passengers faced the nightmare alone.

Although some were separated from their neighbors by less than an arm's length away, they were unable or unwilling to reach out across that chasm.

The flight attendants had the worst of it, scrambling to buckle themselves into an available seat. Dorothy braced herself against the forward bulkhead in first class and struggled to read off instructions from the manual over the PA system. Hopeless at first, she began to sense a pattern to the plane's gyrations.

Nose up for a few seconds, then down. Still too much rolling, and the awkward scary skidding never stopped, but there was some pattern to it at least. She knew the pilots were fighting for control of the ship.

In ten years of flying for Global, Dorothy had never had occasion to read the section of the manual on preparing for a crash landing aloud to passengers before. She had heard the words only in training exercises. She hardly recognized her voice over the PA system. It sounded mechanical, foreign, unreal. Everything seemed unreal. The flapping broken doors of the overhead bins, the gasps of passengers as the ship screeched and groaned, its struts and metal flesh strained beyond their limits.

When there was no more to say, Dorothy strapped herself in to her assigned jumpseat. She and the other attendants had done all they could.

■ ■ ■

The data reception center aboard the Shark was silent, the officers and men watching their screens and monitors and waiting. A few among them prayed. More cursed softly.

Captain Maxwell rubbed his chin thoughtfully and shook his head. Lieutenant Stiles double-checked to make sure their messages had gone out to the Front Office. He knew search and rescue would be ready to launch within minutes, waiting only for Front Office approval to come. If it came.

The crew of the Shark shot quick glances back and forth at each other. A sense of failure hung in the air. Their job had always been primarily to listen and report, but now every man in the ship wanted to do something, anything. And all they could do was listen, wait, and see what happened.

"Can they make it?" Maxwell asked Stiles. "I mean, is there any way the airplane can stay in the air?"

Lieutenant Stiles shook his head. "Not for long."

■ ■ ■

At the Wan Chow radar station, Lieutenant Zhou and Yong watched their antiquated radar screen as the two blips separated, the flight leader's MiG circling as the intruder spiraled down, displaying an erratic circle on the screen. The 757 was still in the air, but they had heard no more from the flight leader.

Lieutenant Zhou picked up the phone and punched the button for the air control tower at the base down the hill.

"Contact flight leader," he whispered hoarsely into the phone. "Advise him I demand a full report."

■ ■ ■

In his window seat, his head bowed and his eyes closed, Bishop Forbes recognized the same old struggle resurfacing and interrupting his prayers. He was still able to say the words, his lips moving nimbly and his voice reciting them in a smooth baritone. Each piece he chose from the Book of Common Prayer warmed and reassured him with its absolute and uncanny rightness for even this occasion. The words comforted him as they always did.

"The Lord Almighty grant us a peaceful night and a perfect end. Amen. Our help is in the Name of the Lord; the Maker of heaven and earth. Almighty God, our heavenly Father," the bishop's lips moved, but the roar of the airplane swallowed his words. "We have sinned against You through our own fault, in thought, word, and deed, and in what we have left undone." He stopped and caught his breath. "For the sake of Your Son our Lord Jesus Christ, forgive us all our offenses and grant that we may serve you in newness of life." He thought for a moment about what he'd just said.

A peaceful night, a perfect end, newness of life, he mused. *What might such things look like right now? Oh Lord, give all of us this newness. And let everything work toward Your perfect end.*

Forbes took another deep breath. He suddenly felt a lightening in his spirit. He knew that he was ready in this moment, but he truly didn't want to die. He'd spent his whole life trying to make amends for causing the death of that boy so long ago. He always felt he could do more, something, anything. Why was he allowed to live, unless it was so he could forfeit his life to make up for the life he took? But, he abruptly realized, the truth was that the issue was actually settled. He'd spent years trying to do a million little deeds that might add up to sufficient repayment of the boy's death. But the whole time, the matter had been settled, finished, done. From somewhere deep within his soul, Tony Forbes knew that he could never pay the price, make the ransom, settle the debt, complete the score. Yet the Lord no longer held that death against Forbes' account. Christ had paid the price for Tony's sin on the cross. The bishop felt a deep and divine sense that he had been forgiven.

But he knew something was still wrong. He thought for a moment and then knew his enemy was still hanging on, hiding in some dark corner of his mind. He had always struggled with this problem. Intellectually the bishop knew that God had forgiven him, but emotionally he couldn't forgive himself. He had to let go of what God had already released. He could never experience the wonderful warmth of divine forgiveness if he didn't.

■ ■ ■

Dorothy wanted to make her way back to coach. She wanted to be with the young mother and her two beautiful children, but she was forced to admit there was no way she could make it that far. Her nausea finally got the best of her. Grabbing an airsickness bag from the seat pouch, she tried not to call attention to herself, turning to shield herself from the passengers as she retched into the bag.

They'll think I'm afraid, she thought. *I have to be strong for the passengers, but I can't help it.*

Dorothy shut the bag tightly and leaned back in the seat. *Maybe, we're not going to survive this flight,* she thought. *It would be easier that way. I've got this child inside me and I don't have any idea what to do. I know what Jack's plans are if we get this plane down in India.* She silently shook her head. *No, a crash might be the simplest and best way to end everything.*

Dorothy closed her eyes and felt the darkness settle over her like a great blanket shrouding her in an endless night.

■ ■ ■

Bishop Forbes watched Dorothy lean over and use the airsickness bag. For several moments he watched her struggle to regain her composure. The bishop had flown for decades and never seen flight personnel get sick. Although, he had to admit, this was certainly a time when all the training in the world wouldn't help.

Forbes studied the young woman. She was no longer retching, but she continued to stroke her stomach with a worried expression on her face. He couldn't be sure, but the cause of her sudden illness seemed clear.

"Poor woman," he said under his breath. "God help her."

Through the years, the bishop had worked with many people facing all kinds of problems. Knowing he was far from perfect, he tried never to judge, always to help. People's problems were his business. He had a knack—or maybe it was something more divine—for identifying what was needed without being told. Forbes had always been a natural at his work.

He had worked hard when he went to the seminary. Feeling sensitive about his time in prison and his crime, he worked harder than his fellow students to prove himself. He was a topnotch scholar, yet the world of academics didn't concern Forbes as much as working with people. He wanted to reach out and bring comfort to the hurting. The work of a minister fit him perfectly.

The bishop knew that it wasn't physically possible for him to get up and offer the flight attendant his assistance right now, but he still wanted to help. He finally turned away and looked out the window. The world was filled with so much heartache.

As the 757 pitched and yawed, the airplane's joints popped and the floor shuddered beneath his feet. Tony Forbes tried to put the woman's problem in proper prospective against the backdrop of what everyone on the airplane faced. The entire airplane was in deep trouble. Nevertheless, he continued to pray for the woman—and the child she was carrying.

■ ■ ■

The flight leader snorted in disgust when Wan Chow air control told him Lieutenant Zhou wanted a report.

"The intruder is doomed," he spat into the microphone. He knew that odds were he was going down as well. Knowing that made him unconcerned with how his report would be received back at Wan Chow. "She's going down. When you use only cannons, it takes a bit longer."

The fighter pilot maintained his broad circle at altitude, keeping the crippled 757 in sight off his dipped left wing as it spiraled toward the mountains below.

He watched as the 757 struggled like a great wounded bird and imagined what it must be like in her cockpit, the doomed crew trying everything they could think of to save her. Even if they were CIA warmongers posing as a civilian transport for their own evil purposes, they were pilots, too. Just like him.

"Good luck," he whispered, with grudging respect for the Americans as he watched them finally fight their ship out of its death spiral.

The fighter pilot planned to maintain altitude to give himself as much of a glide pattern as possible when his fuel was gone, but he would watch the intruder as long as he could, then see what fate had in store for him.

"Good luck to us all," he muttered.

Helen clutched Senator Meyer's arm fiercely and struggled to swallow the scream rising in her throat. She was afraid to close her eyes but unable to bring herself to raise them either. She focused on the senator's chest, the monogram on the pocket of his immaculate white dress shirt, rising and falling with his breathing.

"Hang on, Helen," he whispered, his voice as steady as the rhythm of his breathing. "We're going to be all right. These 757s are built to take it."

"I don't think so," she quipped, the breathless croak of her voice belying her bravado.

Meyer patted her white-knuckled hand with his and smiled down at her.

"We're going to be all right, Helen. Hang on," he repeated.

Helen tried to pull herself together. But she knew that even if they lived through this ordeal, she wasn't going to be all right—hadn't been all right for a long time. In fact, she had wandered so far from all right, following her husband into self-destructive foolishness aimed at extinguishing the pain of their past, that she found herself strangely ambivalent about the outcome of Flight 027's terror.

It's an awful way to die, she thought. *But maybe it's just as well.*

■ ■ ■

Senator Meyer was grateful for Helen. He focused all his energy on the death grip she had on his arm and the look in her eyes when he tried to reassure her. It was obvious what she needed from him.

Decades of deal-making compromises, situational ethics, and pure old politics had left him with little sense of himself. He only knew who to be and what to do by reading others' expectations. Meyer was capable of being almost anybody and doing almost anything, but without an audience to cue him, even an audience of one, he was at a loss.

He patted Helen's hand again and gave her one of his charm-school campaign smiles, glad to see himself in her upturned eyes.

The senator couldn't let himself believe that they might truly crash. The thought that he might die terrified him beyond any capacity of response. He had to force his mind elsewhere, anywhere but on the idea that his life might end in a flash. To keep himself from facing the stark reality rushing toward him, Meyer started to think how he might manipulate the press and turn this situation into a public relations gain for himself.

I could make myself into the hero, the one who pulled things together, he thought. *If I can get myself in the place where I seem to be at the controls, then I'll appear to have turned a disaster around. What great publicity! I'll appear to be everything I want the voters to think that I am.*

■ ■ ■

Odd, Mary Lee McMurray noted, *the tricks your mind plays with time.* She made mental notes about the circumstances of the plane crash. There was too much noise and mayhem in the cabin, too much erratic motion, for her to write anything down. Mary Lee thought about talking into her recorder, but didn't. It would be something for the searchers to find, a part of her left behind for the world to hear and understand who she had been and what she had thought in her last minutes. But Mary Lee didn't care about the world outside or what anyone thought of her after she was dead. She was her own little world, and beyond that nothing really mattered.

Mary Lee had grown up in a black ghetto in Detroit. Her neighborhood was poor, tough—a rough place to live. Mary Lee had lost her parents in an automobile accident and had been passed between her various aunts and uncles. She'd learned before age six that most people weren't to be trusted. The people in the next-door apartment would steal their groceries if they got the chance. Convinced most people were liars, she had learned that she couldn't depend on anyone but herself and doubted most of what she heard. Her cynicism had proven to be an asset when Mary Lee ended up going to college for journalism. Her natural inclination to doubt made her a fierce writer, always going for the extra edge and the hidden truth no one else reported.

When she finally landed a job at the *Chicago Tribune,* Mary Lee quickly moved ahead of many of the other reporters. She took risks to go after the big story and was soon on the inside track. Her reputation had gotten her the special assignment following Senator Meyer to China.

Details were all that mattered to her, the concrete data that could be captured and confirmed. What was said and done. Who did what to whom. The consequences of her prying were unimportant to her unless they resulted in another story. Like insects trapped in amber, she captured her subjects for one moment in time on the slick pages of the magazines that bought her articles.

It occurred to her to lean over the seat in front of her and introduce herself to Senator George Meyer, tell him who she was and how she happened to be in the seat directly behind him in a first-class cabin that would be their tomb in a matter of minutes. However, she didn't do that either. Mary Lee continued to watch and listen, taking in the details as the final moments of Flight 027 passed.

■ ■ ■

Reese gripped the arms of his seat and turned to look at the praying bishop beside him. He cursed through his gritted teeth.

"Guess it was too much to ask," he muttered. "All I ever asked was to go quick."

Reese was a globe-trotter. As a marketing man for one of the world's biggest tobacco companies, Reese flew more miles each year than some professional pilots. It was a long way from the Carolina tobacco fields and hard times he had grown up in, and he had done all right by himself. By anybody's measure, he was a rich man, and the first in a long line of his people who could ever say that.

For generations back, they had been the kind who worked other people's land and filled the ranks of infantry platoons when there was dying to be done.

"Fertilizer and cannon fodder," he had heard his granddaddy say when word came that his father wouldn't be coming back from Korea. "That's all po' folks is good fer."

Flying as often as he did, Reese had always known he was bucking the odds. He had known this day might come.

A gambler at heart, he was willing to take his chances. All he had ever asked was that the end would be quick when it came. He had read with horror about a Japanese airliner that lost part of its tail and stayed in the air for half an hour or more, the passengers and crew all knowing they were doomed, before it finally flew into a mountain.

That's about the worst it could be, Reese had thought. *My worst nightmare. And it's coming true. That's what I get for praying,* he told himself.

■ ■ ■

Jack Harris and Dave Beckman would have sworn in any court they had been fighting for control of their ship for hours before they were finally able to bring her around to the southwesterly heading they hoped would get them to the abandoned airstrip Beckman had spotted on the charts. By the clock, it had been just less than three minutes.

They could deal with the loss of an engine, but that was the least of their problems. The MiG's cannon fire had riddled their right wing. Jack didn't know exactly how much damage it had done to control surfaces and power systems, not to mention the loss of fuel.

The 757 was built to take a lot of punishment, the kind of stress loads wind shears and storms can throw at a plane, and even one-in-a-million shots like lightning strikes or massive system failures. She was tough beyond her specs and blessed with redundancies. Still, no one can engineer for 20-millimeter cannon shells.

Working the airplane's nose up and down by sheer force on the yoke while the controls grew more sluggish and unresponsive from the ship bleeding out her hydraulic fluid, Jack had been able to compensate to some extent for the damage and slow their descent. If they weren't actually flying now, at least they weren't still falling out of the sky. They were winning the battle, for the time being. Using the throttles to shift power and thrust among the remaining three engines, they were able to herd the big ship in a sloppy zigzag along a rough course they hoped would bring them within range of the only chance they had left to save any of their passengers—the abandoned airstrip in the mountains. It would be a tricky approach under the best circumstances, too short for comfort, and easy to miss as darkness and weather closed in over them. All in all, the airstrip wasn't much of a chance, but it was all they had now.

On the plus side of things, the fire suppression system had survived the attack and seemed to be having some effect. Engine number four was no longer ablaze, partly because the fuel had already bled out. Number three was damaged but still responding to the throttles. If they lost number three, it was all over. If it held up, they might get a shot at setting the big plane down.

If the wing doesn't fall off altogether, Jack thought, *landing is a possibility.* He didn't say the words for fear of making them come true.

Navigator Matt Simpson repeated their Mayday again and again. He was relying more on their locator transponders, radar fixes from any other aircraft close enough to have them on screen, or GPS satellite monitoring to give their position than anything he had been able to say over their radio. They couldn't be sure their radio was still working anyway, since they were no longer able to receive Calcutta air traffic control or anybody else. It was all the two pilots could do to wrestle the yoke and grapple with the throttles, never mind barking out their changing coordinates to Matt.

Jack hadn't begun to worry about search and rescue yet. After twenty years of flying and dealing with the kinds of crises that every veteran pilot is faced with from time to time, the seconds of panic that punctuate the hours of routine, he had disciplined himself to rank emergencies and deal with them in order. Search and rescue would be important later, but for the moment, he made himself focus on setting his ship down without killing everybody on board. There would be time enough for all the other crises once he got that far.

In a cubbyhole in the back of his focused and compartmentalized mind, Jack couldn't help thinking about the layover in Delhi, Dorothy Chandler, and the plans they had made. The plans *he* had made, he corrected himself. His plans for the layover didn't seem so important now. He fought the controls and watched the altimeter dial down the margin between him and the rugged mountains in the darkness below.

■ ■ ■

High above Flight 027, the MiG flight leader made his final report to Wan Chow airbase.

"The intruder is bearing southwest, trailing smoke and losing altitude fast. She's in the mountains, and weather is closing in. Low clouds and blowing snow down there. It's getting dark."

He listened with a wry smile beneath his oxygen mask as his engine sputtered and died, leaving him in an eerie silence broken only by the wind whistling over his wings as he began to lose speed.

"That's it," he informed Wan Chow air control. "My fuel is gone. Request you notify our comrades at district."

There was no answer, only the wind.

"Hello, Wan Chow," he said. "Do you read me?"

"Acknowledge you are out of fuel. Will notify district and request search aircraft."

The flight leader sighed. It was all he had expected, but he couldn't help but hope for at least a chance at survival. District command's search planes were almost as old as his Korean War MiG and their all-weather capabilities less than awe-inspiring.

As the nose of his MiG dipped below the horizon that was blurring into the darkening sky, the flight leader looked off his wing to the north at the clouds rumbling in over the mountains below him.

The storm is coming, he thought. *And I am already in it.*

11

"Where are we, Matt?" Jack Harris asked the navigator, his voice flat and calm. "How far out?"

"Educated guess, about twenty miles from the strip."

"Over the border, you think?"

"Probably. In Bhutan, near as I can tell."

"That's good."

"According to the chart, it's disputed territory, Jack. That means..."

"It doesn't matter," Jack cut him off. "It's all we've got."

The sun was gone below the mountain peaks on the horizon ahead and off to his right, casting what little Jack could see of the terrain below in deep shadowy relief. Another minus, he thought. That'll make it even tougher to eyeball a landing.

Snow whipped past the cockpit windshield, blowing hard diagonally. It was a race to make the landing strip ahead of the weather and all-out darkness, and Jack knew they would only get one chance at it.

Fuel had been a problem before the MiG shot up the wing. Now the issue was critical.

Beckman eyed the vertical acceleration indicators, looked out the window for identifiable landmarks, then checked his charts for the thousandth time.

Jack punched up the intercom and felt his stomach tighten when Dorothy answered.

"Get the passengers ready," he told her. "We'll be setting her down in a couple of minutes, and it's going to be rough."

"We're landing? Where?"

"No time to explain, baby. We're on final approach." *In more ways than one,* Jack thought as he clicked off the intercom. He cocked his head toward his copilot. "Give me the altimeter readout."

"I'm reading two niner six zero," Beckman said. "Hang on."

■ ■ ■

Reese looked up when he heard Dorothy's voice echoing through the first-class cabin. *She is a brave woman,* he thought, *risking herself to give us instructions. One way or another, it'll be over soon.*

The bishop turned his attention to his seat companion and put his hand on Reese's arm. "May I say something?" he inquired. Reese turned to the heavyset man in the purple shirt and saw the cross in his fist.

"What did you say, bishop?"

"Make your peace with God, Mr. Reese. I feel obliged to urge you, for the sake of your mortal soul."

Reese nodded with a tight smile, "Reckon I'll play it out like I always have. I don't think that changing now would make any difference."

Bishop Forbes looked at the wiry little man decked out in his Italian suit to look like the master of the universe. "It always makes a difference," the bishop said.

"Humph," Reese snorted.

Forbes leaned closer. "It's never too late," the bishop said in the man's ear. "Did you ever hear the story of the Prodigal

Son? The father standing out on the road waiting for his son to come home?" Forbes spoke louder. "The Father is always *waiting*. Standing there...with His arms open...for us. Mr. Reese, the Father is waiting for you to come home."

■ ■ ■

Senator Meyer pressed the pillow into Helen's lap and tugged her hands free of his arm.

"Put your head on the pillow, Helen. It's the best thing to do."

"Hold me," she whispered. He leaned closer, unable to make out what she had said, and she repeated herself, a little louder. "Hold me."

"I will," he promised.

She leaned forward and pressed her face against the pillow, welcoming the weight of his arm across her shoulders. He was in position, too, both of them braced for impact. "God help us," she moaned. "Please don't let us die, crashing into these terrible mountains."

■ ■ ■

Mary Lee couldn't make out what the flight attendant was saying with all the noise, the engines revving and changing pitch then roaring again, the overhead bins flapping, and the body of the plane groaning. Someone in coach was wailing. She could hear children crying.

Mary Lee knew what to do, and she saw the passengers on the other side of the cabin following the procedure. Pillow on your lap, head between your knees, and brace yourself. The posture was to prevent whiplash, or worse, a broken neck.

■ ■ ■

Dorothy switched off the PA system and made her way back to her seat. She buckled herself in and looked out the window on her left. They screamed past a mountainside, the left wingtip so close that she expected the impact and braced herself for a hard tumbling spin that would be the end of everything. When the crash didn't happen, she made herself look out the window again. At the speed they were going, she could barely distinguish the mountainous terrain. Rocks and boulders blended together with the gnarled little trees perched between them on the harsh slopes.

We're coming in too fast, she thought. *It's almost over.*

She set the pillow between her knees but she did not lean forward and assume the proper position. Instead, she sat upright in her seat and looked down at her body. She put her hands on her stomach and probed gently with her fingers, searching for what she knew was still too small to be found.

"I'm sorry," she whispered, tears welling in her eyes. "I'm sorry, little baby."

Dorothy took a deep breath and began praying. "Oh, Lord, we don't want to die. *I* don't want to die. You're the only one who can save us from this terrible situation. Maybe we can't avoid crashing, but You can keep us from being destroyed." She took another deep breath. "I don't know what the right thing to do about this life inside me is, but I promise that if I live through this crash, I'll do whatever You want. Whatever You show me, I will make sure it happens. God, if I live, I make this solemn promise."

Dorothy looked around and glanced across first class at the people bent over to protect themselves. "God, please help us," she prayed. "Amen."

■ ■ ■

"The weather is getting worse fast," Jack said. "It's moving in quickly and chasing us."

"The wind's blowing off these mountains already, Jack. Wind shear's a given."

"Altimeter," Jack requested.

"Two seven five zero."

"We're wobbling all over the place. We have to get her trimmed out a little better." Jack adjusted the throttles. "We're only going to get one shot at this. I don't suppose there are any beacons?"

"Chart doesn't show any, and I'm not picking up anything."

"Any markers?"

"The place is abandoned, Jack. Since I don't know when." Beckman scanned the mountains below on his side of the ship. "I don't see anything."

"We're good, though, by GPS?"

Simpson checked the navigational readouts and the chart again.

"We're as good as we can be, Jack."

"From these numbers, the glide slope looks good," his copilot added. "We ought to be closing on it. It should pop up any minute but it's pretty much guesswork." Beckman looked across the cockpit at him. "I'm doing the best I can."

"You're doing fine, Dave." Jack looked at him and nodded. "Just keep your eyes peeled. We can't afford a flyby."

"I'd pray if I thought it would help."

Try it, Jack thought.

"Okay, Dave, you've got ignition, radar standby. Auto shutoff armed?"

"Check."

"Waiting on the gear. Got the spoilers?"

Beckman armed the spoilers, and they both heard the system click through its sequence and saw the position confirmation lights pop on. So far, so good.

"Flaps twenty-five degrees."

"Flaps are skewed, Jack."

"Give me what you can. We're coming in hot."

The airplane glided among the mountain peaks now, and Jack hoped Beckman was right about the numbers this time. If not, there'd be no time to react, just a mountainside, coming up fast.

"Correct to heading three two zero, Jack."

"Three two zero."

Beckman took the yoke as Jack worked the throttles, bringing the nose of the 757 around to the new heading. The maneuver was rough, and the plane responded sloppily, but she came around.

A downdraft like the hand of God slapped the big plane hard and both pilots swore in a reflexive explosion of breath before a corresponding updraft tossed them back up and left them drifting off their heading, yawing and slipping crablike between the mountains on either side.

Jack throttled back on the left engines and bumped up number three to correct as Beckman wrestled the yoke to get her back on what they hoped was the proper glide slope.

"We're still too hot," Beckman warned. "Coming in too fast."

"If I cut her any more, we'll stall."

Jack put his hands on the yoke and peered through the darkness ahead.

"I'll take her, Dave. Stand by."

"She's all yours."

"Talk to me, Dave."

"Five miles out, seven hundred feet above, on glide path."

"Come on, baby. We're almost there," Jack cooed to the big ship. "Gear down," he instructed.

"Gearing down," Beckman answered, holding up his left hand with his fingers crossed. The plane's hydraulics were shot, and there wasn't enough time to crank the gear down manually. It was all both of them could do to keep the ship in the air and on course.

"Lord love redundancy," Jack groaned as they heard the backup system kick in and the landing gear rumble down into position and lock in place with a reassuring clunk. The position confirmation lights popped on. "Thank God," he gasped.

Beckman shook his head then went back to his altimeter readouts. "Two miles out, two hundred above, on glide.... There it is!"

Jack saw it, too, and his heart sank. The landing strip was coming up too fast, and there wasn't nearly enough of it.

"Too high and fast," Beckman warned. "We're going to overshoot."

"No we aren't!" Jack spat. "Hang on."

He cut the throttles and shoved the plane's nose down toward the surface of the landing strip rushing up at them. As bad as the strip itself looked, what awaited them at the other end if they went long would only be worse. There was no way they could ever turn the crippled plane around for another try without flying into one of the mountains that towered above them on all sides.

"Hang on, Dave. We're going in."

12

"Yank it! Yank it!"

Jack screamed at Beckman as they both pulled back on the yokes with everything they had, dragging the 757's nose up as the rough and pitted surface of the landing strip rushed up at them. They hit hard, the landing gear hammering into the ground with a shudder that reverberated through the airframe, jarring everyone on board from the cockpit back to the last seat in coach.

Jack heard the muffled screams of his passengers in the cabin behind him as he felt the plane's weight drive down on the gear so hard that the belly of the plane scraped and groaned like a wounded beast. The 757 hit hard enough to bounce, but Jack drove the nose down to get the gear back on the ground, and he felt the tires hit with a shriek and rumble.

"Brakes!"

Beckman hit the brakes as hard as he could as Jack reversed all three engines to slow the careening plane. Unfortunately, the imbalance of power between the two fully operating engines on the left and the overtaxed engine number three on the right required a coordinated touch on the reverse thrusters that was too much to expect under the circumstances.

Cut power to number one, Jack told himself, *reverse two and three, the two inboard engines. That's our best bet to keep her straight until you can get her stopped.*

Jack knew he had to do everything he could to get the airplane stopped before they skidded off the far end of the runway. Getting her stopped was the main thing, everything.

Jack reversed all three engines and felt his weight thrown against the straps of his harness. Out the window to his left, Jack caught a glimpse of a rocky slope scudding by and the silhouette of two ramshackle buildings. *A terminal,* he thought.

Beckman cursed and mumbled as the big ship veered to the left, the imbalance of her reversed engines turning her toward the darkened hulks of more buildings alongside the landing strip.

"Brakes!" Jack barked, reaching to throttle down engines one and two in a desperate bid to correct their heading and bring the ship back on line.

"I'm on them!" Beckman snapped.

"We're gonna hit!"

"I can't do any more!"

Jack saw the left wingtip reaching out toward the nearest building, a square frame hut much too close to the edge of the landing strip. Without hazarding a glance at the instrument panel, he guessed their speed at somewhere near 180 mph. Much too fast.

In the instant before the wingtip clipped the shack, something caught his eye. Jack knew more trouble was coming—the pitted and scarred surface of the abandoned runway crumbled away into blackness in front of them, in a crater the size of a compact car. It was big enough to do serious damage to the 757, but there was nothing they could do now but hold on.

■ ■ ■

Dorothy sat up with the first impact of the landing gear and then winced at the sickening grind of the plane's belly as it hit the ground and scraped along it before caroming back into the air. She braced herself for the crunch as the airplane came down hard again.

Out the window, she saw a shadowy shape in the gathering darkness. A building of some kind. Then she heard the roar of the engines reversing, and her body was thrown forward, the seatbelt biting into her waist. She heard the brakes screeching beneath her as the plane's tires rumbled and bounced over the rough surface.

"Stop," she prayed quietly. "Please, God, get her stopped." Dorothy had no idea where they were, but she knew they were in trouble. She could see no lights of any kind through the window and had never experienced a landing so rough and desperate. "Help us," she cried.

When Dorothy looked out her window again, hoping to see the pulsing strobes of fire trucks and ambulances or at least the lights of an operations building, all she saw was the explosion of a small frame shed as their left wingtip sliced through it, then a ball of fire and shower of splintered wood and hurtling sheet iron from the little building's roof.

The fireball on the left wing blinded her and she threw her hands up over her face just as a maelstrom of shards hit the heavy Plexiglas window. She heard the wing buckling and the scream of the number one engine as it twisted in its mountings.

Screams rang out the length of the cabin as the plane began a hard spin to its left.

■ ■ ■

Jack reached for the throttles to cut all power to the number one engine as he watched the crater in the runway disappear underneath him, his airplane screaming down the runway sideways, turned hard to the left by the impact of the left wing with the building. There was only time to take a deep breath before he felt the landing gear drop into the big hole, and then the thunderous crash as he felt his airplane slam down, the fuselage rolling over on its right side as the damaged right wing sheared off inboard of the number three engine.

He thought they might roll over all the way, but they didn't. The stub of the right wing dug into the runway and the plane listed hard to the right but didn't turn over. The noise was deafening, like the death throes of a great beast, as the landing gear sheared off in the crater and the left wing buckled and slammed back against the fuselage, dumping whatever fuel remained in the cells inside the wing along the left side of the fuselage. The impact was too much for the 757, and she began to break up.

The forward third of the airplane, the cockpit and most of the first-class passenger cabin, skidded down the runway on its belly as the rest of the plane was severed free in a sickening groan of twisted struts and tearing sheet metal. The big ship screamed as the 757 dismembered, the mayhem of tearing steel drowning out the panicked cries of her passengers.

Dorothy heard metal rip apart and felt the plane's skeleton failing around her. She looked up in horror at a jagged wound opening in the ceiling above her. Dorothy turned in her seat and looked behind her. Aghast, she watched the rear section fall away, tumbling off to the right side of the runway as the front section shot forward.

The left wing, its engines still spewing fire, curled up and collapsed over the aft section in a bath of jet fuel. The airplane shook violently again.

Dorothy opened her mouth to scream, but no sound came out. Mute, she watched the sparks of metal grinding along the runway at the open mouth of the aft section. Then the aft passenger compartment disappeared in a stream of fire. She could see the doomed passengers waving frantically before they were engulfed by the flaming holocaust.

■ ■ ■

The forward third of Global 027 skittered down the too-short runway on its right side, with the stub of the wing working like a boat's rudder to keep them from tumbling. Jack Harris sat stunned, helpless, the useless controls in his hands, and watched what was left of the runway rush past beneath him. There was nothing to do now but watch it happen. What was at the end of the runway? Surely not more buildings? More likely a sheer drop off the side of the mountain. Then Jack noticed a berm beyond the runway, the tops of some trees visible beyond the high dirt bank.

"Hang on! We're going over."

■ ■ ■

"That's it. They have to be down by now!" the Shark's radio operator shouted.

The data reception center of the small boat was crowded with sailors. The relief watch had reported for duty, but none of the men wanted to go to the galley for chow.

"Nail down the position, Gates," Lieutenant Stiles called out to his radar operator. "As tight as you can."

"Aye, aye, sir."

Gates read off the coordinates. The sailor at the console punched them in on his keyboard, ready to transmit.

"Rough country," Captain Maxwell grumbled, tracing his fingers over the map of the Chinese border area to find the spot. "Too mountainous for a successful crash landing."

"What's that?" Lieutenant Stiles asked, pointing at a symbol cut into a closely drawn series of lines symbolizing ten-meter increments of elevation in a narrow valley between two high ridges.

"Pei Song. Old airbase, been abandoned for years. That's what they were trying for."

"Whose is it?"

"Good question. That whole area's in dispute. The Chinese claim it from way back. Bhutan's Dragon King says the place is his, and India backs Bhutan like a kid brother."

"The Dragon King?"

"Yeah." Captain Maxwell looked up from the map at Lieutenant Stiles. "Hereditary royalty. It's one of the poorest places in the world, but they've got tradition."

"Talk about the boonies."

"They traded with Tibet until China took over and closed the border. There's no love lost between Bhutan and China."

"Do you think they'll okay search and rescue?"

"Maybe. It's a complicated part of the world, Stiles."

"We could go in now, get permission later."

"That's up to the Front Office. Probably a moot point anyway."

"How's that, Captain?"

"Send it to the Front Office, Sparks, priority relay, copy to the carrier group." Captain Maxwell gave the order to the sailor on the communications console, calling it out over Lieutenant Stiles's shoulder. Then he looked Stiles in the eye and shook his head. "Stiles, it's moot because there aren't going to be any survivors, without some kind of miracle."

■ ■ ■

At the Wan Chow radar station, Yong studied his radar screen carefully. The intruder was gone, lost some time ago amid the mountain peaks near the bottom of the screen, and he had dutifully reported this fact to Lieutenant Zhou. He had reported the coordinates of the American's last position, as well, although both men knew this was only an estimate, given the limitations of Wan Chow's radar equipment.

Now Yong stared at his screen, although there was nothing to see there except the blip that was the flight leader turning back from the mountains. He appeared to be losing altitude fast, but that had been reported, too. Wan Chow air control had relayed to district the flight leader's message that he was out of fuel and requested search planes be sent. District had also been notified of the storm front moving in.

As yet, Yong had heard no radio traffic on the squawk box that would suggest search planes had been sent out from district command to pick up the flight leader. But all those things were of little concern to Yong. They were matters for Lieutenant Zhou and district command. Yong's task was done.

They had accomplished their mission, and Yong was happy when he heard the flight leader report the intruder was going down in the mountains. Lieutenant Zhou had chastised him for his smile and his shout of victory.

"You have no idea what's happening here," Zhou had chided him.

Now Lieutenant Zhou stood at the window, the telephone to his ear. The middle button was lit, a call from district.

"Yes, sir," Lieutenant Zhou had said when he answered the call from district. The colonel had finally called.

Yong kept his eyes on his radar screen because he could tell Lieutenant Zhou was agitated, and he did not want to provoke him by staring.

"Yes, Colonel, I am sure of it. The intruder went down in the mountains.... No, the flight leader was not able to confirm impact because of the storm front moving in. Also, he was running out of fuel.... Yes, a brave sacrifice. But he reported..." A long pause, then, "Yes, Colonel."

Lieutenant Zhou lowered the telephone gingerly into its cradle, then spat a curse. Yong did not look up.

"We are to remain at our posts and await further word from the district colonel," Lieutenant Zhou announced, his voice soft and oddly strained. "We are not to leave this building for any reason, and we are not to contact anyone. Do you understand?"

Yong looked up at his lieutenant and nodded. He fought back an impulse to smile again. He couldn't help it. They were heroes of the people now.

At last, Yong had been given an opportunity, and he had risen to the challenge. Surely there would be a new posting in this for him, a better place with newer equipment and more comfortable quarters. He had dreamed of this moment since leaving his village to join the People's Army. In spite of himself, a smile creased his face.

"What are you grinning at, you fool?" Zhou demanded angrily.

"We stopped the spies, Lieutenant. We have done a great service...."

"We are part of an international incident."

"But..."

"If there's any glory in it, we'll be lucky if we're mentioned in the reports. If there's blame..."

Lieutenant Zhou did not finish. Instead, he frowned at Yong and moved away toward the window. He clasped his fists behind his back, and Yong watched Zhou's knuckles whiten.

Confused, Yong turned back to his radar screen and watched the blip that was the flight leader disappear. He noted the ragged, amorphous line of the storm front moving down the screen toward his last position. The squawk box was silent. Yong's radar screen still showed no sign of search planes being sent from district command to look for the downed flight leader.

13

Dorothy regained consciousness in a cold, smoky darkness filled with eerie stillness. For the first time in what seemed like days, there was no sense of motion. They were down at last, on the ground. Somewhere. Fumbling to free herself from her seatbelt, she tried to look around her, but her vision was blurred, veiled. Her head swam in confusion.

When she got to her feet, Dorothy felt the canted angle of the floor and a sharp pain in her forehead. She reeled and fell in a heap, sliding down the sloping floor to come to rest against a bulkhead. For a moment she struggled to catch her breath.

Awfully cold, she thought. *The wind is biting cold.*

She flexed her fingers and wiggled her toes. Her extremities seemed to be working, but she couldn't see clearly and felt a warm wetness on her face. She brought her hands cautiously to her cheeks and felt upward toward her forehead. Her fingers came away red and sticky. "I'm cut," she told herself. "But it doesn't feel too bad."

She untied the paisley scarf that was part of her uniform and rolled it to make a bandage. She gingerly felt her forehead to find the gash and laid the scarf across her wound, tying it snugly around her heard. *That's it,* she thought. *Keep pressure on it, stop the bleeding.* She rubbed her eyes and blinked away the wetness that remained. She was relieved to discover her vision clearing. *At least I can see.* Dorothy blinked hard. In front of her lay a horror.

From where she lay against what had been part of the forward bulkhead of the first-class passenger cabin, Dorothy looked at the gaping round hole of the truncated fuselage of the 757 where the coach section had been. There was nothing left. Just a dirt slope, and beyond that the swirling snow. In the distance, she could see the fire that marked the remains of the rest of their airplane. A shower of sparks spiraled up into the darkness as the swirl of snow came down.

There were no more screams from the coach section. Only silence.

■ ■ ■

Jack lay slack in his harness, his head lolled to one side within inches of the empty rectangle that had been part of his cockpit window. An icy wind whistled through the cramped and disfigured cockpit, whipping shards of icy rain mixed with snow in through the busted window.

Jack felt the cold and stirred, groaning without realizing the sound was coming from him. He thought it was Beckman making the noise, and looked to his right where Dave should have been.

Everything was wrong, twisted, and collapsed. The instrument panel in front of him was a shattered, crumpled perversion, and he found himself looking down from an impossible angle at what was left of the copilot's seat. As his eyes acclimated to the hazy darkness, he could make out a white shirt with epaulets, the shoulder of a man in the surreal jumble of steel and glass beneath him.

"Dave! Can you hear me?"

■ ■ ■

Reese stood up from his seat and balanced himself on what was left of the cantilevered floor of the first-class passenger cabin. He looked down at himself and rubbed his hands over his face, unbuttoned his double-breasted Armani jacket, and checked inside, feeling for what he was sure were broken ribs or gaping wounds. Nothing.

"I ain't believing this," he announced to the cold darkness and twisted steel. "Not a scratch on me. Not a freakin' scratch." The window seat beside him, Bishop Forbes' seat, was gone. A portion of the ceiling had collapsed, obscuring it, but there was enough of the flooring visible to see that the bishop's seat had been uprooted by the impact and thrown forward somewhere, out of sight beneath the fallen ceiling. Still in shock, Reese had yet to register the carnage around him when he heard noises from the seats directly behind his.

Helen sat still and quiet in her seat, her head resting in the pillow on her lap. Only when she felt Senator Meyer's arm leave her shoulders did she stir.

"Are you all right, Helen?" the senator mumbled.

"Of course," she answered in a flat voice. "Are you?" she asked faintly, almost as if she was disappearing.

"I think so," the senator answered. "I thought I was dead at first, but it was too cold."

"They shot us down," Reese said, as if he still couldn't believe it. "Look, y'all. Not a mark on me."

"You were lucky," someone said behind them.

The three of them turned at the sound of the voice and saw Dorothy making her way past them over the broken and twisted floor of the cabin, lugging a big white first-aid kit with a red cross on its side and carrying a flashlight. Her face was streaked with blood, and she had a scarf tied around her head where she had been cut.

Dorothy had managed to activate a couple of the emergency lights in the cabin, giving a dim, shadowy glow to the interior of the wreckage, in contrast to the darkness that had descended outside.

"There's another lucky one," Dorothy said and pointed beyond the broken seats.

Dorothy reached down behind Helen Bridwell's seat to offer a hand to Mary Lee, who was trying to crawl up out of a hole in the floor where her seat had been. Mary Lee was having trouble because her left arm was broken, the forearm turned at an impossible angle four inches above her wrist.

As Dorothy helped Mary Lee scramble up to sprawl in the buckled aisle, she looked past her, down into the hole in the floor. Mary Lee's seat was cocked at an odd angle, still bolted to the flooring, but what had been the aisle seat beside her hung by a shard of metal against the trunk of a tree.

Dorothy steadied the woman's broken arm and tore the sleeve of her sweater away from the break. Mary Lee said nothing, but just bit her lip to keep from crying out as Dorothy set the broken bones as well as she could. Then she dug a plastic air cast out of the first-aid kit. She worked it up over the broken arm and fired the cartridge to inflate the cast, immobilizing the arm.

"How's that?" Dorothy asked the woman, her baggy sweater black with grease and flecked with bits of insulation from the ruptured bulkhead.

"Better," she groaned, nodding her head. "Thanks."

Smoke filled the cabin, acrid fumes that made the frigid darkness even more oppressive and frightening. As the survivors took stock of the situation, they discovered the back half of the plane was missing. They stared in shock.

"Where's the rest of the plane?" Reese peered out into the darkness.

"Back there," Dorothy said, pointing through the black hole. "Still on the runway."

"We're not on the runway?" Helen asked.

"We went long, off the end of it," Dorothy answered. "Over some kind of ridge at the end."

"I don't hear any sirens." Helen cupped her ear.

"No."

"No fire trucks?"

"There aren't any."

"Ambulances?"

"No."

"Where are we then?" Helen asked. "What kind of airport doesn't have..."

"I'm not sure," Dorothy cut her off.

"You're not sure where we are?"

"No."

"Then ask the pilot."

"I haven't checked, Miss, but I'm pretty sure he's dead," Dorothy said, hoping she was wrong.

"Oh." The woman blinked uncomprehendingly. "I see."

"What's that fire back there?" Senator Meyer asked, climbing over Helen into the aisle. "Behind us?"

"Part of the plane," Dorothy said. "The back half got torn off."

"We have to get back there," Meyer offered, trying to push past Dorothy toward the open end of the fuselage. "See if we can help the survivors."

Dorothy stood up and blocked his path. She looked up into his face.

"There are no survivors, Senator."

"I beg your pardon?"

"There's nobody to save back there."

"They're all...?"

"The fire swept through. It's..." Dorothy stopped and swallowed hard. "None of them made it."

"You can't be sure."

"I'm sure we've got people here who need help." Dorothy pushed past.

Senator Meyer realized she was right. He looked around the cabin and noticed for the first time the bodies of his fellow first-class passengers, all buckled into their seats, not moving. The seats on the left side of the cabin weren't where they should have been. They were stacked and strewn in a jumbled mess where the left side of the plane had caved in on impact. He could finally hear them now, the pitiful moans and cries of the few who were still alive.

We're all in shock, he realized dimly, the awful magnitude of what had happened slowly sinking in.

Senator Meyer looked down at Dorothy, and he knew what she expected of him. *Right,* he thought. *Okay. This will still play in the media. Senator survives crash in clash with Chinese MiGs, rallies survivors, and heads rescue. Yes, that will play.*

Meyer knew what he had to do. There was work to be done.

■ ■ ■

Jack worked free of his seat harness and lowered himself carefully into the dark tangle that had been the right side of the cockpit. In the cold and hazy darkness, he focused on the only part of his copilot he could make out, the portion of his left shoulder protruding from underneath the back of his seat, the epaulet of Global Airlines stained with what might be blood. Jack shot a quick glance over his shoulder at the navigator. Matt Simpson lay on the floor with a long slender metal beam sticking through his neck. No need to look again. Jack instantly knew he was dead.

"Dave?"

There was no answer. Jack felt for solid footing to get down closer. He tried to make sense of what he was looking at, afraid his movement might make things worse for Beckman.

The copilot's seat was turned, facing downward toward the ground, and wedged between the buckled right bulkhead and a portion of the instrument panel and control console that had been twisted by the impact.

All Jack remembered after the landing gear hit the crater in the runway was the plane tipping over and skidding down the runway on its right side. Helpless, he had watched the end of the runway rushing at him, and then...the berm. He remembered the berm. The landing was coming back to him in bits and pieces. They ran out of runway and hit the berm and went airborne again.

Falling. He remembered falling, and looking down at treetops through a hole in the floor of the cockpit. The sound of trees snapping against the hull of the plane, the hull crumpling and making that awful noise. And then the windows exploded. That was the last thing, the windows.

His head cleared as the memories worked their way back. Jack inched his way closer to Beckman, until finally he could reach out and touch his copilot's exposed shoulder.

"Dave?"

■ ■ ■

Bishop Forbes first suspected he wasn't dead when he felt a dagger of sharp pain stab across his chest and slice down his left arm from the shoulder to the elbow.

Until that moment, he had accepted the ebbing and flowing consciousness of the inverted and tightly compressed darkness in which he found himself as some kind of transitional state from which he would momentarily awaken to face the all-seeing God, sitting in judgment. But now he knew it wasn't over. The clenched fist of angina in his chest was proof enough.

The Bishop blinked his eyes and opened them to darkness. He squinted at what he thought at first was a vision, a mysterious figure dressed in gold beckoning to him. As his vision cleared, the image came into focus and he recognized his pectoral cross dangling in front of his face on its chain.

Wherever he was, Forbes felt himself suspended upside down. He could feel the blood rushing down behind his eyes. Able to move only from his shoulders up, he finally realized that his arms were pinned at his sides, still grasping the arms of his seat. When he tried to call out, his voice cracked in his dry throat. He coughed and swallowed, and heard the noises he made reverberate off something solid only inches in front of his face. He had been thrown down into a very snug hole.

■ ■ ■

Dorothy hardly minded that Senator Meyer was being a fool, scrambling around the cabin and striking poses, barking out orders, and playing the hero as if he thought there were cameras taping it all for the evening news. Helen seemed impressed enough for both of them, as she slumped against the back of her seat and watched Meyer in action.

Dorothy watched Helen dig her cigarettes out of her purse and put one in her mouth. As she fumbled for her lighter, she looked up at Dorothy with a wry smile.

"I don't suppose there's any rule against smoking now, is there?"

"Actually, there is, Ms. Bridwell. This is a toxic environment, lots of flammables. There's a high risk of ignition."

"I beg your pardon?"

"You might start a fire," Dorothy snapped. "We have enough problems without *that.*"

"Oh." Helen looked at the cigarette as if she was not sure what to do with it.

Mary Lee struggled to help with the injured. She had sat cross-legged in the aisle for a minute to collect herself but finally got to her feet.

Shamed or shocked out of her inaction by the sight of the injured Mary Lee helping Dorothy with the casualties, Helen offered to lend a hand and struggled to her feet. Dorothy immediately put her to work collecting the things she knew they would need to make it through the night, food and beverages from what was left in the forward storage bins, blankets, and any coats or jackets she could find.

14

Dorothy was thankful there was so much to do. Keeping busy was the only way she knew to keep from going to pieces. There was a chance they were all going to die. But she couldn't stop thinking of the promise she'd made as she waited for the end. She had been unable to choke back the tears of shame and regret as she faced what she had been sure were her last minutes on earth and the problem that had consumed her for weeks.

Her baby.

Yet even trying to help her fellow passengers couldn't stop the thoughts swirling in her head. As she worked, she could not escape the change that facing death had wrought in her. She was riddled with shame that she had never thought of "it" as her baby before. "It" had been a mistake. When she was sure she was pregnant, she had told Jack. Her heart had sunk at his reaction, and "it" had become a crisis.

The baby was her fault. He hadn't said it in so many words, but it was there in Jack's eyes. She knew the rules. His rules. It was up to her to make sure there were no surprises. He had made that clear, right from the start of the affair.

Until Jack, safe sex was the rule. Dorothy couldn't afford to take chances. You never knew where people had been.

But Jack was different. *They* were different, at least as far as she was concerned. When he balked at using a "safe" after their first couple of times together, she relented. She trusted him. She had fallen in love with him.

So, "it" had been her mistake, her problem, her crisis.

But Jack had the answer. He knew a doctor in Delhi, an Englishman with a good reputation. A top-notch medical man, and discreet. Dorothy was still in her first trimester, so it would be quick and easy. A simple solution.

Dorothy had reservations, for sure, though not about "it." She certainly didn't want to undergo surgery, but she worried that the relationship wouldn't survive if she didn't do what Jack wanted. She realized her decision had been selfish.

Dorothy thought about the little life growing inside of her. As long as the baby was an "it," she didn't feel that bad about treating it as an inconvenience, but once she realized that she had...a boy...a girl...a *person* growing in her womb, everything changed. Dorothy saw for the first time that she was pondering the future existence of a human being.

Dorothy realized that she hadn't said much when Jack demanded she get the abortion. Until the plane crash, she had bought the argument that an unwanted baby was a medical problem with a corresponding solution. Dorothy knew that she couldn't say yes with the simplicity and ease that she had just a few hours ago.

Dorothy let her hand wander across her stomach and imagined it rounding and filling out. Life was forming within her. When she had faced her mortality, she hadn't wanted to die, hadn't wanted her baby to die without having the chance to live. If she had pleaded with God to spare the child, how could she heartlessly kill her baby?

God cares for this life growing in me, she thought. *Why else am I still alive? I don't have the right to extinguish it. Did God really answer my prayer? I have to keep the promise I made to Him. What does He want me to do? I know life is much larger than Jack or myself. God wouldn't have let me live without a reason. I can't ignore the possibility that His hand is here and on me.*

"What will Jack say when I tell him?" Dorothy mumbled under her breath. "He won't be happy."

Would Jack still love her? Would things ever be the same between them? Jack's suspiciously ready answer to the problem had given her pause. Had Jack done this kind of thing before, with women who had come before her? Had he used this same doctor before? Where were they now, distant memories scratched out of his little black book? Gone? Forgotten? Oh, God. What was she thinking? Jack! He was probably dead.

Dorothy felt a tear drip down her cheek. She had loved Jack, had convinced herself that Jack loved her. And now he was gone.

"Hey! Hey, back there!"

The voice from the front of the plane shook Dorothy out of her reverie, and she found herself kneeling with a bloody blanket in her hands beside a passenger who stared up at her with eyes that were fixed and dull, unseeing. The eyes of a dead man.

Dorothy laid the blanket over the passenger, covering him and his motionless eyes.

Somebody was alive in the front of the plane, a figure standing in a gaping hole where the cockpit door should have been. "Jack!" she gasped.

"Hey! I could use some help up here," the pilot said.

■ ■ ■

Senator Meyer was the first through the ragged hole in the bulkhead into what had been the cockpit, but Jack knew in a matter of seconds that Meyer was a bumbler, more apt to make things worse than to be of any help.

Reese came after Meyer, picking his way deliberately over the jumble and carnage. Jack liked the look of him better, a wiry little man who could handle himself.

Jack had managed to locate an emergency kit, and he had a flashlight he found inside. He handed it to Senator Meyer.

"Here, sir. Hold this."

Meyer nodded.

"I've got a man down here in a tight place," Jack told Reese. "Can you help me?"

"I'll see what I can do," Reese answered.

"Just ignore him," Jack whispered conspiratorially.

"Good idea, giving the senator that flashlight," Reese said and grinned knowingly. "Where's your man?"

"Down here."

Jack led Reese carefully down through the wreckage of the cockpit until they were positioned on either side of the copilot's upturned seat.

"Dave?" Jack called out.

Beckman answered with a guttural, wordless groan.

"Dave, I'm right here. We're going to get you out. Okay?"

Another groan. Jack and Reese went to work trying to get the copilot out. Behind and above them, the senator fiddled with the light and offered direction.

"Hang on," Reese said as he and Jack worked into the tight quarters at the bottom of the heap of twisted metal. "We're coming!"

Jack watched as Reese peeled off his fancy suit jacket and tossed it aside.

"There, that's better."

"Nice suit," Jack offered. "It'll be ruined."

"No big deal," Reese sniffed. "I've got a walk-in closet full of them back home."

Both men felt the numbing cold whistling into the wreckage from the north, and they were soon covered with a dusting of snow and ice. There was precious little room to maneuver, with even less margin for error.

Jack felt around for the release switches so they could free the seat of its tracks. As he reached down, he discovered that the floor the track should have been attached to was gone.

Searching blindly with his hands through shards of twisted and fractured metal in a cramped space, Jack couldn't help thinking that he might as well be reaching into murky water for all the good the senator was doing with that flashlight.

"Careful, men!" Senator Meyer called out from his perch behind and above them. "Watch your step there."

"Politicians," Jack muttered with a tight, sarcastic smile as he kept reaching with his hand. "They're only good for making speeches."

■ ■ ■

Dorothy's nostrils burned with the scent of electrical fires, singed material, and charred wiring. The stress of heat and impact had been too much for the plane, and the high-tech alloy struts that held the cabin together were exposed like fractured bones.

The fires had died out from the cold wind and lack of anything left to burn, but they left their lingering stench behind. The wind carried numbing cold, thick snow and icy rain into the cabin. Numbed by shock, the survivors struggled to function.

Dorothy and Mary Lee did what they could for the few injured passengers who were still alive, but Dorothy's crude triage, based on little more than her Global Airways first-aid training, classified them all as terminal.

With no idea how long she had been at it, Dorothy was convinced that the only people who had any chance of living through the night were those on the pitifully short list of ambulatory survivors: Dorothy herself, Helen Bridwell, Senator Meyer, Albert Reese, Mary Lee McMurray, and Jack Harris.

Leaving Mary Lee to tend to the dying, Dorothy checked to see what kind of luck Helen was having collecting supplies. She stacked some blankets in a seat and some coats on the deck beside passengers' clothes that had fallen out of overhead bins. The cache of food Mary Lee had scrounged up was pitifully small, but that was no surprise. Dorothy knew most of the food on the plane had been stored in coach, that is, what little remained after dinner had been served. Helen's scant collection was all they had.

The survivors would just have to make the best of it. *Wherever we are,* Dorothy told herself, *somebody knows we're here. Help is on the way. It has to be coming.*

■ ■ ■

Up in the cockpit, Jack Harris and Albert Reese had finally managed to clear a tangle of cabling and conduits and get down alongside the copilot's seat so they could get a better look at him. Beckman moaned occasionally, so they knew he was still alive, though mercifully unconscious.

They were finally able to free Beckman's seat enough to work him back out of the jumble of wreckage that had almost buried him. They lifted him out, and as the senator focused the flashlight beam on him, Jack saw that his copilot was in bad shape. He was bleeding from his nose and left ear, and one side of his face was discolored an ugly dark purple, swollen so badly that his eye was a pulpy slit. His legs were mangled in the wreckage, and his hips appeared to have been crushed.

God only knows how bad his internal injuries are, Jack thought. *It's a wonder he's hung on this long.*

Beckman came to and turned his swollen head to look at Jack with his good eye. Jack hoped the poor man wouldn't see the truth in his face.

"I'm cold, Jack," the dying man murmured.

"They're bringing blankets. We'll have you warm in no time," Jack lied. "Take it easy."

"We screwed up, buddy."

"Hang on, Dave."

"We never should've tried the shortcut. You and your love life." Beckman gasped and struggled to get his breath.

Jack felt Reese's eyes on him as they crouched on either side of Beckman in the closeness of the wreckage.

"What's that about?" Reese asked. "What's he saying?"

"He's delirious."

"Sorry I screwed up...the coordinates," Beckman garbled, blood gurgling in his throat as he tried to swallow. "Forgot... which side of...the world I was on." Beckman coughed, and more blood came up. "Can you believe it?"

"What's he saying?" Senator Meyer asked from above them.

"Something about taking a shortcut," Reese explained, "and screwing up the coordinates. He said..."

Beckman nodded as if lapsing back into unconsciousness, then suddenly straightened with a jolt, his bloodshot eye wide open, his mouth agape.

"Hundred and forty-six..." he babbled, then turned and grabbed Jack's shirt. "God help us, Jack, we killed them!"

"Take it easy, Dave," Jack said, putting his hand on Beckman's shoulder.

Lose consciousness again. Please, just shut up, Jack thought. *Don't make it any worse.*

"What's he saying?" Meyer asked again.

Beckman sagged, and his head rolled to one side. He coughed again and spat blood. "I could use a drink," he mumbled weakly.

Beckman's eyes closed and Jack worked the copilot's bloody hand free of his shirt and laid the hand across Dave's chest.

Jack and Reese both jumped when Beckman suddenly went rigid and let out a bloodcurdling scream that echoed through the cockpit and down the length of the fuselage. The copilot went limp and slumped over into Jack's arms.

Jack pressed his fingers against Beckman's throat to check for a pulse, to make sure. He looked across at Reese and shook his head. "He's dead."

Reese's eyes widened and he swallowed hard. "Oh, my God." He shook his head and mumbled softly, "That's awful. Horrible."

Jack rubbed his forehead. "I can't believe it."

Reese stiffened and pushed past Senator Meyer, hurrying out of the demolished cabin. Meyer quickly turned and followed him. Jack knew to stay close, so he followed, too.

■ ■ ■

Bishop Forbes heard the scream echoing above him and stirred himself. He wasn't the only one. Someone else was out there...somewhere.

Gathering his strength, Forbes took a deep breath and let out his own yell, as loud and long as he could manage.

It echoed off the hard surface inches from his face, and left him dazed and deafened in the close darkness of his hole. The blood rushed to his head. He screamed again, louder this time.

The copilot's scream rang through the remains of the first-class passenger cabin. The three women looked at each other in horror.

"What was that sound?" Helen gripped the back of the seat.

"It came from the front," Dorothy observed.

Mary Lee looked from Dorothy to Helen and listened carefully but said nothing.

"What a terrible noise," Helen said, holding herself against a chill. "Like someone saw the gates of hell opening under him."

"Shh," Dorothy said, looking around the cabin, as she heard another cry, this one closer. "Listen." Mary Lee nodded that she had heard it, too.

"It came from over there," Dorothy said, pointing at the caved-in ceiling against the bulkhead.

She scrambled on her hands and knees to the cave-in, lowering herself onto the floor to look under the hanging slab. At first it was too dark, but then she thought she could make out the shape of a man.

When Bishop Forbes yelled a second time, Dorothy knew who she was looking at.

■ ■ ■

"He said what?" Senator Meyer demanded.

"Something about taking a shortcut," Reese repeated. "It sounded like he blamed our captain here. Something about his love life."

"You took a shortcut across China?" Meyer eyed Jack incredulously.

"Don't be a fool," Jack growled.

"There was something else," Reese went on, "about putting in the wrong coordinates."

"This is incredible!" Meyer exclaimed.

"Senator, the man was delirious," Jack insisted. "He was dying, for heaven's sake."

"Have you ever heard of a deathbed confession?" Reese accused.

Jack and Reese had left Beckman's body strapped in his seat because there was nothing else they could do. The senator stood in front of Jack, blocking his way back to the passenger cabin. Reese was close behind him.

"Somebody screwed up big time," Meyer insisted, eyeing Jack closely. "Are you saying those MiGs attacked us in international airspace? They crossed the border?"

"We were flying around weather," Jack began slowly, trying to choose his words carefully and not condemn himself. "There was a computer malfunction."

"Really?" Senator Meyer wasn't buying the story and had the look of a prosecutor rising to cross-examine a suspect witness. Before he could say anything more, the three men heard the women yelling from the first-class cabin.

Helen Bridwell stuck her head through the crooked hole in the bulkhead that had been the cockpit door. "Come quick, we've found Bishop Forbes." She looked at Meyer and then at Jack, sensing the tension between them.

"Where?" Jack asked.

"Hurry," Helen said. "He's still alive."

■ ■ ■

Aboard the Shark, Captain Maxwell scanned the decoded message he had just received from the Front Office. Lieutenant Stiles stood alongside him, waiting to hear what they had to say.

Communications was a big part of the Shark's business, and they had some of the most sophisticated gear available aboard. By relaying coded messages sent in digitized micro-bursts from the ship to more conventional surface vessels miles away or even land-based transponders far from China, they could get word to the Front Office in a matter of minutes. With this system, they ran only minimum risk that monitoring stations on the Chinese mainland, or even concealed aboard covert Chinese counterintelligence ships, would be able to pinpoint the source of origin. However slight, they had to be careful to avoid any kind of regular or frequent pattern of electronic activity that might raise suspicions.

The Chinese knew the U.S. was monitoring them. They could do little about the intelligence satellites miles overhead, but they spared no effort to detect and intercept any threats within their reach, such as planes and ships.

As Lieutenant Stiles waited for word from the captain, he tried to imagine the situation on the other end of the transglobal communications link. Were they trying to help? How did they view the situation from such a distance? No emergency seemed urgent in a dry, well-lit office back in the States.

"The Front Office" was what they called the command and control center the ship reported to back in the U.S. The vast majority of the information they relayed was technical surveillance that was recorded on board and offloaded by satellite transmission at intervals that might run as long as several days or even a week. Those transmissions, even digitized and compressed electronically, often included imaging too cumbersome for microburst transmission. Consequently, the Shark frequently left the waters of the China Sea near the mainland and found safer locations for extended transmissions. They also hoped that establishing such a pattern of movement made them look more like a genuine fishing boat. Real fishermen went back to port when their holds were full and returned to fish again.

Lieutenant Stiles had often wondered exactly who and what the Front Office was, but in a job like his, everything was on a need-to-know basis. He only had to know how to get the messages through. Stiles and the crew had speculated the Front Office was in some obscure corner suite in the bowels of the Pentagon, or maybe in a suburban Maryland enclave staffed by National Security Center types. It could be in Langley at CIA headquarters, for all they knew. It was best that all they had was speculation.

The crew all knew they ran the risk of capture in such duty, and none of them had forgotten the story of the Pueblo, a Navy intelligence-gathering ship captured years ago by the North Koreans. The crew had been a long time coming home, and what they had gone through in the interim made for a sobering warning for the sailors aboard the Shark.

While every man aboard had wanted to sound the alarm and warn Global Flight 027 directly of the danger they were in, they also knew it couldn't be done that way—for their own good, as well as the continued success of their mission. All they could do was wait for word from the Front Office and follow orders when they came.

"About what I'd expected," Captain Maxwell mused when he had read and reread the Front Office communiqué.

"What's that, Captain?" Lieutenant Stiles asked.

"We're to stand by and maintain cover. Communicate by priority relay only."

"That's it?"

"That's it. We're looking at a rather complicated international problem here. Right now the diplomats are feeling each other out."

"What about the media?"

"Flight 027's not due in Delhi for a while yet. The press won't get involved until Global makes some kind of announcement."

"In the meantime, we just sit here and watch?"

"We're going to do a little more than watch, Stiles," Captain Maxwell assured him. "We're going to downlink satellite imagery, keep an ear out for emergency locator squawks from the 757, and listen in on Chinese radio traffic. Maybe we can find a reason to believe there are survivors out there."

"If there are?"

"If we can prove it, it's a whole new ball game."

■ ■ ■

For the better part of an hour, the survivors tried to pull Bishop Forbes out of the tiny hole he was wedged into. Remarkably, the trauma hadn't killed him immediately, and when Jack learned the bishop had a heart condition, he actually questioned whether excavating the heavy man was worth the effort.

Although his question seemed callous, Harris felt a responsibility as the captain of the downed craft, and the few who had survived the crash were in a tough spot. Night had fallen in earnest now, and the forest was as dark as it was going to get. The storm was on them full force, and they had to rig up some kind of shelter for the night. He reasoned that maybe Forbes was expendable.

Everything was going to be a matter of choices from here on in. Jack knew it was up to him to make the right ones. Every minute, every ounce of energy they spent trying to save Bishop Forbes was a precious, finite resource they couldn't spend on something else. All it would take was a couple of wrong choices and they would be done for.

We can't stand a couple more errors, he thought and shook his head. *There have been enough mistakes made already.*

Jack couldn't allow himself to dwell on mistakes that might be made. There was too much to be done. He could only focus on one crisis at a time.

The pilot was almost glad none of the passengers who had survived the crash with injuries seemed likely to make it. He didn't like thinking that way, but he knew what a drain it would be to care for a half dozen seriously injured people, not to mention sharing rations with them and trying to figure out a way to move them to whatever shelter they were able to build.

All but two of the injured passengers had died since the crash, in spite of all that Dorothy and Mary Lee could do for them. The remaining two were unconscious and fading fast.

When the survivors finally got the cabin ceiling jacked up and braced sufficiently to get to the bishop, Jack crawled into the little space to look the clergyman over. If the bishop were too far gone, it would be up to Jack to call off the rescue and set everybody to building a shelter.

Thankfully, Forbes had rallied. He told Jack about the nitroglycerin in his pants pocket, and Jack fed him one of the capsules. The rotund clergyman's vital signs had steadied.

Forbes probably had a couple of cracked ribs and a broken collarbone, Jack figured from his rough preliminary examination. One of his legs had been twisted awkwardly beneath him, probably tearing ligaments in the knee. There might be internal injuries, too. The bishop's long-term chances weren't as good as the rest of them, but he wasn't terminal by any means. His future would all depend on how long they had to wait for rescue.

In the end, Jack opted to spend the time it took to get the bishop out. They couldn't just abandon him, no matter what Jack's logical side said. He had assigned Reese and the senator to cut or rip out as much of the ship's wiring as they could find, and they used strands of cable to tie off the bishop's seat. Jack had crawled back out of the cramped space and he and the others managed to pull the bishop free of what had very nearly been his tomb. Once out of the confining space, the bishop had looked around him at the faces of his rescuers and then beyond them at the wreckage of the first-class passenger cabin and the gaping darkness where the rest of the airplane should have been.

"Good heavens," he mumbled, his eyes wide and his lip trembling. "Are we the only ones that survived?"

Jack didn't stick around to explain things. He knew Dorothy would do all that could be done for Forbes, and he didn't like the way the others were looking at him. Jack knew that Meyer and Reese blamed him. He couldn't face their stares, the way he caught them looking at him every time he turned his back.

Jack and Dorothy scavenged the wreckage for anything that might be of use to them, but they had come up with a pretty skimpy inventory. They found flashlights that would be useful, along with the blankets and clothes and the food

Helen had rounded up earlier. Jack had located a flare pistol with a couple of rounds in the emergency unit, and Dorothy had the first-aid kit. It might be enough, if rescue was on the way. Jack knew that was an iffy proposition, and the weather wouldn't help.

Leaving the rest of the survivors to organize their supplies while Reese and the senator used some of the cables and a busted seat to rig a kind of litter to take Bishop Forbes, Jack went to scout out a shelter for the night. Wrapping a blanket around his shoulders to protect him from the cold, he took a flashlight and the flare pistol and climbed out of the fuselage over the jagged metal of the open end.

He hoped to find a better place to stay than the wreckage of the passenger cabin. The long jagged hole in the ceiling was letting in snow, and holes in the floor kept a draft running through the plane as well. He knew the cockpit was ruptured in a dozen places, and there were so many structural wounds in the thing that it would let in the wind like a sieve. There was also no way to generate any heat inside. Some fuel remained for a fire, but it would be risky starting a fire in the body of the plane, with so many combustibles in such bad condition. The last thing they needed was an open flame on board. At first, Jack thought that their best bet would be to lash up some kind of shelter along the lee side of the wrecked fuselage, but he quickly discarded that idea when he got a look at it from the outside.

The forward third of the 757 had shot off the end of the runway and over the berm into a wooded area. From outside the wreckage, Jack could see that they had come to rest on a steep slope that ran downward farther than he could see in the cone of light put out by his flashlight. The hulk of the wreckage was resting precariously on a number of twisted and broken trees, and he didn't think the trees would hold the weight for long. Then the hull would continue its slide down the slope to who-knew-where. There wasn't much time to find a suitable place, and it was already much colder than it had been before dark, with the storm raging around him.

As he trudged up the slope toward the top of the berm and the runway beyond, Jack thought about the buildings he had seen flashing by alongside the edge of the runway. Maybe one of them was still sound enough to serve as a rough shelter.

Within a hundred yards of the wreckage, Jack stumbled over something on the ground. He turned his light on the *thing,* and immediately wished he hadn't. Laying before him was a body, one of the passengers thrown free of the wreckage during the crash landing. Looking around him, Jack saw several more people scattered up the slope.

Keeping his light shining on the ground immediately ahead of him, Jack tried to force the images of the bodies out of his mind as he made his way up the slope to the level top of the berm. From there, he could see the runway and the smoldering ruins that were all that remained of the rest of his airplane.

"God, help us," he gasped, his knees buckling. He knelt on the flat top of the berm and watched the hungry fire devouring the heap of twisted metal and everything inside it. "Gone. All gone," the pilot muttered.

What had Beckman said, one hundred forty-six? One hundred forty-six! Jack shook his head. A hundred forty-six lives.

That's a lot to have on your conscience, Jack thought. He abruptly remembered what Beckman said before he died. "I could use a drink," he'd said. *I need one right now,* Jack reflected.

It had been dark for three hours by the time the survivors finally gathered everything they thought they could use and managed to push Bishop Forbes in his makeshift seat-sled up the slope of the berm and down the little road toward the dilapidated shelter Jack had found at the other end of the runway. The temperature was falling fast, and there was still a lot to be done.

As he had knelt on top of the berm and looked down the runway at the burning wreckage, Jack had forced himself to put everything out of his mind except what they had to do to stay alive. He had struggled to his feet and struck out down the flat top of the berm to his right, in the direction of the buildings he had seen earlier. He could make out some of them in the flickering light of the big fire on the runway. He wanted to scout a route for the others in case his idea panned out. The top of the berm proved to be a rough road, little more than a graded strip gouged in the rough soil of the little plateau that clung to the side of a mountain.

Chinese must have built this place, Jack thought as he slogged along through the snow that was piling up on every flat surface. More than a dusting now, it was really beginning to stick.

At the end of the berm, the road turned sharply to his left and paralleled the edge of the runway. There was nothing but rocks and scrubby brush for a few hundred yards, then a collection of dark shapes materialized out of the swirling snow and darkness alongside the crude little road.

Half an hour of exploration had satisfied him that the hangars weren't sufficient shelter. They blocked the wind a bit, but they were too open to keep in much heat. He checked out the dilapidated barracks next, but the ceiling had caved in on one side, letting in the wind and snow. Beyond them, he found the shards and debris that remained of the building that the left wingtip of the 757 had demolished. Back farther from the edge of the runway, Jack found another structure.

Firelight from the burning wreckage on the runway played in the two small windows in the front of this building. The roof was still in place, and the walls looked solid.

Yes, Jack thought. *I think this building will do.*

The door resisted at first, and Jack had to put his weight into a series of shoves that finally broke through. With his flashlight, he was able to make out a good-sized room with a fireplace in its rear wall, and doors that led to a couple of other rooms beyond.

Must have been their ops center, Jack thought. *Probably offices in the back there.* He didn't waste time exploring further. Jack had found what he was looking for.

As he made his way back to the others, he couldn't help thinking the fire on the runway was a blessing. The flames gave no sign of burning out yet, and he knew there was enough fuel to keep the fire burning into the night. He could feel a tinge of warmth from the blaze as he retraced his steps through the accumulating snow on the little road. The wreckage gave off enough light that the others could make their way without exhausting the flashlights. They'd have to conserve batteries, save everything.

Senator Meyer hadn't cared for the idea of moving up the slope and all the way across the runway. He thought the smart thing was to stay with the plane. Jack had made an attempt to explain things rationally, but his patience was running thin and time was not on their side. When Jack made it clear he was willing to fight the senator, Meyer pushed for putting the issue to a vote.

"Vote all you like," Jack had grumbled at him menacingly. "In the meantime, round up this stuff, and let's get started."

As he had expected and secretly hoped, the last of the critical survivors had succumbed to their injuries while he was out on his scouting expedition, and when Jack surveyed his little party, their number was down to seven. Except for Mary Lee McMurray's broken arm, the bishop's injuries, and an assortment of lacerations and abrasions, the rest were in relatively good shape.

That was good, Jack knew. It was going to take all of them working together if they were going to get off this mountain.

Bishop Forbes at first insisted he could walk if he had something to use as a crutch, but his left knee was swollen and would not bear his weight. Jack didn't want him to risk the strain on his heart, trying to make it so far over rough ground in the freezing cold. Forbes finally relented, apologizing for being a burden.

The bishop suffered a good deal, being strapped into a broken seat and pushed and pulled up the slope of the berm, then bounced along the rough little road alongside the runway. Yet he silently endured the discomfort, grateful to be alive. Having spent so long jammed headfirst down a hole, he was happy simply to find himself breathing fresh air, no matter how raw and cold it was.

Jack, Reese, and the senator took turns, two of them at a time, dragging and pushing the bishop in his makeshift sled. All the women carried supplies wrapped in blankets and thrown over their shoulders. They had parceled out some of the passengers' clothing among themselves, since none of them were dressed for the snow, and the men made do with blankets tied around their shoulders.

■ ■ ■

Lieutenant Stiles hovered over the sailor examining the first of the satellite images downloaded into a bank of computers aboard the Shark. What he saw on the screen looked like an aerial photograph to Lieutenant Stiles, blacks and grays suggesting mountainous terrain, all obscured by an overlay of white and lighter gray. He couldn't make anything out of it.

"What're you looking at there?" he asked.

"Mountains, sir," the sailor answered, not looking up from his screen as he tapped in commands on his keyboard in an effort to step up the contrast in the images. "With a storm front moving through. Heavy clouds, lot of snow."

"I don't see anything."

"No, sir. It's a big mess."

The sailor clicked out a quick staccato rhythm on his keyboard and the image shifted, the grays and blacks interlaced with splotches of color.

"What's that?" Lieutenant Stiles asked.

"Scan for infrared." The sailor studied the screen. "See that?"

He pointed at a light orange blotch near the center of the screen.

"Yeah."

"It matches the coordinates from radar, sir. Near as I can tell, that should be Pei Song. See the color?"

"Yeah. What's that mean?"

"Fire, sir. A big fire, very hot."

Stiles cursed.

■ ■ ■

Dorothy helped Bishop Forbes from his makeshift sled on the floor in front of the blackened fireplace, put down a blanket for him to lie on, then covered him with another blanket. "Thank you," he smiled. "But do you mind if I sit up?"

"Sure, if you'll be more comfortable."

"There, that's better," Forbes grunted as Dorothy helped him into a sitting position, his back against the wall beside the fireplace. "I think I can breathe better like this."

"I'm going back to the plane," Jack announced, "to round up anything we left behind and check one more time to make sure we got everything."

"Need any help?" Dorothy offered, looking up from the bishop.

"No, I want you ladies to stop up any leaks in the windows. Around the door here, too. Use clothes, anything you can find. It's probably better to save the blankets for sleeping."

"What about us?" Reese asked.

"Firewood. We need to gather up all we can find before the snow buries it. There should be some in these other buildings, the barracks and whatever that was we hit coming in. You should be able to find kindling in there."

"Okay." Reese looked at Senator Meyer, who was holding Helen under the pretext of trying to warm her. "Come on, Senator. Let's go."

"I'll be right with you."

Meyer whispered something to Helen and she looked over at Jack and nodded.

"Here, Senator. You may need this." Mary Lee held out a coat for him to try on.

"That's a woman's coat," Meyer objected.

"I know."

"A fur."

"That's right. A mink."

"I can't wear fur. It's not..."

"Politically correct, I know," Mary Lee snorted. "Who cares?"

"Nobody's going to see you in it," Reese added. "You don't have to worry about getting your picture in the paper out here."

"It's better than freezing to death," Mary Lee added. "Here, Mr. Reese. I think this one will fit you."

"Thank you, ma'am."

Reese took the coat she offered and pulled it on.

"It certainly beats wearing a blanket like some kind of homeless person," Reese observed, stretching his arms and testing the fit.

Meyer relented and put on the woman's fur coat.

"Yes," he said, nodding at Mary Lee. "I have to admit, it's warmer. Thank you..."

"Mary Lee."

"Thank you, Mary Lee." Meyer nodded and smiled at Mary Lee, then turned to Reese and the others. "You all know who I am, of course." He offered his hand to Reese. "But I don't believe I got your name."

"Reese, Albert Reese."

"That sounds familiar. What line are you in?"

"Smokes."

"I beg your pardon?"

"Tobacco. I'm with American Amalgamated Tobacco."

"Oh, I see. I guess that's where I've heard of you. You testified on the Hill, didn't you?"

"Yeah, and I'm not any more politically correct than that fur coat you're wearing." Reese shook his hand. "But don't let that bother you."

"Not a bit, under the circumstances."

"Would you two please shut up and go get some firewood?" Dorothy said. "It's not much warmer in here than it was outside, and it's going to get worse before it gets better."

"We're on our way."

The two men tugged the door open and disappeared into the darkness. Jack had been looking over the selection of coats piled on the floor but found nothing big enough to fit him. He untied the snow-soaked blanket from around his shoulders and picked up another one from the floor. At least it was dry.

"Wait a minute, I'll go with you."

Jack turned at the sound of the voice and was surprised to see Helen bundling herself up and moving toward the door.

"There's plenty to do here," Jack said.

"Dorothy and Mary Lee can stuff the holes. It's not that big a place. You may need help carrying stuff back here."

Jack looked at Dorothy, and she nodded.

"Go ahead," the exhausted flight attendant said. "I'll put some coffee on, and fix something to eat. You'll need a bite when you get back. We all will."

"Okay," Jack relented. "After you."

Helen buttoned the coat she had found on the plane tight under her chin and stepped through the door into the snowy night.

As Jack and Helen made their way back toward the wreckage on the other side of the berm, Jack expected her to explain why she had insisted on coming with him, but she trudged along beside him silently. The thought never occurred to Jack that there might be a connection between Helen's offer to go back to the wreckage and the brief whispered exchange between her and Senator Meyer in the shelter.

■ ■ ■

"That was a nice bit of playacting back there, Senator." Reese laughed. "'Reese? That name sounds familiar.' Whose benefit was that for?"

"For the record," Meyer said. "I think our secret's safe, but it only makes sense to play the game out all the way."

The two men located the small shed splintered by the impact of the 757's wingtip during the landing. Meyer scrambled around, picking up shards of kindling, trying to hold the pieces in his arms. He soon had an armful and couldn't pick up any more without dropping pieces from the load he was carrying.

Reese found a couple of long boards and produced a length of cable from the interior of the plane from under his coat. He tied the two boards together, leaving a length of cable at either end of the tie.

"See," he instructed the senator. "We stack the wood on these two pieces, then we use the loose ends to tie the load on."

"Good idea."

"Better than trying to carry it all in your hands. You make a lot of trips that way before you got enough wood to make a fire that'll last the night."

"All right, I said it was a good idea. Leave it to a Carolina redneck to know how to gather firewood."

"At least I know how to do something besides talk," Reese retorted, unfazed. "You really think our secret is safe, Senator? You think we can pull this off?"

"If we play our cards right."

"You got something in mind?"

"As a matter of fact, I do. For one thing, I want to get my hands on that little black box."

"That what? Oh, the flight recorder?"

"That's right. I know about these things, from committee hearings. I know where it is, and it's not that big a deal to get it out."

"Yeah? Where is it?"

"Under a panel in the cockpit, right under the pilot's seat."

"Oh, I see. That's why you sent Miss what's-her-name along with the captain."

"Exactly. To make sure the good captain didn't pull the box and toss it down the side of the mountain."

"Why? What do you want it for?"

"Leave that to me, Al. You may be handy out here, but I'm the expert on survival when it comes to the Washington press corps."

17

In the makeshift accommodations that the survivors had constructed out of the battered old terminal, Dorothy shuffled back and forth between the piles of goods on the floor, straightening up the foodstuff and trying to get a kitchen work area laid out. The strange assortment strained her imagination, but she could see a few options emerging. It would take some doing, but she'd make meals by adding a bit of this and that together. As she turned the lid on a canister of dried coffee, the smell assaulted her and brought another wave of nausea.

Dorothy gritted her teeth and bent over, nearly buckling at the knees. For a few moments, Dorothy was certain that she wouldn't be able to stifle the impulse to gag. Slowly, the horrible sensation decreased.

Dorothy slid down on the cold floor, breathing hard. She had just been thinking that if she could live through a plane crash, she could certainly survive an abortion. Was it fair for God to expect her to live up to a promise she made when she thought she was going to die? Dorothy felt as if her body was shouting at her and demanding she pay attention. The baby was asserting its life by making her sick. For several minutes, Dorothy laid on the floor, thinking about what an abortion would have been like. Jack said the operation was nothing. A simple "procedure." Easy enough for him to say! He didn't have to do anything but pay the bill and leave. She was the one left on the operating table, the one who would struggle with the cramping and the pain when everything was over.

Her conscience pounded the thought into her head—yes, *she'd* made the mistake, and she would have to live with it. Dorothy shivered. She couldn't escape the consequences if she chose to kill her baby. She realized how painful it might become, remembering day after day she had taken the life of a child growing inside of her. Jack would walk away without even thinking about what had occurred, but she would carry the weight, the pain, the inner accusation every day for the rest of her life.

For a few moments, Dorothy huddled in a ball with her knees pulled up tightly under her chin. "Dear God," Dorothy prayed. "I'm the one who got myself in this fix, but I know that You created this life I'm carrying. You love this little child and have a future planned for this small life. I need Your help. I desperately must have Your strength." Dorothy sighed. "God, please help me."

After a few moments, Dorothy struggled to get to her feet, and she began organizing their supplies. The tasks weren't hard, but it wasn't easy for her to do anything. She just wanted to curl up in her own bed, in her own room, and sleep. Her mind wasn't on the tasks. After a couple of minutes, the flight attendant stopped and took a deep breath. "Thank You, God," she abruptly said and smiled. "Regardless of the past, I know that You are with me."

She suddenly remembered the conversation she had overheard just before they crashed. Bishop Forbes had quoted the Bible saying, "We know that all things work together for good to those who love God, to those who are the called according to His purpose." The words reassured her. Possibly...maybe... hopefully...some divine purpose rested at the bottom of this terrible tragedy. In a way that she couldn't fathom at that moment, it just might be that God did have some purpose for her life. The thought almost took her breath away.

■ ■ ■

Jack felt his way through the tumbled wreckage of the plane to the cockpit and stood beside his seat for a moment, trying to get his bearings. The instrument panel was so badly warped and disfigured that it wasn't easy to find what he was looking for. He tried not to look at Dave Beckman's body lying in the rubble.

After some work, Jack finally located the device. He switched the toggle to the test/confirm position and saw the transponder light blink on. Relieved, he turned around to make his way back into the passenger cabin and found himself face-to-face with Helen Bridwell.

"Is everything all right, Captain?"

"Yeah, I was checking to make sure our emergency position transponder was working."

"Is it?"

"Yes. It'll let them know where we are."

"Who?"

"Search and rescue."

"Oh."

"How about you, Ms. Bridwell? Are you okay?"

"I'm fine.... Well, you know what I mean."

"Yes, ma'am. Come on. It's not safe up here."

"I...don't like to be left alone."

"I understand. Let's move back into the cabin then, okay?"

Jack and Helen worked their way back into the first-class passenger cabin, and Jack told Helen to look around for any clothing, blankets, or food they might have missed earlier. He was thinking some of the passengers may have stored something in the overhead bins, or had snacks in their carry-ons. He decided to rifle through the passengers' belongings himself. He didn't want Helen to get upset. She didn't seem too steady, and he didn't want her coming unraveled on him this far from the shelter.

Helen hadn't brought a flashlight, so he clicked on the emergency lights again and told her to check up and down the aisle where there was enough light to see.

Jack scrounged more thoroughly, holding his breath as he went through some of the passengers' possessions. By the time the cold started to get to him, he had found a few things he thought would be useful and figured it was time for them to start back. Jack had enough odds and ends that he needed something to carry it all in. He emptied one of the larger carry-ons and filled it with his finds and some pots, pans, and utensils from the cooking galley. As he packed the bag, he watched Helen. She hadn't had much to say and didn't seem very interested in helping him search.

She doesn't seem with it, Jack thought, *but we're all still in shock. Who knows what's going through her mind after what she's been through? Let it go,* he told himself.

Jack was glad Helen was quiet and didn't make any demands on his attention. Her silence gave him time to think as they trudged back up the hill toward to their shelter. Now that they had food, shelter, and soon, a fire, he turned his thoughts to the next crisis. He had plenty on his mind.

It was no good replaying the flight in his mind. That was a fool's game, good for nothing but driving himself nuts. He knew what had happened, and there was going to be a price to pay for it. An awful lot of people were dead, and he would have to answer for that. Beckman had screwed up. The truth was that the man was a drunk.

He has it easy, Jack told himself bitterly. *He won't be around to face the music like I will.*

Above all else, Jack was a proud man, and his pride was bound up in his being a pilot, a top-of-the-line senior captain on a 757, the best of the fleet, over twenty years in the air. Never had there been a blemish on his record—but now his record was shattered. All he'd ever wanted to do was fly. He'd fallen in love with the freedom of it from the first time he ever looked down from the sky at the people scurrying around in their little world far beneath him. Nothing matched the thrill of takeoff.

Maybe he'd never fly again, certainly not at the top of the heap as a 757 captain. That single thought galled him most, as he and Helen started back toward the shelter. Jack held a small suitcase in one hand and had a bulging carry-on slung over his shoulder.

Jack knew what they'd say, the brass at Global and the feds. He was the captain and that meant he was responsible for everything that happened, no matter whose fault it really was. Never mind that Beckman was half in the bag and forgot what side of the world he was on.

"You should have double-checked," they'd say. "You should have put Beckman on report the first time he showed signs of a drinking problem."

There was no getting out of it. The "big boys" would make him the fall guy.

All he had done was adjust course to avoid bad weather. If they hadn't crashed, the airline would be commending him for making up the time. The passengers would all be grateful. True, he had personal reasons for wanting to get there faster because of his layover plans in Delhi. But it wasn't like he was hurrying so he could party. He and Dorothy had a problem to deal with, and he wanted to take some time with her. The abortion would be tough for her, and he hadn't wanted to rush her through it. Was that so wrong?

If Beckman hadn't screwed up the coordinates, none of this would have happened. They'd be setting down in Delhi right about now, and he and Dorothy would be resolving their crisis soon after that.

And I'd still be a pilot, Jack thought bitterly.

■ ■ ■

Bishop Forbes had the oddest feeling. He seemed to be an island in a sea of movement. He leaned back against the rough stone wall beside the fireplace and watched the others busy at their chores. Dorothy and Mary Lee had gone around the place, stuffing bits of clothing into chinks under the doors and around the windows to keep out the wind while Meyer and Reese were bringing in wood. The men made three trips, dragging the firewood behind them on a frame they had made that looked to the bishop like a travois. He alone did nothing as they hustled by.

By the time the men unloaded their third load of wood, they were obviously exhausted and on the brink of hypothermia. Forbes was glad they decided to call an end to their wood-gathering for the evening. The result of their labors was impressive, a bank of firewood stacked halfway up the wall on the other side of the fireplace.

Dorothy had built a fire as soon as Reese and Meyer came back with the first of the wood. She had first crumpled paper from magazines brought from the plane, then stacked bits and chips of wood, and finally piled small pieces on top of that heap as kindling. Within minutes, she had a roaring fire going. She had even managed to clear the old flue enough that most of the smoke was going up the stone chimney and not backing up into the room.

"Well done," the Bishop congratulated her. "Very efficient work."

"Once a Girl Scout, always a Girl Scout," she smiled at him, her green eyes catching the luster of the fire.

A beautiful woman, the bishop thought. *And a trooper.* He could see how tired she was and knew she shouldn't be overdoing things in her condition.

"How are you feeling?" Dorothy asked the Bishop. "I'll have some food in a minute."

"I'm getting by. Thank you."

If there was one thing he might have asked her to do differently, it was change how she looked at him. Dorothy made him feel like a seriously ill patient. He appreciated the concern, but he couldn't help feeling that he was much worse off than he hoped was true. Then again, maybe he was in bad condition.

Forbes knew all about his heart. He'd been told by experts what to expect and what he had to do to keep it from getting worse. Of course, he had done none of it and went back to his old ways as soon as the doctors let him out, clearing his palate of the bland hospital food with generous portions of the rich food he loved so well. He didn't question his lack of ability to follow the diet and exercise program they spelled out for him.

But now the Bishop wished he had listened to medical advice. Forbes knew how many nitroglycerin capsules he had with him and how long he could expect them to last under the circumstances. He also had a good idea that his knee wasn't the worst of his injuries. If he was not mistaken, he had suffered internal injuries as well. He had enough knowledge of these things to know his wounds would take their toll sooner rather than later. All of which did not dim the warm sense of peace he found springing up within him. Feeling warmed within by this unusual feeling, Forbes began to think that he had been pulled out of that hole for a reason.

At Dorothy's insistence, Reese and Meyer were taking off their shoes and putting on dry socks. Mary Lee McMurray, in spite of her broken arm, was helping Dorothy make dinner.

She's a curious one, the bishop thought. He noticed Mary Lee had her earphones on and idly wondered what kind of music she was listening to under these circumstances.

■ ■ ■

The trek up the slope of the berm to the road and then along the road to the shelter seemed much longer to Jack Harris this time. Counting his scouting trip, this was his third round trip on the route. His hands and feet felt numb, and he had to stop more than once along the way to set down the bags he was carrying and breathe on his fingers and stamp his feet in an effort to keep his blood circulating.

Jack knew about frostbite and how it could sneak up on a person, skewing his judgment and crippling him before he knew it. Jack was cutting it close, and knew he might have stayed too long in the plane this last time before starting back.

The first couple of times Helen offered to help him carry the bags, Jack insisted he could handle it. The third time, he let her take the carry-on while he struggled the rest of the way with the larger bag.

When they finally reached the shelter, Jack let the big bag fall at his feet and shoved on the door but he didn't have the strength to force it open. The thought occurred to him that the others might have locked him out to die in the snow. The paranoid tic passed in a moment as soon as he heard voices inside and hands pulling out the fabric they had stuffed in the cracks of the door.

■ ■ ■

Mary Lee left her earphones on long after she stopped listening to the voices being fed into the recorder clipped to her belt because she wanted the others to get used to seeing her wearing them. She didn't want them to make any connections between her earphones and anything besides listening to music.

When Reese and Meyer stomped into the shelter with their third load of wood and kicked their feet against the doorframe to get the snow off, Mary Lee made a point to help them unload the wood from their improvised sled and stack it against the wall. When they decided they were done for the night and Dorothy told them to change into dry socks, Mary Lee offered to take their coats and shake the snow off them in one of the other rooms, so they would be dry to sleep in that night.

In the little room behind the fireplace, Mary Lee ran her hand along the fur coat she had given to Meyer and retrieved the tiny microphone she had planted there.

Mary Lee had heard what the two men had said to each other as they gathered wood. She had been right about them all along.

18

Jack was a broad-shouldered athlete, easily a head taller than Reese and stronger than Meyer. Neither of them had been willing to cross him back at the wreckage when he had insisted they make a shelter out of this hut, and they grudgingly admitted he had been right. As rough and run-down as they looked, the stone walls of the hut made a good windbreak, and the fireplace was a lifesaver. It was already much warmer inside than they ever could have managed inside the wreckage.

Still, Jack's third round-trip between the hut and the wreckage with only a blanket for protection against the cold had taken its toll on him. He stumbled through the door into the warmed fire-lit darkness of the hut and tried to collect himself. Hypothermia and exhaustion were getting the best of him. He couldn't make himself think clearly and, when he tried to talk, his words came out in a thick-tongued mumble.

Dorothy saw the look on his face as he staggered into the hut. She left the fireplace and went to him. His lips were bluish and his eyes had a glazed look. She unwrapped the wet blanket from his shoulders and led him across the little room to stand near the fire. Shaking out a dry blanket, she made him a pallet on the floor between the fireplace and the stacked firewood, opposite Bishop Forbes.

"Sit down, Jack," she said.

Harris knew he had to stay on his feet and keep moving, although he couldn't remember where he was going. In a dull haze, he resisted at first as Dorothy tried to get him to lie down.

Mary Lee understood the condition Harris was in and tried to help Dorothy. Between them, the two women finally wrestled him down onto the blanket, and Mary Lee wrapped another blanket around Jack as Dorothy knelt at his feet, tugging off his wet shoes and socks.

Helen came through the door after Jack, toting the carry-on bag, and Reese stepped outside to drag in the larger suitcase. He placed the suitcase on the floor and leaned on the warped door to close it, stuffing scraps of clothing into the cracks between the door and the frame to keep out the wind.

Meyer set down his coffee, eyeing Jack closely. Helen came over to Meyer and wrapped her arms around his waist. The senator looked down at her with his automatic campaign smile and put his arm around her shoulder, but it was Jack he was interested in.

"All right, Captain," Meyer began, the smile gone from his face. "We're all in for the night. Let's hear your version of what went wrong up there."

"Not now, Senator," Dorothy said over her shoulder, as she held Jack's foot and worked a dry sock up over it. "He's in no condition to talk."

Dorothy put two pairs of socks on Jack, being as gentle as she could with his swollen and discolored feet. The legs of his pants were soaked up to the knees but she didn't have anything else he could put on, and that was the last of the socks.

She would have to take the wet socks everybody had taken off and dry them by the fire.

"Right now," Senator Meyer insisted. "Before there's any more time to come up with a story. You owe us an explanation, Captain."

Meyer shrugged Helen aside and moved closer to Jack, standing over the larger man on the pallet. Dorothy stepped in front of Meyer and glared up at him.

"I said he's not in very good shape right now. Let him warm up and clear his head."

"No, I want to hear what he has to say right now, when he's not up to lying," Meyer insisted.

Dorothy shook her head at the senator disapprovingly and went back to the fireplace.

"How about it, Captain?" Meyer bored in, leaning down over Jack. Mary Lee was still holding the pilot in her arms, trying to warm him with the dry blanket. "What went wrong up there?"

"Weather," Jack muttered thickly, his eyes unfocused. "Computer...malfunction."

"I don't believe you." Meyer turned toward Reese, who was standing near the door, drinking his coffee. "Mr. Reese, what was it the copilot said before he died?"

"Something about a shortcut," Reese said. "And putting in the wrong coordinates."

"There was something else too, wasn't there?" Meyer pressed.

"Yeah." Reese looked around the room at the others. "He said something about the captain's love life."

"What did he mean by that, Captain?" Meyer glowered down at Jack. "What does your love life have to do with what happened?"

Dorothy came back with a cup of coffee and knelt on the floor between the senator and the pilot, her back toward the senator. She held the cup to Jack's lips, and his eyes flickered as the smell registered.

"He needs to rest," Dorothy insisted, not looking up at Meyer. "How about a recess, Mr. Prosecutor? You can cross-examine him some other time."

Meyer looked around the room at the others and saw Helen looking at him with her sad, lonely eyes. Reese was almost casual, with a bemused air about him. The bishop was taking it all in, but with a look Meyer couldn't make out. Dorothy was busy with the pilot. Meyer abruptly switched agendas. The pilot was out of action, at least for the time being, and this was his chance. There were a couple of things he could be sure of. Someone had screwed up royally, and if what the copilot had said wasn't pure delirium, he had a pretty good idea what had gone wrong. Harris had a hot date in Delhi and took a shortcut to make up for the time lost in the delay in Hong Kong. On top of that, they somehow had wandered into China. The navigation error was the main thing to make sure everybody remembered, the lead for the press corps. "Pilot blunders into China and triggers tragedy."

Meyer could see that line as the focus. In the resulting media circus, nobody would concern themselves too much with what a U.S. senator and a key tobacco executive happened to be doing on the same flight. A coincidence, a sidebar without meaning. Enemies at home, allies in a time of crisis. Yes, that would make a good angle.

Meyer was fashioning himself into the hero as he thought it through, and the plan was all coming together for him. He could see the subplot of the in-depth pieces the big papers would run about the crash, the articles in the news magazines.

"Senator is hero in Chinese shoot-down, rallies survivors and uncovers pilot error that led to tragedy." The publicity could only be good for his reputation.

Meyer turned to Reese, deciding it was best to leave the pilot alone for the time being. The man was in no shape to cough up any answers, and Meyer didn't want the others to turn on him for badgering Harris. There would be time to lean on him later. Besides, there was another angle. A foolproof way of knowing exactly what had happened up there. "We have to get our hands on that black box," he whispered.

"If you say so," Reese shrugged. He knew the senator and had seen him pull his chameleon act before. "But if you're talking about going after it tonight, you're going by yourself."

"But..." the senator started to protest.

"It's snowing heavier every minute out there," Reese put in, cutting the senator off. "And getting colder, too. It's a wonder they made it back at all. The captain must have broken a trail for Helen, or they'd still be out there somewhere."

"All right," Meyer growled. "In the morning, then. But we have to keep an eye on him, make sure he doesn't get to the box first."

"He doesn't look like he's going to be going anywhere for a while," Reese assured him.

Meyer went over to Helen. He needed to know what she had seen. "What did he do on the plane?" he asked.

"He went into the cockpit...."

"What? Why?"

"I'm not sure."

"What did he do there?" Meyer demanded, an edge to his voice. "It's important, Helen."

"He...fiddled with a switch, something on the control panel. I saw a light flash on. That's all."

"Then what?"

"We went through the plane and gathered up that stuff." She gestured toward the two bags they had brought back. "Then we came back here. He got very tired on the way back. I thought we weren't going to..." Helen trailed off.

"It's all right," Meyer told her. "You're all right now."

"Yeah, we're all okay now," Reese said, making his way around the senator and Helen toward the fireplace where Dorothy knelt, tending to the fire and boiling more water in a little saucepan from the plane's galley. "But for how long?"

Dorothy looked up at him as he loomed over her, looking down at the fire.

"What I'm asking is, how long do you figure before they come to rescue us?" Reese asked.

"You're asking me?" Dorothy answered without looking up.

"I'm sure not asking him," Reese said, pointing at Jack, who lay against the woodpile, swathed in blankets, with his eyes closed and his chest rattling as he breathed heavily. "He's conked out."

"I'm not sure," Dorothy hedged. "Search and rescue's a little out of my line."

"I'll take your best guess."

"Well, I don't expect to see anybody flying in this storm at night. Tomorrow probably, if there's a break in the weather."

"Helen said the pilot fiddled with a switch in the cockpit and she saw a light come on. What would that have been? Do you know?"

"It sounds like he was checking the emergency position transponder. It would broadcast our location so they can find us."

"What would a flashing light mean?"

"That it was working."

"Good. That's good. But who are *they*?"

"They?" Dorothy frowned.

"Who'll be coming? Do you have any ideas about our rescuers?" Reese pressed her.

"What do you mean?"

"We're just paying passengers, lady. For all we knew, we were nearly to Delhi. It turns out we were really somewhere over China. See? We don't have a clue where we are right now. I guess I'm asking you whose turf we're on. Is it going to be the Chinese coming to take us out of here, or who?"

"What difference does it make?" Dorothy snapped up at him. "As long as we get out of here!"

Her answer seemed to satisfy Reese for the moment, and Dorothy went back to her chores. It was the best answer she could give him, but the truth of the matter was, she didn't know any more about where they were than the rest of them.

No matter what she did, Dorothy could not get Reese's question out of her mind. His questioning irritated her, but the man was right. How long would they be there before help came? She knew enough about the politics of the Far East to understand how desperate their situation was. The eternal wrangling between China and its neighbors made for constant instability and uncertainty. Anything could happen. The truth was that they might go undiscovered for weeks.

Dorothy shuddered and worked faster, but Reese's question still lingered. What if help did come quickly? Then she'd be faced with the dilemma that Jack would put before her in New Delhi. He wasn't an easy man to argue with, and she knew that his mind was made up about the abortion. Dorothy's mind was made up, too. He would find out how tough Dorothy could be.

I won't cave in to him, even if he pressures me, she told herself. *It's my decision. I'll just tell him that he doesn't have to worry about anything, but he has to realize that it's a person growing inside me. It's a baby, and now that I know that, it affects my choice. Let the rescuers come! Bring them on!* She knew she wouldn't be bullied into changing her mind. She would do what she had to do.

Dorothy slowed down the pace of her feverish work and took a deep breath. She suddenly felt better. Maybe she was more in control of her life than she thought.

19

Aboard the Shark in the China Sea, Lieutenant Stiles was trying to make a case for launching search and rescue, and never mind the politics. The task wasn't easy.

"We have confirmation on their emergency transponder," he pointed out to Captain Maxwell. "That fact alone ought to be worth something."

"And confirmation of a fire too, Stiles." Maxwell reached into a shirt pocket and produced a cigar, one of the thick black ones he was always smoking, but he didn't light it. Maxwell just rolled it in his fingers and held it under his nose for a second, savoring the aroma of the leaves. "The signal means the transponder survived the fire, which almost certainly means a crash. With our information, the crash is the only thing we're sure about."

"Somebody has to get in there and check it out, sir. There's no sign the Chinese are making any effort."

"I wouldn't expect them to unless there's a break in the weather. Their search and rescue people aren't exactly famous for success with foul weather operations."

"I guess that's why they haven't been out looking for their downed pilot, the MiG that ran out of fuel," Lieutenant Stiles added. He had mixed feelings about that MiG pilot. The man had shot down a 757 full of innocent civilians, but that had been on orders. For all the MiG pilot knew, the airplane was a CIA provocateur. He had to hand it to the pilot, sticking with the assignment like that, right down to the end, even when he knew his fuel was low and there wasn't much hope of rescue if he had to bail out over the mountains. "Bhutan doesn't want the Chinese in there, and the Chinese don't want to see any third parties in there either."

"Meaning *us*."

"Does Bhutan have an air force, Captain?"

"In a matter of speaking. But *nobody's* flying in there until there's a break in the weather."

"What's the word on that, sir?"

"It may be better tomorrow. That's the word from fleet."

"Have we heard anything from the State Department?"

"The diplomats are working it, but it's a tricky situation. Everybody suspects everybody else of staging some kind of provocation, or setting up the whole thing as an excuse to send in troops. Our people are trying to convince the Chinese that a U.S. senator was on board. Maybe that will loosen them up."

"Are the Chinese denying the shoot-down?"

"Yeah, they're blaming it on the weather. They're calling it a spy plane, too."

"That's crazy, sir. We have it all on tape."

"But we can't go public, Stiles. All we can do is wait and watch."

"It's a bad deal, sir."

"Yes, it is. The best thing you can do is find me some evidence of survivors. Then maybe we can make something happen."

"Aye, aye, sir."

■ ■ ■

The survivors were starving after their exertions in the cold and snow. The dinner they had eaten aboard Global 027 seemed a lifetime ago. Dorothy laid out some dinner rolls and bagels to warm in front of the fire and located some soup cubes in a bag she had salvaged from the galley.

"Bread and soup will be ready in a few minutes," Dorothy announced to the group.

Dorothy had dragged the two bags Jack and Helen brought back from the wreckage over by the fire and opened them up to see what she could find. Jack had included some small pots and pans in with the other stuff, and Dorothy was glad to see them. She asked Reese to step outside and fill them with snow to be boiled down for water. At least dehydration shouldn't be a problem. The rest of the contents of the two bags Dorothy separated into stacks on the floor with some clothing and a few more blankets. These items she handed out to the group, with instructions for each of them to make a place to sleep.

Dorothy found odd bits of food—snack food and candy, even a box of chocolates. Her stomach tightened as she realized Jack must have gone through bags from the overhead bins and underneath the seats, the first-class passengers' carry-ons. He had gone through their pockets, too, she thought. There were cigarette lighters and packs of cigarettes, some of them opened. She couldn't figure out at first why he had included the cigarettes, although she figured out the reason for the collection of liquor bottles, the single serving size they used for drinks in flight.

Maybe he thought we could use it for a disinfectant in case of wounds, she thought. *Or as a painkiller if the first-aid kit runs low.* Mary Lee had taken aspirin for her broken arm, and Dorothy had wished there were something more she could give her.

Dorothy stacked all the food in the corner and started calculating how long the pile would last them. Seven people, three meals a day. Twenty-one meals a day total. She worked out in her mind how much would make a meal, enough to keep strength up without depleting their stash too quickly. The best she could figure, subtracting the soup and bread they were about to eat, they had enough for only three more meals for the seven of them. That amount would get them through tomorrow and that was it. They wouldn't be hearty meals by any means, mostly bread and soup and some sweets, enough to keep from starving but not enough to sustain any vigorous activity in this cold.

She could only hope it would be enough, that she had been right about rescue coming tomorrow if there was a break in the weather.

■ ■ ■

In Thimphu, the capital city of the small nation of Bhutan, the Dragon King waited for the consul from India to arrive in the king's private library. Because they had both studied at Cambridge, the king gave the consul far more latitude than he did other diplomats. Nevertheless, he didn't like being dragged out of bed for any sort of "special talk." The king turned slowly and glared when the small dark-skinned man hurried into the room.

"Please forgive me, my good friend," the consul began before he was even halfway across the room. "I must apologize profusely for awakening your majesty at such a late hour."

The king said nothing but stood with his hands behind his back, waiting.

"The matter has become extremely urgent," the consul continued as he hurried across the room. "For this reason and this reason alone, I have come to talk with you at this inconvenient hour of the night."

"And what is this earth-shaking emergency that you seem to think is so important?" The Dragon King took several steps forward but kept his hands behind his back and did not offer to shake hands. "Surely the matter must be of considerable consequence."

"Please understand that I am here at the urging of my government," the consul continued. "Because there are no diplomats here from the United States of America, the government of India has sent me to explain the current dilemma that is unfolding within your borders."

"You think that I have no information about what is happening within my own country?" the king snapped.

"A thousand pardons." The consul bowed humbly. "I did not mean to leave such a clumsy implication in what I was saying."

The king gave a curt nod. "Continue. What is it that the diplomats in Delhi have to instruct me about?"

"We are both aware that India is not in the habit of running errands for the government of the United States of America," the consul sounded apologetic.

The king sighed. "The United States certainly has a propensity for involving itself in the affairs of Asian countries in a manner that does little to endear them to a country like Bhutan. Why would you choose this hour of the night to remind me of this fact?"

"You see," the consul's voice shifted and he sounded more professional, "there has been an airplane crash in the mountainous area along the border adjacent to China. A commercial 757 airliner was forced to crash land by a Chinese jet. We believe some of the passengers survived and are making shelter at the abandoned airfield where they were forced down."

The Dragon King's face froze. He was completely aware of the crash landing but had not received information on possible survivors. Only a few hours earlier he had been pondering whether his government should take any steps to investigate the wreckage in the near future. The matter was quite sensitive. The king didn't reply while he thought through the situation.

"The Chinese are making threats of retaliation if third parties attempt to enter the area and explore what has occurred." the consul said carefully. "I am sure that they are attempting to intimidate your country." He bowed his head ceremoniously.

"Do you think the Chinese can frighten me?" the Dragon King asked peevishly. "You've come to make sure that I am not losing my sleep because of their threats?"

"Listen, Darmark," the Indian consul said with clear coldness, "I am here because this simple matter could explode into a full-scale war. We both know that is a possibility."

"We are not back in Cambridge," the king responded with equal frigidness. "Do not call me by the name we used back in those days. Let's keep this conversation on a diplomatic level."

The Indian consul ground his teeth. "I'm here to warn you. The Americans are threatening to investigate. They claim it's humanitarian—to search for survivors—but China will see it as an aggressive act."

The king pulled at his lip and stared out the window again for a moment. "Do you think they'd actually enter our airspace without permission?"

"What have you got to stop them?" The diplomat shrugged. "Do you have enough airplanes to turn the Americans back?"

The ruler of Bhutan stiffened. "You know our military situation as well as I do. We cannot stand up against the most powerful nation on the earth."

"That's my point," the Indian consul shot back. "You must prepare. We believe they are coming. And China won't like it."

The king shook his head. "I see," he finally answered. "You are telling me that a confrontation is about to occur?"

The consul nodded his head. "Definitely."

■ ■ ■

There was no way for him to know what time it was, but Bishop Forbes imagined it was around midnight when he awoke from a restless sleep to the sound of the wind whistling outside and someone snoring. He found himself, as he had dreamed, lying on the stone floor of the hut with his back against its rough wall beside the fireplace.

So, it was real after all, he told himself. *The crash and everything else all really happened.*

All the others were asleep, huddled shapes buried under coats and blankets on pallets in a rough semicircle in front of the fire—except Dorothy. Forbes watched her drag two splintered boards from the stack of firewood to the fireplace and cross them, laying them on top of the fire so they would be fed into the blaze as it burned down, ensuring that the fire wouldn't go out for some time.

"Are you are still up?" Forbes whispered.

"I'm sorry. Did I wake you?" Dorothy asked quietly.

"No." The Bishop shook his head and readjusted his blanket. "I've been dozing off and on. You'd better get some sleep, too."

"We're taking turns standing watch and making sure the fire doesn't go out."

"Oh, I understand."

"I just relieved Reese. Helen's up next, then the senator."

"I see. You've got everything organized."

"It's by committee, really."

"Nonsense. I've been watching you. The dry socks and food, the peacekeeping. You're the one holding everything together."

"How are you feeling?" Dorothy asked to change the subject, uncomfortable with his praise.

"Good. Better than I expected."

"I just realized that I don't know what to call you. Bishop? Your Eminence?"

"Tony."

"That's simple enough."

"It strikes me this is a time for simplicity."

"I guess so." Dorothy smiled weakly.

Forbes watched the firelight play over her face as she squatted on the rough stone floor and reached out to poke the burning wood with a stick to keep it going. He saw the neat row of socks she had laid out on the hearth to dry.

"How are you *actually* feeling, my dear?" he asked.

"Tired," she sighed, turning to him with another smile. "But I'm okay. We're lucky to be alive."

"Certainly." Forbes wasn't actually sure he agreed with her. Earlier, before drifting off into one of his fitful naps, he had been thinking that the opposite might be true. "We're alive anyway," he mumbled. "How far along are you, if you don't mind my asking?"

"What?" Dorothy's eyes widened in shock.

"The baby. How far along?"

"How did you..." Dorothy's voice faltered. "How did you know?"

"You have a glow about you."

"Really?"

Forbes knew he had a sense about these things, an instinct for people's secrets. He couldn't tell her that God had revealed it to him. And there *was* a glow about her, even if it was nothing more than the firelight.

Dorothy stared at the ground, blinking away the tears.

"Is it a secret?" he asked.

A tear ran down the stewardess' cheek.

"Come here," he whispered. "Sit by me."

Like a brokenhearted child, Dorothy walked over to the bishop. Something about his sincere round face made him easy to trust. She wedged herself between him and the fireplace and felt the warmth of the wall at her back.

"It is a secret, then," Forbes murmured. "I'm sorry. I didn't mean to upset you."

"It's..." Dorothy choked back a sob and brushed at her eyes with the backs of her hands. "It's more than that, I'm afraid. I'm..."

"You're not married, are you?"

She shook her head.

"I see."

"If...all this...hadn't happened, I'd be in Delhi right now. Having an abortion."

"I see." The Bishop nodded his head, no reaction on his face.

She looked up at him, searching for condemnation in his expression. In the flickering firelight and deep shadows of the little hut, he somehow gave the impression that this conversation was the most normal thing in the world.

"There's that to be thankful for, then," Forbes whispered. Groaning with the effort, the bishop freed his right arm from his blanket and reached out to her. He put his arm around her shoulder, and she sagged against him.

"I've been trying to make sense of all this," she said softly, "It's stupid, I know, but I've been thinking, maybe..."

When her voice trailed off, Forbes nodded. "Maybe there's a reason for crash, for the way the wreck worked out?" he offered.

"Yes. I know it's silly to think like that, but...I prayed. Can you imagine? I actually prayed."

"You prayed?" he prompted her.

"Yes. When I knew we were going down. I prayed my baby would live. Isn't that..."

"Perfectly natural. It seems natural to me, at any rate."

"But I'm not the praying type, Tony. You don't know me. I've been...I don't know how to say it. I'm not...religious. Let's just put it that way."

"I feel the same way sometimes."

"What do you mean?" Dorothy frowned. "You're a bishop."

"We all have times when God seems to be a million miles away. If He's calling, we don't answer. Sure. I know how it feels when you seem to be totally out of touch with the Almighty."

Dorothy blinked uncomprehendingly at the bishop.

"Long ago I learned a little secret that comes back to help me during the hard times." Forbes held up his finger like a lecturer, starting to teach. "God is often the closest...when He feels the furthest away."

Dorothy put her hand to her mouth. "That's an amazing thought. I'd like to think He's watching out for me."

"Have you heard of the great Old Testament king, David? He once wrote that in his relationship with God he felt like a sparrow alone on a rooftop. We certainly have those moments when it feels like God is a million miles away, and the whole world is against us. But the truth is that God cares for the raven and the sparrow, so how much more does He care for us? He's always closer than the next breath."

For a moment Dorothy thought about what he was saying. Finally she asked, "How in the world can we know He cares about us if we can't feel Him near us?"

"Oh, I understand," the bishop nodded his head. "We have to learn to tell the difference between faith and feeling. Quite a disparity." He looked thoughtful.

Dorothy pulled on his arm gently. "The difference between faith and feeling?"

"Feelings are purely emotional. They bubble up and down, depending on what's happening to us or around us." Forbes cleared his throat. "Faith doesn't have anything to do with how we feel. God's purposes, intentions, and love go right on regardless of whether we're frightened or excited. Faith stands straight and tall when our feelings drag us to the ground. Faith is believing, no matter what the circumstances."

"I would never have realized what you've just explained, Bishop. It's really important not to base our faith on mere feelings, then, right?"

"Right. Our relationship with God often inspires feelings of joy and peace, but even in the absence of these 'warm fuzzies,' we must go on believing He's close at hand, whether we are aware or not."

They were quiet for a moment, both thinking. The fire crackled and the wind whistled outside, showing no signs of abating.

Dorothy let his answer settle. "I thought the clergy were different," she finally said. "Never out of touch with God."

"We put our pants on every morning like everyone else in the world does," Forbes answered. "No, we struggle to work out our salvation like anyone else."

Dorothy nodded her head. "I have to be honest. On some days, it doesn't feel like God wants to hear from me." She ran her hands through her long hair. "I mean...I simply feel a very long way from Him, and I really don't want to be close."

Forbes nodded his head. "I know exactly what you mean. There's a reason for that distance. We have a not-so-nice theological word for the problem."

"What is it?"

"We call the condition sin."

Dorothy blinked several times and shook her head. "Sin? You mean that list of bad no-no's you preach about on Sunday?"

Forbes smiled. "Most of us don't preach much about sin." He stroked his chin in thought. "*Sin* is a word for the state of being we're in, which results in our separation from the Almighty. The truth is that we've all done something—usually many little things—that separate us from the Lord."

Dorothy thought for a moment. "You're suggesting that my actions cut me off from God?"

"That's about it."

Dorothy took a deep breath. "Yeah, I see that. Does living life on my own terms without much interest or concern for what God wants count as sin?"

Forbes nodded his head again. "I'd say that's about the heart of the problem. You've put the matter quite well."

Dorothy patted her stomach. "What can I say? You've obviously seen my problem. You know the truth. I had an affair, and now I'm paying the price. I'm sure God isn't happy with my lifestyle."

"Unfortunately, Dorothy, God *is* displeased with us when we sin. And we all sin. He's completely holy, so He can't associate with the unholy. But He still loves us." Forbes cleared his throat. "One of the good things that I've learned from my years of study is that facing the problem head-on is all you need to get the lines of communication connected again."

Dorothy leaned closer. "How can I do that?"

Forbes smiled. "We must say that we're sorry and that we want the Lord to allow us to come into His presence. It's as simple as admitting our sin and asking for forgiveness. In the church we call that *repentance,* changing our mind. We decide that we want to do things God's way from now on, and we tell Him so."

Dorothy lowered her head and looked at the floor of the old building.

"I guess my life isn't in very good shape," Dorothy finally said. "I admit that fact. I have sin in my life."

"Dorothy, it's a major step to realize you're a sinner. Many people go through life never realizing that God has a better way. That's all you need to admit to God. We call that making a prayer of confession. If you are sincere, God will forgive those sins. That's why He sent His Son—to die on the cross as the ultimate sacrifice for our sins. He took those sins upon Himself, but He rose again the third day so He could reign in our lives," the bishop explained. "Let me tell you something that I experienced many years ago when I was in prison. It happened in a dream one night. I saw the hand of God coming down to me from above and I reached for it. But I couldn't touch Him no matter how I strained. I prayed for God to help me, and immediately I felt strong fingers close around my hand. You can't imagine the overpowering love I felt. But when I looked down, I realized that I hadn't touched God's hand directly. A man stood in the gap, joining us together. As I looked at His hands, I discovered that they were both nail-scarred." The bishop smiled. "That's what the death of Jesus Christ did for us. He connects us to God. All we need to do is make the admission that you just gave."

"Really?" Dorothy looked hopeful.

"You need to simply tell our heavenly Father how you feel. Why not do that right now?"

Dorothy took a deep breath. "Okay," she said resolutely. "That's exactly what I'll do." She swallowed hard and closed her eyes.

The bishop watched as Dorothy prayed silently, her lips moving slightly. Tears began to run down her cheeks. He smiled. After a couple of minutes, Dorothy reached up and wiped her cheeks. She finally opened her eyes and smiled.

"From here on out, I think you'll find that God is listening to you."

Dorothy reached out and squeezed his chubby fingers. "Thank you," she said. "I know God was listening."

20

When Helen woke Senator Meyer for his turn to stand watch over the fire, she made it clear he didn't need to be alone. As he crawled out of his blankets and wrapped himself in the woman's fur coat Mary Lee had given him, Helen stood close and made no move to go back to her own little bed.

"Mind a little company?" she asked.

"Not a bit." He smiled.

Meyer squatted on the floor in front of the fire and gestured for her to sit beside him. As she knelt close and leaned against the senator, he studied her face in the firelight and caught the scent of her hair.

"Aren't you exhausted?" Meyer whispered in her ear.

"I don't want to be alone," she answered, then looked into his eyes with a warm longing that matched the fire in front of them. "I want to be with you."

"Good." A grin crept across his face. "Great."

What exactly did she mean by that? Meyer wondered. *Did she actually mean what I think she said? Something intimate? Under these conditions?*

Meyer had lain awake, in spite of the aching tiredness in his arms and legs, worrying about how all this was going to play out back home, not just in the press and on Capitol Hill, but at his house. In the darkness of the little hut, alone with his thoughts, Meyer had no one to convince him that he was on top of things. When he was alone, doubts crept in, and he imagined the worst. In those lonely moments, he found himself considering the unthinkable, the possibility that he wasn't going to make it off this mountain.

What would his wife do, facing life without him? He had pondered that possibility, and it had been less than gratifying for him to admit that she would get on quite nicely.

His wife had long since lost her appetite for listening to his speeches. "His *speech!*" she often pointed out rudely, the one speech he rewrote and put a new spin on to match any occasion. She was no longer impressed with Washington and the corridors of power or in awe of the famous names and faces on their social calendar. Why she stayed with him was something of a mystery, but he was inclined to put it down to the rut of familiarity that long marriages develop. Of course, he pandered to her lavishly, knowing she was an integral part of his public image.

No, he had been forced to admit in the lonely darkness that she would not miss him unduly, certainly not as much as he would miss the theater of politics. His mistress was another matter.

The senator had always promised to provide for her, but he had never gotten around to making the arrangements. It wasn't a simple matter, diverting funds from his estate to see that she would get what she needed to continue in the style in which he had kept her. But of course, she was not understanding about any of those issues. It would not sit well with her to lose her condo and the furnishings. He could easily imagine her in some trashy tabloid, on some sleazy talk show, or selling her story to a publisher for a fat book contract. Such a possibility was troubling.

Meyer had imagined a nation in mourning when his time came. Not any time soon, of course. He still had hopes of making his party's presidential ticket. If he won the senate re-election and handled this situation just right, this thing with the Chinese would be a feather in his cap. The truth was that he had much to live for.

As he looked into Helen's affectionate eyes in the dancing firelight, he felt the chill of self-doubt ebbing away. It was enough that she needed him right now. He could be strong for her—a hero.

This is more like it, he thought, pushing the doubts aside. "Everything will be all right," he assured her.

■ ■ ■

On a rocky ridge somewhere in the mountains north of Pei Song, the MiG flight leader lay burrowed deep in a snow bank underneath the sheltering branches of a gnarled pine tree, the fur collar of his quilted flight suit pulled up around his ears and his parachute wrapped around him like a shroud as he made the most of the meager protection he could find from the icy howling wind.

He had switched off the locator that was part of his survival kit, designed to lead search planes to his position. There was no use sapping the battery in this storm because he knew there would be no planes out looking for him until the weather cleared. If then.

As he lay on the verge of sleep in his snowbound cocoon, the flight leader tried not to think about what might be going on back at district headquarters. He had done his duty and followed orders. He had to believe the intruder was a spy plane, a CIA provocateur or a probe of their defenses. They had every right to defend themselves against such aggressors.

And yet, he could not put out of his mind the ugly possibility that it had all been some horrible misunderstanding. *No airline pilot could have been so lost,* he tried to tell himself. Not these days, with their computers and satellites.

The flight leader knew that if it had been a mistake, district would be in no hurry to find him. Better a dead pilot than a witness to the downing of a civilian airliner. He had done his duty. He didn't deserve to die in a crash, but the flight leader had been a soldier a long time. He knew how things were done. As he drifted off into sleep, he thought of his young wife. He hoped there would be a widow's pension for her after all.

■ ■ ■

In the China Sea, activity aboard the Shark had settled into its night rhythm. Below deck, the blue light of radar and computer monitors bathed sailors in its eerie glow, and the ship's electronic eyes and ears still reached out over the horizon toward China and Bhutan. There was little to see or hear.

There had been no radio traffic from Wan Chow for hours, and while Global 027's emergency location transponder kept beeping its signal into the night sky, there was no sign of human life from the vicinity of Pei Song.

Satellite images continued to feed into the computers for analysis, but the snowstorm was heavier than ever, and the images showed nothing but a blanket of swirling gray and a few jagged mountain peaks.

■ ■ ■

Bishop Forbes woke from a doze and blinked in the darkness. After Dorothy's watch was over, she had returned to sit beside him, but now she lay sleeping next to him, snuggled against the priest for warmth and, he hoped, a bit of comfort.

Forbes glanced around the room and noticed the senator and the American woman cuddling underneath the incongruous lady's mink coat. He closed his eyes again to block out the sight and give them some privacy. Forbes' thoughts drifted to Dorothy and her baby then to Jack Harris. Jack's conduct since the crash had been heroic, but Forbes worried about him. How could he live with the blood of so many on his hands?

Forbes was shaken from his thoughts by the renewed snores of someone across the room. He identified Reese as the source. Forbes classified him as an overdressed country boy far from home, although he had to give him admiration for his politeness. Reese slept farthest from the fire, in deference to the women.

Sleeping like a baby, Forbes thought. Was he the simple man he portrayed himself to be? Forbes thought there was more to the man than an earthly gambler who took his chances.

His eyes roamed across the room again. The inscrutable Mary Lee wore her earphones even in sleep. He mused that her eyes appeared devoid of emotion. What had brought her to this place?

The churchman considered the six survivors with which his lot was cast here at the top of the world and closed his eyes as the angina gripped his chest again, sending little lightning bolts down his left arm.

Careful not to wake Dorothy, he worked his hand gently beneath his blanket into his pocket and found his nitro. Placing a capsule under his tongue, he tried again to compute his odds. Would the nitroglycerin last long enough for him to die of his internal injuries? Maybe long enough to be rescued, if his ears did not deceive him. The winds sounded as if they were lessening as morning drew near. The storm might dissipate tomorrow, and the sky clear enough for rescuers to find them.

But that was not what he prayed for. What he prayed for was the hand of God to open his heart and give him understanding. He requested some meaning behind these strange circumstances. Finally, he prayed for the peace that had welled up in him to stay. In the deepest part of the bishop's soul, he discovered that he had slipped past that invisible barrier that had turned him back so often in the past. He had forgiven himself this time. He knew the peace would stay with him.

Long ago Tony Forbes had memorized, "All things work together for good to those who love God." The hand of God had surely placed a new and deep love within him. No questions there. Even with his problems, Tony knew that he had spent his life trying to make good out of evil. There had been plenty of evil to work on. He remembered reading that if we tried to make good out of good, we'd soon run out of material to work on. Well, Tony knew he'd not wasted any time playing with the good. He'd spent his days trying to turn evil situations into positive possibilities. No, the truth was clear. He had not misspent his life.

■ ■ ■

Dorothy's sleep became increasingly restless as the night progressed. Twisting and turning, she felt her dreams becoming stronger and more troubling. Near dawn, a particularly violent dream gripped her, sweeping her away into a maelstrom of emotion.

Dorothy found herself in front of a beaten down house that was badly in need of repair. She entered timidly and slowly, edging her way through the dusty, dirty rooms. Cobwebs hung from the ceiling with a dim light barely illuminating the center of the room. The distant corners disappeared into blackness. Dorothy tiptoed through the living room into a large dining room, lit only by a candle sitting in the middle of a large table. The ancient candelabra was tarnished with large drips of wax hanging down from the arms.

Dorothy heard crying coming from a far-off room in another part of the house. Abruptly the dining room disappeared and she was standing in a bedroom. In complete contrast with the rest of the house, the bedroom sparkled with life and brightness. A wide wallpaper border depicted animal scenes and made the room look like a nursery. Dorothy discovered that the crying had turned into laughter. She tiptoed toward the baby crib.

When Dorothy looked over the crib, a small baby lying on soft blue blankets waved and cooed at her. The child's innocent beauty invited her to come closer. Dorothy reached out and picked up the baby.

At that moment Dorothy heard footsteps behind her and turned. A pilot in his flight uniform towered behind her, his frame filling the doorway. The man looked vicious, his anger evident in his menacing eyes. The man reached out a hand with gnarled fingers, curling fingernails. When the pilot opened his mouth, fangs suddenly grew out of his mouth making him look like a vampire.

Dorothy grabbed the baby and ran. The wall disappeared, and she plunged into a churning ocean that tossed her around like a small ship on the waves. The baby disappeared, and Dorothy struggled for her life. Suddenly a huge hand reached down from the sky, extending its giant fingers toward her. The ocean slowly disappeared, and Dorothy woke up.

For a few moments, the stewardess stared at the ceiling. Dorothy's heart beat frantically and confusion gripped her. Dorothy wanted to scream, but she stifled the urge. Instead, she concentrated on the snapping and popping of the fire.

21

Dawn found the survivors in the hut at Pei Song slowly waking from their troubled dreams one at a time as the two small windows in the front of the hut brightened slightly to announce the new day. Meyer had served on the last watch before daybreak, and with Helen's help, he had stayed awake until sunrise. A heavy cloud cover still hung across the sky so the sun was not visible, but the darkness had lifted.

"It's stopped snowing," Meyer announced, rubbing his hand back and forth on the glass to clear the heavy frost and peer outside. "About time."

Helen joined him at the window and let out a gasp when she looked outside.

"What's the matter?" Dorothy asked, looking up from the hearth where she was boiling water for coffee.

"Look how deep the snow is," Helen said, turning toward the others. "It's almost up to the window."

"The wind blowing across the runway made a drift," Meyer tried to reassure her. "It won't be that deep everywhere."

"What's all the conversation about?" Reese asked, poking his head out from under his blanket. "What are y'all doing up?"

"It's morning," Meyer said, "and it's stopped snowing."

"Okay." Reese looked out at the others. "So what?" He shook his head to clear away the sleepiness.

Senator Meyer and Helen stayed at the window while Dorothy divided up the food she had rationed for their breakfast and heated water for coffee. Bishop Forbes was still upright against the wall beside the fireplace and seemed to be sleeping, oblivious to the noise.

Jack hadn't moved since the night before, still flat on his back under a couple of blankets beside the pile of firewood. Mary Lee's makeshift bed was empty, but she was nowhere in sight.

"Where's what's-her-name?" Reese asked abruptly.

"Mary Lee's in the back room," Dorothy said.

"Doing what?"

"Changing clothes, freshening up, none of your business," Dorothy laughed, taking the sting out of her reproof. "Take your choice. Okay, who wants breakfast?"

Reese couldn't help noticing how their supply of firewood had dwindled during the night. He knew it wouldn't be as easy to find more of it under a blanket of snow. He and Meyer had already scrounged the easy pickings. The next time out, they would have to dig for it. Even if they could find some in the barracks, they'd still have to haul it back through the drifted snow. He scrambled out of his blankets.

Meyer grabbed Reese by the arm. "We have some business to take care of."

"It can wait till I've had breakfast," Reese grumbled. "Coffee at least."

"Now," Meyer hissed under his breath. "It has to be now, before the snow starts again or the good captain wakes up."

"Maybe later the sky will clear and the snow will melt a little," Reese offered halfheartedly. He had no stomach for tromping through snow all the way back to the wreckage.

"Don't be ridiculous, Al. It's not getting warmer, it's getting colder."

"You're sure we have to do this? That thingamajig is that important?"

"Absolutely vital. Come on, let's go."

"Okay, okay. Dorothy, save me some coffee, will you? And a helping of whatever we're having for breakfast."

"Are you leaving?"

"Yeah, the senator and I are going out for a bit."

"You're kidding."

"Nah, with the break in the snow, we figured we'd..." He saw Meyer shake his head almost imperceptively. "...see if we could round up some more wood for the fire."

"Okay. You don't want to eat something first?" Dorothy looked at the two of them, skeptically but not with suspicion.

"It'll do us more good when we get back," Reese said.

The survivors had all slept in their clothing underneath their blankets, and the two men buttoned up their coats and turned up the collars.

"Here," Dorothy called out to them as they were about to yank out the rags packed around the door. "Take these."

"What's that?" Reese asked.

"Scarves and sweaters. We didn't find any gloves, but I thought you could wrap the scarves around your hands. Maybe tie the sweaters on your heads. You don't want any exposed skin out there for very long."

"Right. Thanks, we'll wear them."

If the situation hadn't been so serious, the two men would have looked comical when they opened the door of the hut a couple of minutes later and scrambled out through the snow bank that had drifted halfway up the front of the little stone building. Both had sweaters, one argyle and the other an expensive cream-colored cashmere, doubled and pulled down on their heads, the sleeves wrapped around and tied to hold the makeshift headpieces in place. Their hands were wrapped in the scarves, making it look like they were wearing fingerless mittens. It was bitterly cold, and neither of them gave a thought to how they looked.

"Geez," Reese muttered after they had finally struggled free of the snowdrift in front of the hut. "This stuff is deep."

"Yeah," the senator grumbled.

As far as the two men could see, the world was a blanket of white, the deep snow undulating across the ground obscuring any landmarks. The burned wreckage of the airplane on the runway was all they could recognize to get their bearings. Both men stood gaping at the twisted metal as the image sunk in.

What had been a roaring bonfire the evening before had been transformed into a bizarre tangle of cold steel, like an enormous ice sculpture.

"It's like a..." Reese struggled for a word. "...tombstone. Only enormous. You know what I mean, like a giant memorial or something."

"It's hard to believe it's the same thing," Meyer muttered, "the same place. It's...weird."

"Yeah."

Reese looked around him at the field of snow, glistening in the dull light of morning. Above them, a solid sky of gray glowed thinly above the horizon where the feeble sun was almost breaking through.

"You were wrong about the snow," Reese carped.

"What do you mean?"

"I heard you tell Helen it was only deep in front of the hut because it drifted with the wind. It won't be that deep everywhere, you said. Well it is."

"Let's get going before it gets any deeper."

"It's deep enough already," Reese complained

"I can't help that. Come on."

The two of them trudged off in the direction of the berm at the end of the runway, Reese knowing better than his politician friend how easy it would be for them to lose their way and flounder off into deep snow. They wouldn't survive long if they got lost.

"I'll go ahead," Reese offered.

"Why?"

"To break a trail for you to follow. We'll take turns. There's no use both of us wearing out."

"Makes sense."

"I'm glad you think so," Reese laughed bitterly, listening to his voice boom out across the winter stillness. "I wish I thought it made sense to be out doing this in the first place."

"You'll thank me for this, Al," Meyer said. "You just wait and see."

■ ■ ■

Bishop Forbes had been awake before the rest of them, but he let them think he was still sleeping so they would go on with their business and not worry about him. Dorothy had fed them breakfast while Mary Lee remained in the back room. When Dorothy knelt beside Jack to wake him and feed him some broth and coffee, Forbes stirred and caught Helen's eye.

"Oh, you're up," Helen said. "Would you like some breakfast?"

"No, thank you. Some coffee, if you don't mind."

"Sure. I hope instant is okay." Helen realized how silly she must sound and laughed.

Forbes laughed too and smiled as she poured hot water from the saucepan into a cup and stirred the mix, then brought it over to him.

"Would you mind sitting with me for a bit?" Forbes asked.

"Not at all." Helen wrapped a blanket around her shoulders and lowered herself to the floor beside him. "Mmm. This is a nice, warm spot you've got here. I can feel the heat in the wall."

"Yes. I'm quite comfortable."

When his left arm wasn't aching from his angina, he could feel it growing numb and cold, beginning at his fingertips and working up toward his shoulder. His chest felt increasingly congested, making breathing progressively more difficult. He had begun to lose sensation in his legs during the night, as much a blessing as a curse since his swollen knee had ceased to torment him.

Forbes knew he was bleeding internally; his broken ribs must have done some damage somewhere. He suspected a lung was in danger of collapsing and had generally come to terms with the pessimistic prognosis. His breathing was difficult and his body ached. His time was running out.

And yet his prayers had been answered, at least in part. The mysterious sense of peace had not deserted him, had, in fact, remained with him in such measure that he looked forward to the fulfillment of the rest of his prayer. He wanted desperately to come to terms with this crash, to find some sense of meaning, and he prayed silently for God to be with him, to give him insight.

For the first time, the bishop sensed that God might have some important purpose for each of the survivors. Maybe, these moments in this frozen wasteland were a final testing time for each of them. Some of them might fail, but they still had been given a wonderful opportunity to think about their lives in a way that could affect them eternally. *Yes,* he thought, *each moment has divine potential.*

He took a drink of the coffee Helen handed him, then balanced the cup in his lap, freeing his one good arm. He reached out to Helen and took her hand in his. Helen looked at him kindly, and he saw compassion in her eyes as well as a deep sadness.

"A human touch," he said softly. "It's the best medicine, isn't it?"

Helen nodded, looking from his face to their clasped hands.

"Sometimes I think loneliness is the worst disease in the world. It's at the heart of all our ailments. The fear of being cut off, losing the sense of connection and purpose. The pain has the power to stop me in my tracks," he said.

Forbes watched a single tear trace the curve of Helen's cheek. She nodded silently and gave his hand a gentle squeeze.

Her hand rested in his, their fingers intertwined, and he couldn't help noticing the telltale line on the ring finger of her left hand, a silent pale band of flesh that spoke a thousand words.

■ ■ ■

Dorothy let her thoughts drift as she cleaned up their breakfast. She mused that Tony Forbes carried an unusual ambiance, a special thoughtfulness that the others lacked. Whatever his shortcomings were, the bishop genuinely seemed to care about the pain his fellow survivors were feeling. He dealt with his own injuries without the self-pity Dorothy had observed in the rest of the group. Bishop Forbes had a strength the others were lacking.

She had watched the clergyman slip off into a gentle sleep, looking tranquil and at ease, although his injuries would probably take his life in a short time. He wore no expression of worry or fear on his face.

It must be his spirituality, Dorothy concluded. *I've rarely seen a man who so obviously believes in the faith that he proclaims. I'm sure that he has his limits, but he hasn't shown them yet. I hope I can draw such strength from my faith.*

That's what she needed. Strength. Dorothy didn't know if they'd make it out of the mountains alive, but she was more terrified to face life with her unborn child than death. Where would she get the strength she needed to be a good mother? She needed the fire that Tony Forbes had. Yes, God was exactly what she needed in her life.

For a long moment, Dorothy thought about her need for something transcendent, personal, meaningful. She didn't know the right words, the proper expression to explain what she lacked, but she knew that a divine touch would make a tremendous difference. Dorothy remembered praying at mealtime as a child. Could she need something as simple as praying again?

Dorothy looked at the bishop's cross hanging around his neck. The plain gold crucifix seemed to be screaming a message at her. She could almost hear the words, "I AM the Way. Follow Me."

Taking a deep breath, Dorothy bowed her head and closed her eyes. *Are You out there?* she prayed silently. *I mean, are You really there? Closer than my next breath, like the bishop said? Because*

I need Your help more than anything in this world. I am desperate, and You can make all the difference. Please, give me the strength to face this child inside of me. O Lord Jesus, You came to help lonely people like me. I'm alone, and I have no one to turn to but You. I can't think of another time in my life when I've needed You like I do this very minute.

"Please," Dorothy whispered.

■ ■ ■

Reese cursed and flailed through a snowdrift so high that he lost his footing and crashed down in the white powder piling up to his chest.

It was taking much longer than it should have, much longer than it had taken them to make it from the wreckage up the berm and down the little road to the hut the night before. The snow had only begun to fall then, and the trek had been much easier. The snow had been bad enough coming from the hut to the flat top of the berm, but it was much worse on the down slope as they floundered toward the wreckage.

"Meyer, if we ever get out of this," Reese wheezed as he battled through the drift and found solid footing again on the rocky slope buried under the snow, "I'm gonna kick your face in."

"We're almost there," Meyer panted behind him.

"It's more like swimming than walking," Reese growled. "Swimming in molasses."

Reese had taken the lead at first, then Meyer had broken trail part way down the road to the berm. Reese took over again then, afraid that the senator would stumble off into trouble in his eagerness to reach the wreck of the plane and get his hands on the black box.

The trek was even tougher going than Reese had figured. He was a Southerner, used to hard work under the Carolina sun, coping with heat, humidity, bugs, and snakes. This was a completely different ball game, and he had begun to worry that they were more overmatched than he had feared at first.

"This walk is the kind of stuff that can get greenhorns in serious trouble," Reese groaned.

"Yeah," Meyer answered painfully.

Reese's breath was ragged, and it burned in his chest as he panted and heaved through the snow. His breath hung in the air like cigarette smoke. He cursed himself for not indulging in a smoke before they left the hut. Now was no time for it, he knew. He needed all his lung power just to keep trudging ahead.

When they finally covered the last few yards to the wreckage, Reese thought something was out of kilter. The heavy snow changed the look of everything, but he thought there was more to it than that.

"It looks different," Reese gasped, fighting for breath. Every deep breath he took seared his lungs, but he couldn't help gulping in the frigid air in hungry mouthfuls. As hard as he tried, he couldn't seem to get enough, and he could feel his hands and feet growing number by the minute. "Don't you think?"

"It's the snow," Meyer panted as he pushed past Reese and reached for the jagged metal of the severed end of the fuselage. It was less of a reach now, the snow built up under it. "The amount makes everything look different."

"Nah, I don't think so," Reese muttered, eyeballing the amputated airplane. "It's lying at a different angle this morning. Last night it was more..."

"What difference does it make? We're here now. Let's get inside."

Meyer clambered up from the clutching sea of snow into the remains of the first-class passenger cabin and kicked a seat to knock off the snow that clung to his shoes and pant legs. Both men were wearing the suit pants and dress shoes they had worn aboard the flight. They offered little protection from the cold that cut through to the bone.

As he followed Meyer up into the first-class cabin, Reese sensed movement underneath him, as if the plane were shifting. What had the pilot told them the night before about why he hadn't wanted them to make a shelter in the wreckage? It wouldn't be safe to build a fire, and there were too many gashes and holes in the fuselage that would let the wind in. But he'd said something more.

Meyer rushed up the aisle and disappeared through the crooked hole in the forward bulkhead into the cockpit. Reese followed more slowly, his lack of enthusiasm for the quest compounded by a queasy sense of unease. The rattling in his chest triggered a fit of coughing just as he reached the front of the aisle, and he doubled over into a red-faced crouch and almost retched.

"Eureka!"

Reese heard Meyer in the cockpit and the sound of metal clanging like a door banging open. Just as Meyer appeared in what had been the cockpit door, proudly wielding an odd-looking orange thing that looked like a tackle box, Reese remembered the other reason the pilot hadn't wanted to make a shelter in the wreckage. Harris said it wasn't steady. It was resting on top of some trees on the slope. He'd said it might work loose and go sliding down the slope during the night.

"I've got it!" Meyer exulted.

"Let's get out of here," Reese grumbled, turning for the open end of the fuselage as he felt the floor shift again, more noticeably this time. "We'll freeze."

"While we're here, I thought we might look around for a minute," Meyer protested. "See if there's anything we can use."

"This airplane is moving!" Reese yelled, looking back at Meyer as he hustled down the aisle. "We've gotta get out, right now!"

"Moving?" Meyer looked around him as if he thought Reese was losing his mind. "What are you talking about?"

The shift was hardly subtle this time as the wreckage groaned and flinched beneath them with a crack that Reese knew was a tree trunk splitting.

"Hurry!" Reese called out, turning to look back at Meyer from the open end of the fuselage. "Get out of there!"

Meyer suddenly realized that the plane was actually rising on one side as it began a slow but inexorable roll down the slope.

"Oh my God! It's rolling over!"

"Come on, you idiot! Run!"

Meyer flashed back to a scene, a midway ride at the state fair. He was trying to run in a straight line in a tube that was spinning around him. The seats on one side of him rising, first slowly and then much faster, and he heard the shrieking and groaning of metal all around him, gaining momentum as the wreckage worked free of the trees underneath it and began its final flight down the slope into oblivion.

22

In New York City, a senior member of the American U.N. delegation called on his counterpart from the People's Republic of China, receiving a cool though outwardly polite reception.

"You are here about the intruder aircraft," the Chinese diplomat said, uncharacteristically dispensing with ceremonial tea and small talk.

"The American airliner, yes."

"That is yet to be confirmed," the Chinese diplomat objected.

"No, as a matter of fact, it has been identified. It was Global Airways Flight 027 out of Hong Kong, bound for Delhi and then on to Frankfurt."

"We received information to that effect, but we have reason to doubt its authenticity."

"Not anymore. Global Airlines has confirmed the plane is overdue at Delhi and reports radar contact was lost about here, in Bhutan." The American offered his counterpart a map and pointed to a red circle drawn on it in northern India, near the Chinese border.

"This map is hardly proof."

"Global is holding a press briefing in Delhi now and offering counseling for family members of the missing passengers. There will be another press conference at their international headquarters in New York within the hour. We wanted you to know so you could prepare to deal with the inquiries."

"It was an intruder," the Chinese insisted. "No modern airliner would be so far off course by accident."

"I'm sure we both wish that were true," the American said, nodding grimly. "But the fact of the matter is it happened." He cleared his voice. "There's another matter."

"Oh?" The Chinese diplomat's eyes narrowed.

"One of the passengers happened to be a U.S. senator."

"Really?" The Chinese did not sound convinced.

"Yes. Senator George Meyer. I believe you know him."

"Meyer?"

"Yes. He had just left the Peoples' Republic after a round of talks with your senior leadership. You are aware of that, of course."

"Of course."

"You can see the problem we have." The American paused. "That we all have."

"I will inform my government of these allegations."

"Please do. And there is one final problem," the American added.

"Yes?" The Chinese sighed.

"We have reason to believe there are survivors."

"May I inquire upon what this belief is based?"

"I'm afraid this matter is technical. However, a beeper on the plane was activated."

"I see. Aren't those automated?"

"I'm sure I don't know."

"If so, that would hardly seem to offer proof of survivors. It is my understanding a fire was reported at the crash site."

"Really?"

"That is what I was informed." The Chinese shook his head sadly. "I am afraid it is extremely unlikely that there were any survivors."

"You're right, of course. Even if anyone did live through the crash, it's clear they wouldn't last long under those conditions. However..." The American let the thought dangle in the air for a moment. "If there were survivors, and if Senator Meyer happened to be among them.... You can see how regrettable it would be if no attempt were made at a rescue."

"I understand the weather is very bad in that region at the moment."

"Yes, so do I. However, I'm told there may be a clearing today or tomorrow. We propose to be prepared in case the weathermen are right for a change."

"This is an area of international boundary dispute."

"I understand, but that's not the issue here. My government is only suggesting a quick search of the crash site to put everyone's minds at ease about any survivors. We'll have done all that could be done. In and out. No lingering, establishing bases, or anything of that sort."

"Examination of the wreckage might confirm the plane was an intruder, a provocateur."

"Or an innocent civilian air transport."

"Such an examination might also establish that the intruder crashed due to weather."

"Or was shot down by your MiG interceptors," the American returned, "but that's not our concern either. We are only interested in survivors."

"Perhaps even our humble air force would be capable of such an operation," the Chinese suggested. "For humanitarian purposes."

"Of course it would be," the American smiled. "But as you say, that area is in dispute. I'm afraid the Dragon King's feelings about these matters are not entirely clear at this time."

"You would know much more about that part of it than I would." The Chinese diplomat sat silent for a moment, as if hoping the American would feel obliged to say more, but he didn't.

"Your government is proposing a limited operation," the Chinese said at last.

"Very limited, in scope and duration," the American confirmed. "No more than a couple hours at the site."

"I will inform my government."

"Please do."

"Tea?" the Chinese asked.

"Thank you, but I must leave now. This airplane problem has created urgent business."

■ ■ ■

Aboard the Shark, things were picking up in the data reception center below decks. CPO Gates had reported during his watch that the radar screen showed the skies clearing in the vicinity of Pei Song, and the sailor on the satellite imaging console reported he was getting better detail from the intelligence satellite locked in geo-synchronous orbit over China to provide 24-hour coverage.

Lieutenant Stiles hadn't slept well. Something had been gnawing on his mind, and he couldn't seem to get the picture of the 757 crashing out of his head. He dressed quickly and took a slow walk, trying to give himself some energy to face the day. He went up the steps to the deck above.

Worrying too much about that downed airplane, Stiles thought as he strolled along the side of the upper deck. *That's what's getting to me. I have to stop thinking about all those people out there in the snow.*

The lieutenant knew that worry was the key to most of his insomnia problems. Periodically insomnia would strike, and he'd struggle with getting his internal clock back on schedule. Usually a few days would go by, and then everything would become normal again. He walked faster, hoping that a quicker pace might energize him, but it didn't help. Eventually he slowed back down again.

On the second time around the deck, Stiles decided to try a cup of coffee and went back down below. The caffeine surged through his system with the first swallow of the thick black swill. He strolled on down to the message center to see what had come in during the night. As he walked along, the lieutenant unconsciously matched his gait to the roll of the sea. He was feeling better already.

Lieutenant Stiles found the fast pace of the communications hub to be running at the usual frantic speed. For a moment he watched the men working and then called out, "Hey guys, morning has come. You don't have to work so hard."

A couple of the men cursed, and no one seemed to find Stiles to be as clever as he considered himself to be. "Just trying to say hello," he confessed. "You don't have to take it so seriously."

No one answered.

Stiles ambled over to watch the data rolling in over one of the computers. Nothing looked particularly unusual.

"Lieutenant!" the sailor working on the satellite imagery called to Stiles. "Come here!"

"Yeah?" Stiles answered. "What have you got?"

"I think I've got something you'll want to see," the sailor yelled back.

■ ■ ■

Dorothy was worried about Reese and Meyer. They'd been gone much longer than she would have liked, but she didn't dare send someone out to check on them.

Helen and Bishop Forbes had been whispering together for what seemed like hours, and Dorothy could see the woman was in tears, leaning on the poor churchman and listening closely to whatever he was saying in that hushed cathedral tone of his. Sometimes Helen shook her head, and sometimes she nodded, as if agreeing with him. Whatever they were doing, it seemed too intimate for Dorothy to intrude.

Mary Lee had been out of sight most of the morning, doing something in the back room behind the fireplace, and Dorothy had been too concerned with the two men in the snow and with tending to Jack Harris to worry about what she was doing. Although Dorothy worried about the black woman's arm, Mary Lee could take care of herself.

Jack was coming around. After Dorothy had propped him up and spooned two cups of hot soup down his throat and practically forced him to drink a cup of coffee, he looked around the room, blinking in the relatively bright light coming through the two small windows in the front of the hut. He gazed up at Dorothy as if he had almost forgotten who she was.

"Hi, baby," he said softly. "How long was I out?"

"All night and then some," Dorothy answered. "You needed the sleep. You were in rough shape last night."

"I feel better now. I'm not in any pain, anyway."

"That's not necessarily a good sign," she reminded him. "Let me take a look at you."

Jack grumbled but let Dorothy undo his blankets to check his feet. When she saw them, Dorothy knew there was reason to worry. Both of his feet were swollen and discolored. His toes had an ugly blend of blue and gray under the skin, edging toward black at their tips.

"What's the verdict?" Jack asked.

"Not great."

"Let me see."

The pilot shoved his feet out onto the floor and looked at his legs. His face sagged and he cursed.

"Give me my socks," the pilot snapped.

"You'll never get your shoes on, Jack."

"Just put my socks on, baby. One pair this time."

Dorothy did as he demanded, but she knew what the swelling and discoloration meant. Frostbite had set in from being out in the snow so long last night with nothing on his feet but his uniform Oxfords and thin dress socks. He had done more walking than any of the others, and apparently the additional exposure had been too much.

Dorothy handed Jack his shoes but didn't stay to watch him try to get them on. She turned away and went to one of the windows, hoping she would see Reese and Meyer making their way back.

"Where are they?" Jack called out. "Reese and Meyer."

"They said they were going for more wood, but..."

"But what?"

"They've been gone a long time. I went out to check on them a while ago, and their tracks led off toward the berm."

"Why?"

"I don't know, Jack. The barracks are on the other side. That's where they would have found firewood. If there's any left to find. If..."

"If the snow didn't bury whatever's left," Jack cut her off. "What time is it?"

"Almost ten o'clock."

"How long have they been gone?"

"I didn't check my watch when they left, but I'd guess a couple hours."

Jack cursed and struggled with his feet, letting out a short scream as he jammed his swollen right foot into his shoe. Grimacing and squinting, he forced his left foot into the other and tried to stand, but he didn't make it.

"Jack!" Dorothy rushed to him. She could see his shoes were stretched, the strings dangling untied. "Don't try to get up. You're in no condition..."

"I have to go see if I can find them."

"What's all the yelling about?" Mary Lee appeared in the doorway of the back room, her earphones in place. "What's going on in here?"

Jack tried again to get to his feet. He pushed himself up the wall into a standing position, but when he took a step and put his weight on his right foot, his leg buckled and he went to his knees.

"That's enough, Jack," Dorothy demanded. "Mary Lee... Helen...I have to go look for Reese and Meyer. Will one of you take care of Jack?"

"I will," Helen offered.

"You take care of him," Mary Lee said. "I'll check outside."

"No, I'll go," Dorothy insisted.

"Dorothy," Bishop Forbes called out in his most authoritative pulpit voice. "You stay with Jack. Helen and Mary Lee, if you don't mind, I think both of you should go outside and see if you can see anything of our two friends."

"Okay," Mary Lee shrugged.

"I'm worried about him, too," Helen said and then caught herself. "About *them,* I mean. Of course."

Bishop Forbes smiled and nodded. "Of course."

"I should be the one to go," Dorothy protested.

"On the contrary, Dorothy," Forbes contradicted her. "You least of all."

Whatever Forbes meant was of little consequence. Mary Lee was perfectly willing to go even with her broken arm, and Helen preferred searching to waiting without knowing.

"Bundle up, as much as you can layer," Dorothy cautioned them. "Don't go too far, and don't stay out there long. Just look down the trail they made going out and see if you can see anything of them."

"Yes, Mom," Mary Lee cracked, with the closest thing to a smile any of them had ever seen on her face.

"Their trail leads off to the left, toward the berm."

"Berm?" Helen asked, looking puzzled.

"The bank at the end of the runway," Dorothy explained. "Where the wreckage is."

"Oh. Right."

"No, left," Mary Lee joked. The joke fell flat, and she shrugged.

"Wait," Dorothy said. "Try them with these." She gave Helen a second pair of socks. Helen had changed from her dress flats into more sensible shoes, but they were too big.

Dorothy noticed that Mary Lee was wearing hiking boots. *At least one of us dressed for this,* she thought.

"Be careful," Dorothy admonished them after they were finally bundled up enough to suit her. They cleared the door of rags and pushed out into the snowdrift blocking the door.

"I should have gone," Dorothy muttered after she had shut the door. She looked at Forbes. "I don't know why I let you keep me from going."

"Why are you so concerned? Because you're crew and they're passengers?" Forbes asked.

"That's right!"

"Admirable, but you have a higher responsibility now. Beyond your passengers and even yourself."

Still on the floor and trying to gather his strength for another stab at standing, Harris looked up at Forbes.

"What are you saying?" the pilot demanded. "What are you talking about?"

"Her baby," Forbes explained.

"You told him?" Jack's mouth dropped, and his face twisted in a mixture of pain and anger.

"I didn't have to," Dorothy said, looking from one man to the other. "I don't know how, but he already knew."

23

Captain Maxwell was at breakfast aboard the Shark when he heard himself being paged to the data reception center. Hurrying down the passageway, he bumped into Lieutenant Stiles. The young officer reached forward, too excited to wait for him to reach the center.

"What's up, Stiles?"

"Look at this, Captain." Lieutenant Stiles shoved a piece of paper in front of the captain, a printout from the satellite imagery computer. "Read it."

"Okay, what am I looking at here?"

"Right there. See?"

"I don't see anything."

The whole picture was shades of gray, with the black contours of the mountains and ridges etched more sharply than before. "Rough country," Maxwell said. "Wait. What's this here?"

"Exactly."

"Exactly what, Lieutenant Stiles?"

"A column of smoke."

"There was a fire," Captain Maxwell reminded his subordinate.

"On the runway, sir. This is the runway, over here. We've confirmed wreckage there. This is something else."

"What do you think it is?"

"Secondary heat source. Look at this."

Lieutenant Stiles jammed a second print in front of his commander. The picture was color-coded for infrared, but almost as thoroughly gray and black as the first one—except for a smudge of orangish red in a spot corresponding to the column of smoke in the other print.

"I'm amazed," Captain Maxwell said. "Stiles, you've got something here!"

"Aye, sir."

■ ■ ■

Mary Lee and Helen stood in the tracks Reese and Meyer had made, shielding their eyes against the light reflected off the surface of the snow. The cold air stung their faces and lungs when they breathed, but there was only a light breeze compared to the previous night's driving wind. Overhead, the membrane of gray clouds stretched thin over a pale sun, temptingly offering the promise of direct light.

With no wind driving the snow and no fresh snow falling, the path Reese and Meyer had beaten out earlier remained much as they had left it. Mary Lee and Helen didn't start out right away. The immensity of the rugged mountains around them and the huge, open sky frightened them—they were stuck in the middle of nowhere, in the snow, with little food or fuel. Mary Lee and Helen struggled to find courage to look for their missing companions.

The wreckage on the runway was impossible not to stare at. The twisted steel filled them with conflicting feelings of sadness for the loss of life, gratefulness that they were still alive, and despair that the looming structure might be their memorial as well. With a few remarks on how the snow had transformed the sight, the women struck out.

The ice crunched brittlely under their feet as they walked. By the time they reached the point where the little road turned at the corner of the runway and headed out across the top of the berm, they were both considering turning back.

"Come on," Mary Lee said, summoning her courage.

At that moment something in the trail ahead caught Helen's eye, and she grabbed Mary Lee by the arm and pointed. "Is that them?" she asked.

"I don't know who else it would be."

"Hello!" Helen cried out, her voice echoing across the plateau. "Why didn't I think of that before?" she asked Mary Lee. "We should have been calling out to them all this time. Hello!"

The answer came back sounding weak and indecipherable. Less than fifty yards ahead, the two men lay, cold and exhausted, in the snow. When the women came up to them, Helen gasped and threw herself on the still form of Senator Meyer.

"Careful there," Reese cautioned. "Watch out for his leg."

"George, George! Meyer!" Helen screamed. "Are you all right?"

"His leg's torn up pretty bad." Reese's breath rolled up like smoke. "It's busted...I think."

"What happened?" Mary Lee asked frantically.

"The plane—what was left of it—rolled over with him inside."

"Rolled over?"

"Yeah. It must have shifted in the night, with all the snow." Reese explained. "The trees holding her up must have broken or something. I had just dragged him out the back, and over she went, all the way down the mountains. He caught his leg on a jagged edge of the fuselage and nearly tore it off."

"You saved his life," Helen rubbed her hands over George's face. The senator rallied and looked up at her with his campaign smile.

"Not yet I haven't," Reese said. "It's still a long way back to the hut. It's taken forever to get him up this slope."

"What's that?" Mary Lee asked, pointing at the orange object in Reese's hand. She knew perfectly well what it was but wanted to hear what Reese would say.

"Beats me," Reese lied. "But Meyer wouldn't let go of it until we fell down here in the snow."

"Must be important." Helen warmed Meyer's face with her hands.

"Expect so," Reese drawled. "Now that you ladies have rescued us, I'd appreciate it if you'd help us get back to the hut. I haven't had my breakfast yet."

■ ■ ■

At the Wan Chow radar station, Lieutenant Zhou heard the sound of vehicles pulling up on the hilltop outside the ramshackle building. Brakes squealed and doors slammed. He heard the clambering of boots and footsteps leading to the door.

Lieutenant Zhou got up from the chair at his desk and pushed aside the partition that separated his office from the room where Yong sat.

Yong looked up from his empty screen as the lieutenant reached behind the partition for his uniform cap. Running one hand over his hair to flatten it, Zhou set his cap in place and tugged at his army tunic.

"Soldiers are outside, Lieutenant," Yong said.

"That's right." Zhou looked solemnly straight ahead. "We have company."

"Perhaps we are to be relieved at last," Yong offered.

"Yes, I'm sure that's it." Zhou looked at the young soldier. He saw Yong start to rise from his seat. "Remain at your post," he ordered.

"Yes, sir."

There was no knock, just the scuffle of boots and the door swung open. Colonel Qong stepped inside and ignored their salutes. Yong arose out of respect for the colonel, ignoring his lieutenant's order to remain at his post.

"Lieutenant Zhou," the colonel said, his face devoid of expression.

"Colonel Qong."

Zhou and Yong held their salutes.

Colonel Qong strode into the room and took it in with a quick glance. He stepped in front of the lieutenant, still pointedly not returning their salute.

"You have involved the People's Republic in a regrettable international incident with civilians."

Lieutenant Zhou knew there was nothing for him to say. It did not matter that he had tried desperately to reach Colonel Qong for instructions, that he had kept the command center at district headquarters scrupulously informed of developments that they almost certainly were following anyway. It did not matter that, had he failed to take action in the absence of orders and allowed the intruder to escape unscathed, he would have been tried and found guilty of dereliction and a failure of revolutionary fortitude. None of it mattered.

"But Comrade Colonel," Yong sputtered, "the lieutenant and I did our duty, sir. We detected the intruder and reported it to district. We...did our duty. Sir."

"The airplane was a civilian air transport," the colonel said in a flat tone hardly more than a whisper. "The pilot panicked and crashed in weather trying to make it back over the mountains."

"Our interceptors could have shot him down with missiles, Comrade Colonel." Zhou made his case, even though he knew the matter was already decided. "But in the absence of orders from district, I instructed them to disable the aircraft with cannon fire only. My intent was to force him down within our borders."

"He crashed in a disputed border district instead," the colonel noted dryly.

"Perhaps if we had received a more timely response from district, Comrade Colonel, we might have acted more promptly and avoided that unfortunate development."

Colonel Qong stood directly in front of Zhou and looked him in the eye. The lieutenant returned his stare, knowing he had nothing to lose.

Zhou saw the colonel's lips curl almost imperceptibly at the corners, the merest suggestion of a smile.

Without another word, the colonel stepped aside and, with a gesture to the squad of soldiers, turned, walked out the door, and climbed back into his staff car.

The soldiers formed on either side of Lieutenant Zhou and Yong, leaving the way open for them to follow the colonel outside.

Yong looked at the lieutenant in bewilderment, but Zhou said nothing and did not look at Yong. Yong lowered his salute and stepped between the soldiers with their rifles. Yong followed, and the two marched out of the Wan Chow radar station to the waiting truck and climbed into the back, where they were joined by the soldiers for what Lieutenant Zhou knew would not be a long ride. He understood there would be no search planes sent out for the MiG flight leader, and he knew the soldiers Colonel Qong had brought along with him would be their firing squad.

Zhou looked at Yong, seated beside him in the back of the truck. The radar operator looked frightened and uncertain. Zhou could neither do nor say anything to comfort Yong, the simple villager, who had only done his job.

■ ■ ■

The senior American member of the U.S. delegation to the U.N. found it unnecessary to call again on his counterpart in the Chinese delegation. The Chinese diplomat, however, found it neceassary to drop by his office. The American greeted the man civilly, and the diplomat immediately got down to business.

"The People's Republic of China requests that I express its appreciation for your government's offer to conduct a rescue operation in the disputed border region related to the alleged spy plane. However, given the unlikely prospects that there are actually any survivors, my government regrets that it must restate its objection to any third-party intervention in this disputed area. We, of course, do not suspect that your government's motive in this matter is any form of subterfuge aimed at embarrassing the People's Republic, or that your government is motivated by anything other than the highest degree of humanitarianism. Still, we must decline. This is my government's official response to your proposal."

"Thank you for bringing me this response so promptly," the American smiled. "However, I suggest that your government may wish to reconsider."

The Chinese was obviously offended, though he controlled his reaction.

"May I ask on what grounds you make such a bold suggestion?"

"Here, you may have these," the American said, pushing two computer printouts across his desk. The pictures were the two satellite images recently received from the Shark via the Front Office, showing Pei Song airbase with the column of smoke rising from what appeared to be a hut alongside the runway on one image, and the smudge of heat as color on the infrared version of the same image. "To forward to your government."

"I am afraid this is technical..."

"And I'm no more qualified than you are to evaluate such data," the American diplomat said with a smile. "But I have it on good authority that dead people don't make chimney smoke."

The Chinese diplomat took the two printouts and studied them closely.

"Coffee?" the American offered.

"Thank you, I'd love some." The Chinese diplomat kept staring at the pictures.

Reese thought one of the women should go back to the hut and get the makeshift firewood rig he had lashed together the night before, the two long boards tied together with cable from the wreckage of the plane. Because Helen wanted to stay with the senator, Mary Lee volunteered. She made good time on the way back and only stayed at the hut long enough to grab Reese's contraption and tell Dorothy what was going on. Jack wanted to go in her place to help bring Meyer back, but he only made it as far as the front door before Mary Lee was gone through the snowdrift and down the trail.

Half an hour later, Dorothy stood watch at one of the front windows and saw the little party come into view around a cluster of pines buried in snow. By the time they punched through the snowdrift in front of the door and set Meyer down, they were exhausted. Dorothy immediately had them out of their shoes and wet socks, putting on dry ones. Outside, the sun was still hidden by clouds, and the time was well past noon. Reese optimistically suggested that the clouds were higher than they had been and that they didn't look as thick as they actually were.

"Good enough weather to fly in, I guess," Reese said, aiming his remark at Jack. "With instruments and everything, they could find us in this, couldn't they?"

"Probably," Jack grumped.

Dorothy bustled around, making sure everybody got into dry clothes, offering whatever was left from the collection of passengers' clothing they'd salvaged.

"Don't worry about the fit," Dorothy warned. "Just put the dry stuff on. You men, wear dresses if you have to, or wrap sweaters around your legs and bundle up in blankets till your things dry out."

Dorothy had a meal ready for them, too, the rest of the rolls and all the snack-sized wedges of cheese she had hoarded, topped off with bits of chocolate. The survivors were exhausted and hungry, their bodies craving nourishment. They ate frantically, even Jack and the senator.

Reese's feet were bad, but not as bad as Jack's had been. The Southerner had been out a long time, and the temperature was deadly. He would limp for awhile, but Dorothy knew he wouldn't lose any toes. She couldn't say the same for Jack.

Helen had come through the ordeal in pretty good shape, thanks in large measure to the scarves Dorothy had insisted she wrap around her feet before going out. Mary Lee, dressed in jeans and hiking boots, seemed none the worse for wear.

Senator Meyer was in serious trouble. His leg was fractured below the knee, and he lay on the makeshift travois at an odd angle. To complicate things, the man had suffered a gash from the jagged metal of the airplane. The wound was deep enough and big enough that Dorothy knew he would likely have bled to death if it hadn't been so cold that the blood in the cut congealed, effectively cauterizing the wound, at least temporarily. Everything Dorothy had in her first-aid kit would be required to clean and dress the gash and to make sure it didn't start bleeding again. Whatever Dorothy did, she wasn't sure they could save the leg. It might come down to an amputation to save his life, and she knew even that might not be enough. Plus, they didn't have the equipment.

At least we won't make it long enough for gangrene to set in, Dorothy thought bitterly.

Dorothy had listened and waited all day for the sound of an engine, an airplane or helicopter, some sign that someone was out there. She didn't care if it was the Chinese, as long as somebody was looking for them. A Chinese prison camp didn't sound all that bad to her at the moment.

"What in God's name did you two go back there to find?" Jack demanded angrily. "Tell me."

Reese, who had been warming his hands over the fire, turned to look at Meyer before he faced Jack. Meyer was rolling his head and mumbling as Helen leaned over him, stroking his face.

"It was his idea," Reese said, pointing at Meyer with his thumb.

"Sure it was my idea," Meyer said, his voice surprisingly strong. He abruptly sat upright and rolled on his hip, turning to face Jack. His face was red and his eyes showing their whites. "This whole thing was my idea."

Meyer raised the cockpit data recorder he clutched in both hands. He had held it on his chest all the way back to the hut while Reese and the two women took turns dragging him along.

"That's...why, you crazy...that's the..." Jack stuttered.

"The black box," Meyer shouted triumphantly. "That's right. That's what you call it, hero. Know what I call it? I call it the eye of God!"

"Computer malfunction, you said," Meyer was livid now, and Jack was his target. "Weather, you said. Is that your story, hero? Well, I guess we'll see about that, won't we?"

"Senator, you need to calm down," Dorothy cautioned, kneeling beside him with the first-aid kit in hand.

"That's right, Meyer," Helen chimed in. For some strange reason, she had taken to calling him Meyer, as if it were his first name. She didn't seem to be able to bring herself to call him George. "Lie down and take it easy. Let Dorothy take care of that leg for you."

"The eye of God, hero!" Meyer continued, ignoring the women's concerns. "This little baby doesn't lie. The black box won't cover for you or anybody. It sees all, and it tells all. We're going to know what happened up there. I promise you that!"

"You two idiots tramped all the way out there in snow up to your waists," Jack groaned, burying his face in his hands, "for that?"

"You didn't think we would, did you?" Meyer taunted him. "Didn't think we could. Didn't think we knew about the black box, huh?"

Dorothy put her hand on Meyer's face to calm him and felt for fever. "Senator, please. You need to lie down."

"What's your story now, hero?" Meyer demanded. "Huh? Why don't you tell us what really happened, how we wound up here and all those people out there wound up dead?"

Meyer looked from Jack to Helen, his eyes sparkling wildly. "You can't hide any of it," he said and shot a glance at Reese, still standing by the door. "With this tape, I have you trapped in every lie you told us."

Jack stared at the senator but said nothing.

"See!" Meyer waved the box in the air once more. "We have the recording of everything that this man and his copilot did wrong. He won't be able to cover up what happened."

Jack shook his head and looked at the floor. Everyone in the room was staring at the senator. Meyer stopped waving the box and slowly lowered it to his chest again, waiting for someone to say something. No one spoke.

Maybe I overplayed it, the senator said to himself. *Nobody seems to be doing anything...saying anything. They just look at me like I'm a clown or something.* He hugged the box to his chest and gritted his teeth.

"Are you going to lie down now so that I can fix your leg?" Dorothy asked.

Meyer looked down at the gash on his leg. "Humph!" he grunted.

"You're bleeding again, Senator," Dorothy said without much emotion in her voice. "Stop acting like a victim, and let me try to fix your leg."

"Sure," Meyer said and took another quick glance around the room. No one seemed any more impressed with his heroics than they had been seconds earlier. "Go ahead."

"Hold still," Dorothy warned him and reached inside the first-aid kit.

Victim? Meyer thought. *Ridiculous. I'm a hero. A wounded hero. That one will play in the press. I can see it now. 'Senator hero of tragic shoot down. Senator solves mystery of pilot error.' I'll be in fine shape when the papers get this story.*

■ ■ ■

Air traffic controllers at the airport in Calcutta cleared the two big HU-53 helicopters to land on a remote part of the property where no one would bother them. They didn't know who was on board, but the word had come down from Delhi to clear them and leave the helicopters alone. Within the hour, another aircraft with a special clearance from Delhi came in for a landing. This craft was a big multiengine job with a tall tail that made it possible to get in and out of places where a plane that size had no business landing.

The whole thing was obviously military, but no one in the Calcutta tower had been told who they were or where they were from, and nobody was in the mood to ask questions either. Everything had all come down from Delhi, and that was all they needed to know. They had an airport to run.

■ ■ ■

"What's the word, skipper?" Lieutenant Stiles caught Captain Maxwell in a passageway below decks on the Shark, a fresh communiqué from the Front Office in his hand.

"You wouldn't believe me if I told you," Maxwell answered.

"Don't tell me they said no."

"No, it's not that," Maxwell answered. "That's the good news." Captain Maxwell was twirling one of his black cigars around his fingers, as usual. "Your men did a tremendous job, Stiles, and I'll see they get credit. Identifying that chimney smoke is what turned the whole thing around."

"So what's the bad news?"

"Not so fast. Let the good news breathe a while. When the Chinese saw proof that somebody was alive up there as of this morning, they started backpedaling. Our diplomats had already told them Senator Meyer was on board. If there's a chance he's still kicking, that's big leverage. He just left China, and they don't want any negative repercussions from the U.S. government."

"So, they're going to let us go in, right?"

"We're going in regardless. Two Huey 53s and a C-130 are staging in Calcutta even as we speak."

"Good. So what's the catch?"

"It's going to be an international operation."

"A what?"

"I told you that you wouldn't believe me."

"But how..."

"Simple. Our choppers, crews, and marines. One Chinese and one of the Dragon King's men on board each chopper. International."

"I don't get it."

"Simple. Bhutan doesn't want the Chinese in there messing around with the evidence, maybe knocking off any witnesses, much less establishing a precedence for military operations in the disputed zone. Conversely, China can't hold still for an American force invited by Bhutan, which would read like they were abdicating their territorial claims. Not to mention that they don't want us finding proof they shot down our airliner. Therefore, we go in with chaperones from both sides."

"I don't..."

"The deal is, we swoop in, grab any people still breathing, and we swoop out. No crash investigation, no collecting evidence. How's that grab you, son?"

"I can live with it, as long as we get the people out."

"Good answer," Maxwell said.

"Is all this international red tape going to slow things down?"

"No. If anybody's late, they get left behind."

"That's from the Front Office?"

"Not exactly," Maxwell shook his head. "But they picked a Marine bird colonel I know from way back to run the show. That's how he operates."

"Good. Will they get up there before dark?"

"No, too far and too rough," Maxwell explained. "They'll launch from Calcutta tonight sometime, arrive at the site as soon as they can after first light, as soon as they can see to pick their way through the mountains."

"Those people have to spend another night up there?" Stiles groaned.

"I'm afraid so. We need the weather clear enough for the choppers to get in tomorrow. Today was probably the best chance we're going to get." Maxwell shook his head.

"And there's nothing else we can do?"

"You could say a prayer, son, if you were raised that way. I get the feeling you were."

Her earphones hanging down around her neck and her recorder clipped to her belt, Mary Lee slipped off her blanket, walked over to Senator Meyer, and crouched down beside him, on the other side away from Helen and Dorothy.

"Are you still awake?" she asked.

Meyer looked up at her, a puzzled look on his face. He couldn't imagine what she wanted from him. He nodded his head.

"Good," she said. "I want you to hear this."

She disconnected her earphones from the recorder and adjusted the volume on the recorder, then pushed the play button and held the little black machine up so everyone in the room could hear it. What they heard were two voices, a little cramped and tinny, but clearly the voices of Reese and Meyer.

"I dropped a microphone in the pocket of that fur coat you're wearing, Senator, when you and Reese went out to gather firewood last night. I got it back when you came in and I took your coats in the back room to dust them off," Mary Lee explained.

"What?" Meyer looked up at her dumbfounded. "Why?"

"It's my job," Mary Lee said with a self-depreciating half-smile. "It's what I do." She flipped on the recorder again, loud enough for everyone to hear.

"What's that?" Reese muttered from across the room.

The survivors all heard Reese on the tape: "That was a nice bit of playacting back there, Senator. 'Reese? That name sounds familiar.' Whose benefit was that for?"

The senator's voice immediately answered, "For the record, I think our secret's safe, but it only makes sense to play the game out all the way."

"Their secret," Mary Lee explained to the whole group, stopping the tape, "is that they've known each other for years. Reese and the senator have been coconspirators in various felonies since Meyer's first term."

"That's a lie," Meyer protested, struggling to sit up so he could refute her properly.

"Reese is in charge of dirty tricks and shady deals for one of America's largest tobacco companies. Among other things, he bribes politicians."

"That's an ugly word, *bribery*," Reese argued. "There's no law against campaign contributions."

"How about obstruction of justice?" Mary Lee charged. "Perjury? Conspiracy? Embezzlement? The senator's saved your company millions, tipping you off to committee subpoenas, helping you hide research reports and memos. He's been part of your cover-up for years."

Mary Lee fast-forwarded past the two men's conversation about how to gather firewood, then let the tape play again.

Reese's voice boomed, "You really think our secret is safe, Senator? You think we can pull this off?"

"If we play our cards right."

"You got something in mind?"

"As a matter of fact, I do," Meyer answered. "For one thing, I want to get my hands on that little black box."

"The what?" Reese asked. "The flight recorder you mean?"

"That's right. I know about these things, from committee hearings. I know where it is, and it's not that big a deal to get it out."

"The reason the senator was so dead set on getting the flight recorder," Mary Lee paused the tape again and explained, "was to deflect any attention away from the fact that he and his buddy Al Reese were traveling on the same flight. That would have raised some eyebrows in the Washington press corps, without a bigger story to throw them off the track. He explains a little later on in the tape that he's an expert at survival when it comes to the Washington press corps."

"That's...that's illegal to tape us!" Meyer growled.

"I won't bore you all with the whole thing," Mary Lee said, turning off the tape player. "But they were out there picking up firewood quite awhile, and they talked about a lot of things."

"Like what?" Helen asked nervously.

"Like what they were doing together in China. Their dealings were supposed to be top secret, but of course all their dirty dealings are."

"You're moving from gossip to slander, young lady. You'd better be careful," Reese charged with a look in his eye that he meant business. "That could be dangerous."

Mary Lee popped open the little tape recorder and removed the tape. She slipped it into the pocket of her jeans and deftly loaded the machine with a fresh tape. She held the recorder up toward Reese.

"Was that a threat, Mr. Reese?" she asked. "I'm sorry, could you say that again, on the record?"

"What are you after?" Reese didn't raise his voice, but his tone was hard. "What do you want?"

"The same thing the senator was after when he risked all our lives to get the black box off that airplane. The truth. That's all, Mr. Reese. Just the truth."

"Don't toy with me," Reese snapped.

"I'm not playing," Mary Lee waved her tape recorder at him. "Just keep talking."

"What were they doing in China?" Helen asked.

"Reese was setting up production agreements to use slave labor in Chinese prison camps to make cigarettes for Asian and Mideast markets. Right, Al? That's hush-hush, of course. As Al says on my tape, 'Slave labor don't make for good headlines back home.'"

"But what about Meyer?" Helen persisted, her mouth dropping.

"For public consumption, he was delivering a message on human rights from the President and promoting trade agreements to open markets for American exports."

"I am the champion of the working class and the small farmer," Meyer mumbled from the floor, delirious now with the pain in his leg. "Everybody knows that's true."

"You are the champion of the tobacco lobby and now the Chinese government," Mary Lee countered. She looked around the room at the others. "They were setting up a scam worth millions to export Chinese cigarettes to neighboring countries then smuggle them back in tax-free on the black market. They'd all get rich."

"That's a bit much, don't you think?" Jack spoke up from his pallet. He didn't mind the unexpected turn of events or seeing Meyer take his own medicine. The reporter had deflected everyone's attention from him and what went wrong on the flight. "An agent of the Chinese? Come on."

"I'm not making this up, Captain Harris. I've got it all on tape, in their own voices. Tobacco owns Meyer and they could ruin him if they wanted to, but he's worth more the way he is. They're settling public health and Medicare class action suits all over the U.S.—costing them billions of dollars! So, the tobacco boys are taking their act overseas to jack up profits. People like Meyer are good for that approach, good for business."

"You've got us on tape talking about stuff like that?" Reese laughed as if it was ridiculous. He didn't sound convincing, but he knew the tape recorder was still rolling, and he wanted to get on the record. "I don't think so."

"Meyer didn't have a lot of choice, really," Mary Lee went on. "Tobacco wants him to front for them in China, the world's biggest market and cheapest labor pool, and he pretty much has to play along. In return, not only does he keep getting his allowance from Reese, but arrangements are made for the Chinese to chip in big cash donations to his campaign fund. He won the last election in a landslide, by the way. Outspent his opponent four to one and had plenty left over for a slush fund, with a little creative bookkeeping."

"Lies, all lies," Meyer mumbled.

"I think that's quite enough," Helen told Mary Lee. "The poor man's not well."

"And a major priority for his slush fund is to make arrangements for his mistress, to make sure she's set for life so he won't have to worry about the woman selling her story and smearing his family-man image." Mary Lee looked down at Helen and shrugged. "That's about all. I just wanted to get that in."

At the mention of his mistress and the slush fund to set her up for life, Meyer groaned and cursed under his breath. He hadn't taken care of that problem, and if he died on this godforsaken mountain, there would be the devil to pay.

"Okay, missy, that's about enough." Reese's voice raised and he uncoiled from his slouch, getting to his feet. "I'm going to have to take that tape."

"That's right," Mary Lee said, nodding defiantly. "You're going to have to take it in front of these witnesses."

"What are you talking about? Witnesses?" Reese laughed. "We're all gonna be dead in another day or two."

"Then my tape's not a problem, is it?"

"Depends on who finds it."

"You are a company man, aren't you, Mr. Reese? Covering for your bosses even after you're dead."

"That's my worry. Now, you just hand over the tape, and I won't have to do anything ugly."

Reese moved toward Mary Lee, and she backed away. Dorothy and Helen both looked up at the two of them.

"Mr. Reese," Dorothy bristled, "we don't need any struggle now."

"That won't be necessary if this little lady will just be reasonable."

"Reese, leave her alone," Jack demanded, still sitting on his pallet on the floor by the stacked firewood.

"Captain, I don't want any trouble with you. You've got enough problems already."

"I said *leave her alone.*"

"Or what, man? If you get up from there, I'll stomp on one of them swollen feet and put you out of commission."

Jack winced at the thought but kept his eyes locked on Reese's as he fumbled under the blanket with his right hand.

"I know how bad my feet hurt," Reese went on, "and yours look a lot worse. So you just keep your seat, Captain."

Mary Lee backed away toward the door to the back room, but Reese took a quick long step and cut her off, trapping her against the wall.

Reese looked around the room at his fellow survivors. He held up his hands in an apologetic gesture.

"Now folks, I'm not a particularly bad man. I've never killed anybody on purpose, and I don't go around beating up women or anybody else, but this girl here is messing in some powerful business. I'm telling y'all, she has no idea." He turned back to Mary Lee. "You should have kept your secret to yourself," he chided her. "And waited until you get out of here to play that tape for people. If you get out of here."

"I wanted to give you and the senator a chance to respond, on the record," Mary Lee shot back. "I'm giving you a second chance."

"What a joke." Reese let out a bark of laughter.

"It's only fair."

"When did fair ever get in the way of the news?" Reese snarled. "Who do you work for, anyway?"

"I'm a reporter. Got me? A journalist."

"A big one?"

"National."

"That's what I figured, you trailing after us all the way over here. How'd you get wind of the China deal, anyway?

"A leak in the Justice Department." Mary Lee smiled and raised one eyebrow.

"Figures."

"Don't you want to know where my leak got his information?"

"I'm guessing you wouldn't tell me."

"Sure I would. He got it from the senator."

"Meyer?"

"That's right."

"Now I know you're lying. Give me that blasted tape, and your recorder, too."

"I'm not lying. Meyer stumbled into a Justice Department sting operation. When they confronted him, he started talking, trying to save his hide."

"You're nuts."

"Reese!" Jack demanded again, still sitting in the floor by the firewood, just at the edge of Reese's peripheral vision.

"Captain, I'm busy right now, if you don't mind."

"Leave her alone, Reese. Or I'll kill you."

"Come on, now." Reese half-turned toward Jack. "How are you gonna..."

What he saw brought him up short. Jack held a bright red pistol, a pistol with an enormous bore, like something out of a cartoon. Reese couldn't believe it, wasn't even sure what he was looking at.

"You know what this is, Reese?"

Reese shook his head.

"It's a flare pistol. You know what a flare is, don't you? An aerial flare?"

"Yeah."

"Well, this is where they come from. Up close like this, it'll burn you good. You understand?"

Reese blinked several times.

"Now go sit down and leave the girl alone."

"I can't help wondering if you'd really use that thing, Captain. I don't think killing somebody is all that easy."

"According to your friend Meyer, I killed almost a hundred and fifty people yesterday. What's one more?"

Reese took a deep breath and acknowledged with a wry smile. "Yeah, maybe so."

"Is that a chance you want to take, Reese?"

"You two stop it!" Dorothy looked up from the senator's mangled leg, her face ashen and her lips taut. She struggled to fight back the nausea triggered by the sight of the wound she was trying to treat. "There's no point in anybody getting hurt over that tape, unless you're prepared to do away with the rest of us, Reese. We've all heard it now."

"Yeah," Reese nodded, eyeing Mary Lee. "I guess that's the real reason you played it, huh? So you'd have witnesses, just in case?"

Mary Lee said nothing. She cringed against the wall, holding the tape recorder in both hands, still getting the entire conversation on tape.

Reese looked around the room at his fellow survivors. He smiled a tight smile at Jack, who still held the funny-looking gun pointed in his direction, and stepped back from Mary Lee. He threw up his hands and shook his head as he turned away and went back to his place by the door.

"What're you going to do, Captain?" Reese asked. "You going to hold that cannon on me twenty-four hours a day until one of us dies or until rescue comes? You have to sleep sometime."

"Don't talk like that," Helen chided him. "You sound like some kind of tough guy in the movies or something."

"Fact of life, Miss Helen. I really want that tape, and Captain Jack can't hold me at gunpoint forever."

"I want your word," Jack said.

"I beg your pardon, Captain?"

"Give me your word that you'll leave Mary Lee alone, and I'll put the flare gun away."

"You think a lot of my word, I guess."

"I figure it means something, to a man like you."

"Do you?" Reese frowned, staring at Mary Lee and then at Jack. "As a matter of fact, it does. You could say it's about all I got left, except for a bunch of money and some trinkets like this Rolex watch."

"Do you give me your word?" Jack insisted.

"I hate to, because if I do, I'll have to keep it, and I really ought to get a hold of that tape."

"Not if I can help it," Jack said, still holding the flare pistol leveled at Reese's face. "I guess we can do this one of two ways. It's up to you."

"All right," Reese said, nodding slowly in what looked like resignation. "I give you my word. I may try to buy it off of her, but I won't try to take it away from her by force. Satisfied?"

"Mary Lee?" Jack asked.

"What makes you think his word's worth anything?"

"Like he said. It's all he has. And then again...I might shoot him anyway."

"And that makes you the better judge of character, Captain," Reese said with a wry smile in place as he leaned back against the wall beside the door. He laughed softly. "I told Meyer we should have taken separate flights coming out of there. You know what he said? 'What could go wrong?' Can you believe it? That's what he said. And now look at us."

26

Dorothy hurried to bandage Senator Meyer's leg and then dashed outside, battling through the snowdrift. The drift was trampled down now from the others going in and out, and she was able to make it through easily enough. A few yards beyond the drift, she succumbed to the wave of nausea and retched in the pristine whiteness.

The others inside the hut watched her leave, but only Mary Lee went after her. She sidled warily around Reese sitting by the door as she passed to stay out of his reach, just in case, then disappeared through the door, calling Dorothy's name.

Outside, Mary Lee found Dorothy standing in deep snow, doubled over with her hands on her knees.

"Are you all right?" she asked.

"Yes, I'm just..." She retched again, "a little queasy, I guess."

"You don't look good," Mary Lee noted in her flat-toned voice, as always more attuned to facts than feelings. "You ought to go curl up in the back room if you need to, instead of coming out here."

Mary Lee wrapped her arms around herself. She shivered in the biting cold, the wind picking up again as the sky darkened. "It's going to storm again," she said.

"I'm pregnant," Dorothy said, looking up at the waifish woman. "Can you believe it?"

She found it odd that she would tell Mary Lee about the baby. Mary Lee was the least likely to care. But after pouring her heart out to Bishop Forbes, it didn't feel like a secret anymore. She was tired of hiding the truth from everyone except Jack.

"All the more reason you should stay inside," Mary Lee said, unconcerned with the news. "And push fluids. You'll get dehydrated if you don't. You need to eat something, too, keep your strength up."

"I ate when everybody else did," Dorothy said, nodding as she straightened and looked out at the forbidding scenery.

"A piece of roll and some coffee," Mary Lee said, shaking her head. "I wouldn't call that eating."

"With the trouble I've been having keeping food down, it seems like a waste when there's so little of it."

"Sure."

Dorothy felt better now. She straightened up and was suddenly painfully aware of the cold and the gathering darkness. *Daylight doesn't last long up here,* she thought. She turned to Mary Lee with a skeptical look.

"Are you keeping track of what I eat for some reason?" Dorothy asked suspiciously.

"No," Mary Lee answered, then smiled sheepishly. "Consider me your friend."

"Thanks." Dorothy smiled. "I need all the friends I can get."

"You have a room full of them in there." Mary Lee pointed toward the house. "Those people have seen your strength, and you've cared for us like no one else. Don't you worry about a little problem like having a baby."

"I think that you're overstating my case," Dorothy protested.

"No." Mary Lee shook her head. "I watch people. Make a note of what they do. Keep conversations on my tape recorder. I may be a snoop, but I'm great at it. That's what I do, how I write my stories. You're the only person in this whole place who cared for the rest of us. That's what you do. Take care of people."

Dorothy frowned and shook her head.

"We're the ones eating the food you put together," Mary Lee pressed. "I've watched the rest of this group moan and groan. We've all been figuring out how to get ourselves out of here, meet our own needs." Mary Lee pointed her finger in Dorothy's face. "You've been the only individual to take care of our cuts and scrapes. You bet I'm your friend."

"Thank you," Dorothy answered softly.

"Now let's go back in there and make sure the boys are behaving before Sheriff Jack has to shoot one of them."

Dorothy laughed. "Thank you, Mary Lee. Thanks for your support. Let's keep my problem between us for the time being. I don't want anyone to worry."

■ ■ ■

Bishop Forbes stirred a little as the two women came back inside, shivering and brushing the snow off their legs as they pushed the crooked door closed and replaced the rags around the cracks.

Have we sunken low enough yet? he wondered. *Is it time now?*

His sense of peace had opened his heart to a deeper understanding than he'd ever known and a new inkling of divine purpose, but he knew that timing was everything. That much of his old cunning remained, and he hadn't the strength for a false start. He had to conserve his energy and make his words count when it was time to speak.

When Reese pushed himself up off the floor and began bundling up to go back outside, Forbes knew it was not yet time. Not while there was still enough pride left in any of them to rely upon.

■ ■ ■

"Where are you going?" Jack asked suspiciously.

"Out for a smoke," Reese turned toward Jack with a smile. He added, more seriously, "I'm worried about our supply of firewood."

"Yeah. Me, too," Jack admitted.

"We've used up two-thirds of it getting through last night and so far today," Reese continued. "I'm not sure if we have enough to get us through another night."

"It won't be easy finding any out there, as much as it's snowed," Jack pointed out.

"Tell me about it."

"Wait. I'll go with you."

Reese watched Jack struggle to his feet and saw the look in his face when he put his weight on his feet.

"I don't think so," Reese said. "I spent most of the day out there with Meyer and his bad leg. No offense, but I'd end up trying to bury you in the snow." He chuckled. "My own feet are sore enough already."

"I can take care of myself," Jack countered.

"Jack, don't be a fool," Dorothy cut in from the floor in the corner, taking stock of their food. "If you go out there for more than a couple of minutes, you'll never walk on those feet again. We'll have to come out and get you, and you'll only make it worse."

"I'll take my chances," Jack insisted, still struggling to make his way to the door.

"You'll die, Jack," Dorothy said softly with an undertone of feeling that stopped Jack. "Maybe you want to go, but I'd rather you didn't."

"Baby, I..."

"Please don't call me that."

"Huh?"

"Don't call me baby, Jack, and don't throw your life away trying to be a hero. Trying to make up for..." Dorothy's voice trailed off, and she looked away from Jack. After a moment, she regained her voice and added sharply, "Just sit down, Jack. *Please.*"

"Next time, Jack," Reese said. "I'll need some help in the morning. You'll be back on your feet by then, I imagine."

"Yeah," Jack muttered bitterly. "Next time."

■ ■ ■

Reese was surprised the light was going so quickly. He checked his wristwatch, tugging his Rolex out from under the cuff of the coat Mary Lee had given him to wear. *I guess it's because we're so high up, and the mountains all around us block the sun,* he thought. *Keep walking.*

Taking the optimistic view that he would find enough firewood somewhere under the snow or in the barracks to make a full load, Reese had brought his travois rig along with him. It had meant helping Helen and Mary Lee lift Senator Meyer up to slide the two boards out from under him, but if he got lucky and actually found some wood, it would come in handy.

Meyer had been out of his head, delirious, and Reese had felt the fever when he touched him. *Where'd the infection come from so quickly?* Reese wondered. *It would be awful to live through a plane crash and then end up like that. Too bad. Glad it's not me.*

Maybe it served him right, Reese thought as he stumbled through the snow and made his way inside one of the two dilapidated barracks not far from the hut where the survivors waited, *if that reporter, or whatever she is, really knew what she was saying. I can't believe that George Meyer would spill his guts to those creeps at Justice.*

On the other hand, Reese knew Meyer well enough to know the senator could and would do anything under the right circumstances. They didn't call him the Chameleon for nothing. If Meyer had sold him out to federal prosecutors, it would mean the end of things for both of them. No matter what promises the Feds made Meyer, he had to know that it would all come out sooner or later. The voters back home wouldn't forgive Meyer, and nobody was going to forgive a man like Reese.

Mary Lee had been right. Reese was in charge of dirty tricks and shenanigans for a corporate board that played tough and didn't mind getting their hands dirty to wring every last ounce of profit out of a deal. Reese had grown up hard, scrambling, and felt himself lucky to have found a niche where he could make a comfortable living and stay within the law—most of the time.

Along the way, he had learned not to demand too much of people he considered friends, like the senator. People could say Meyer was a crooked politician, but up till now he'd always been what Reese considered "an honest crook." Once someone bought him, he stayed bought and would deal straight with. He wouldn't double-cross the buyer or sell out behind his back to a higher bidder. In Reese's world, that meant something. Now Reese knew that even that degree of honesty had been too much to expect.

In a corner of the barracks sheltered by its walls, Reese had a stroke of luck. He found the remains of several rafters lying in a heap and spent longer than he realized collecting them and loading them onto his improvised sled. Exhilarated at his find, he worked feverishly to tie down the load before starting back. He and Meyer had brought in three full loads the night before that had lasted them through the night and all day, with some left over. This pile was hardly a full load, but he figured it might get them through until morning. After that, he knew, they would be in serious trouble.

Oh well, he told himself, *I'll just have to come back out here and find some more. When the plane crashed and the back end broke off, stuff was slung all over the ground. Maybe there's something left on the plane that will burn.*

When he dragged his sled out through the door of the old barracks, Reese got a sinking feeling as he braced his knee against the side of the door to get leverage for pulling the sled. He felt nothing in the knee jammed against the doorframe, even through his thin dress pants. He reached down and touched his knee, pinched it hard. Nothing. He felt nothing from the knee down. *How long have I been out here?* he wondered.

■ ■ ■

Back at the hut, Bishop Forbes watched Senator Meyer sink deeper and deeper into a feverish sleep bordering on coma. *I feel bad for the senator,* Forbes thought. *Delirious, mumbling something he probably thinks is a speech to his colleagues in the Senate and all the time clutching that gadget, that black box, to him like it's his salvation.*

Poor man.

The wind had picked up again, howling around them. Dorothy was at the window, watching for some sign of Reese.

She's the best of us, Forbes thought. *For all she's done and intended, she's the best of us.*

■ ■ ■

Dorothy stood at the window, listening to the wind and watching the snow fall. She remembered watching the snow drift down when she was a child. Those moments always seemed special, unique, as though God was sending His love in cleansing flakes. The vast covering of white turned all the dirty blemishes of the earth into a new world. The flakes transformed the bare trees and hard, frozen ground into something pure. Once again, a layer of promise covered the whole world with new hope.

For a moment, Dorothy looked at the unending white and knew that was the way she wanted everyone to see her life. If only grace could immerse her like the snow-covered wreckage on the runway, covering her jagged edges. Her errors, mistakes, and flagrant sins required a blanket of kindness extended back over the past. At this moment, the time had come to reach out for the possibility. The bishop had told her that three thousand years ago a man named Isaiah had promised that though your sins be as scarlet, God's forgiveness will make them white as snow. She wanted everything that promise from the Bible offered her.

"Dear Lord," she whispered, "please forgive me for what I've done in the past. I want to be like a beautiful endless white field from which new life can grow. I want this child within me to be able to come forth with the same purity that I want others to find in me. Please, please, lay a blanket of grace and worthiness over me."

Dorothy knew that she would not and could not terminate the life growing inside of her. No matter what Jack or anyone else said, Dorothy knew that she would protect her baby with everything she had.

"Thank You, God," she whispered again. "Thank You for this gift of new life. I promise that I will not bend. Whether I live or die in this place, I will love and care for this person growing inside me to the very end. Amen."

27

When Bishop Forbes saw Reese stagger stiff-legged through the door and fall to his knees with his makeshift sled wedged in the open door behind him, he knew that the time had very nearly come. The end wouldn't be long now. Dorothy and Mary Lee hurried to drag the sled inside and close the door, then Dorothy turned to help Reese onto his pallet.

"Stayed out longer than I meant to," Reese mumbled, his wry smile in place but his breath ragged and rattling deep in his chest. "My feet are...numb, kind of."

Dorothy stripped off his shoes and socks and swabbed his swollen and discolored feet with a rag before putting dry socks on him.

"How bad are they?" he asked.

"Not good."

"As bad as the captain's over there?"

"Just about."

"We'll see about that," Reese groaned. "I bet I'll be up and around before he is."

Mary Lee untied the boards Reese had brought back from his sled and stacked them against the wall by the fireplace to dry out. When she had stacked the last of the wood, she took the two long boards that made up the sled and stacked them against the wall, too.

"What're you doing there?" Reese asked.

"We might as well burn them, too," Mary Lee answered.

"Not hardly. What am I gonna use in the morning to bring in some more?"

"We'll worry about that in the morning," Dorothy said gently. She smiled at Reese and brushed snow out of his hair, off his shoulders. "You did good, Mr. Reese. I'm surprised you found so much."

"It was inside the barracks, the far one. Meyer and I didn't go in there last night, because..."

Reese seemed to suddenly realize something was different in the room, but it took him a minute to figure out what it was. Dorothy had taken the food from the stack in the corner and divided it evenly into seven smaller stacks. She had placed these small stacks beside the survivors' pallets.

"What's this?" Reese asked, struggling to focus on the handful of food on the floor beside him.

"We're almost out of food," Dorothy explained. "That's your share."

"Oh." Reese reached out to touch his stack, and they all saw the shape his hands were in with the fingers curled and the color unnatural. "Is this all there is?"

"Yes."

"I could eat all this in a gulp," he said, trying to smile.

"That's all there is."

A gust of wind rattled the hut. "Hear that?" Senator Meyer bolted upright from his pallet so unexpectedly that he knocked Helen aside. "An airplane! They've found us!"

"Hang on, Meyer," Helen cooed, trying to get him to lie back down. "You mustn't get excited."

"Can't you hear it?" Meyer yelled, looking around the room wild eyed, his face flushed and rigid.

"He's burning up with fever," Helen said to Dorothy. "Isn't there something we can do for him?"

"I've done all I can," Dorothy answered. "I'm afraid his leg's infected. Without medicine, there's nothing any of us can do."

■ ■ ■

Aboard the Shark, Lieutenant Stiles stood behind CPO Gates and looked over his shoulder at the over-the-horizon radar screen. He didn't like what he saw.

"Is that bad weather?" he asked.

"Yes, sir. It doesn't look good."

"What's fleet say about it?"

"They called it, sir. Front moving down from the north. High winds, moderate to heavy snow, dropping temperatures."

"Any hope for a break in the conditions?"

"Maybe. Looks like there's a gap between fronts." Gates pointed at an amorphous circle that looked like an amoeba on the screen. "See that?"

Lieutenant Stiles nodded.

"If that cell holds up, and the front maintains direction, there should be a little window up there sometime in the morning."

"How much of a window?"

"An hour, maybe a little more," Gates offered. "If the cell holds up."

"We should've been up there today. It was the best chance we had."

"Yes, sir."

Stiles shook his head and walked away.

■ ■ ■

"Iron Mike" Hawkins, the helicopter pilot, watched the ground fall away beneath him and felt the rush that always came with the launch of a mission. This one was not exactly what he was used to, but it had an edge of its own. He watched the members of his aircrew doing their jobs and was mindful of the grunts aboard, the infantrymen who would disembark and conduct the search. They had been briefed, knew what to expect and where to look. The men would start with the hut where the chimney smoke came up and hope there was still smoke coming out of the chimney when they got there.

The Chinese colonel and the Bhutanese major had taken seats in the body of Hawkins' HU-53 as far from each other as they could get, and that suited Hawkins. The less trouble either of them stirred up, the better.

"Linus, this is Magic."

"Come in, Magic."

"Vector three-six-oh for traffic and stand by for course heading."

"Roger, Magic. Three-six-oh."

"Magic" was the AWACS radar plane circling somewhere thousands of feet above where they could see everything. Magic would be their air traffic controller, directing them to the site and back, alerting them to weather and anything else that posed a threat.

"Linus" was the call sign for Colonel Hawkins' helicopter. He had long since resigned himself to the name.

The HU-53s were equipped with Forward-Looking-Infra-Red, or FLIR, optics, and all the rest of the latest technology, but there was no replacing the eye in the sky.

If this had been a standard military search and rescue mission, going after a downed pilot in enemy territory, there would have been a pair of Cobra gun ships along to provide cover when they went in, but this wasn't a standard mission, military or otherwise. This was a humanitarian outing, Hawkins had been told. An international humanitarian lash-up.

If they caught any luck at all, Hawkins' 53 would fly through the night and arrive within a few miles of Pei Song at first light. Allowing for a break in the weather, they could go in between the mountains and set her down at the abandoned airstrip.

On the assumption that Murphy's Law would prevail, Hawkins had planned for *everything* to go wrong. His second HU-53 was stripped down to the flight crew only and loaded with all the fuel she would carry. The second helicopter would land well short of Pei Song and establish a second staging area. If need be, Hawkins could have his pilot turn back and land there to refuel should the weather not cooperate or any one of a number of other things go wrong. If Hawkins pushed his luck with the weather and they got in trouble, the second HU-53 could off-load the extra fuel and come in for them. Hawkins was thinking through all the possible scenarios as he worked his way back through the body of the 53 to the burly marine manning the .50 caliber machine gun aft near the ramp that would open downward to unleash his marines for the ground search. Nothing sounded good.

"Everything all right back here?" Hawkins asked conversationally.

"So far so good, sir."

"Keep your eye on the foreigners," Hawkins said, as softly as he could manage while still making himself heard over the roar of the engine. "Watch them. Especially the Chinese."

"Aye, aye, sir." The big marine looked forward, then back at Hawkins. "And which one would that be exactly, Colonel?"

"The one on the left. Come on. The other one's Bhutanese."

"Got it."

■ ■ ■

All the survivors in the hut were desperately hungry, but no one felt like eating. The sight of the meager individual rations of food had an effect on them, along with the shrieking wind from the mountaintops surrounding the hut.

Reese and Jack were both too sick and exhausted to squabble any more, although Jack kept the flare gun close. They had agreed that the wood would be enough to last through the night at least, maybe until morning, possibly even until around noon. Reese had assured the survivors that he would be back on his feet in the morning and would go out for more wood then. They pretended to believe him.

Secretly, the women knew it would be up to them to go out the next time, and Mary Lee had already told Dorothy and Helen that she would go. They both thanked her but no one talked about the fresh snow outside or the fact that she wouldn't be able to manage much with her broken arm. The additional snow would make it even more difficult for anyone to find whatever scraps of wood were left and get back with them without ending up in the same shape as Reese and Jack.

The hut grew dispiritedly silent except for the wind, as each of them settled into his or her own thoughts.

"Have we sunk low enough yet, I wonder?" the Bishop asked in a low tone.

The other survivors looked up at him in surprise because Bishop Forbes spoke for the first time in hours, and his voice was strong.

"I believe it is not until we have exhausted our own resources," Forbes continued, "until we are absolutely without hope, that we are willing to listen to the still, small voice of God."

"Are you okay, Bishop Forbes?" Dorothy asked, looking up from Meyer in surprise.

"I am not delirious, Dorothy," the bishop promised her. "I have been biding my time, until our hearts were ready to listen."

Forbes dipped his head and cleared his throat. The survivors looked at him with curiosity.

"I know what I'm talking about," Forbes continued with a smile. "I had to be thrown headfirst down a hole to pay attention. We're all headfirst down a hole now." He looked at each of their faces and saw that they were listening.

"Senator Meyer said that the gadget he and Reese dragged back from the wreckage was like the eye of God. The black box. Miss McMurray has her own little black box, her recorder. It acts as the eye of God as well."

Senator Meyer stirred, hearing the bishop saying something about the black box. "The box?" he mumbled nervously.

"I'd like to point out," Forbes continued slowly, "that these are only machines, but the real eye of God is turned upon us now in this hour of peril. You accept that the flight recorder knows the truth about what happened up there and how we came to be where we find ourselves tonight. You accept that Mary Lee's tape recorder accuses Mr. Reese and the senator with their own words, captured from life. But can you also accept that God is infinitely more omniscient than these mere machines? He hears everything."

"Time to get religion, is it?" Reese moaned from his pallet, leaning against the wall beside the door. "You figure we're that far gone, Your Holiness?"

"Your courage in this time of trial has been remarkable," the Bishop answered Reese.

Reese nodded and took half a bow with a comical smile on his face. "I only did what anyone would do," he said, obviously pleased with the compliment even though he played it off.

Forbes turned to their pilot. "Jack, you saved us, at the risk of your own life, by finding this shelter and leading us here."

Jack eyed the bishop but said nothing.

"And, Dorothy, you have been marvelous."

Dorothy shook her head, not looking up from tending Meyer's leg.

"But we are at the end of our own endeavors here," Forbes said. "We've reached the limit of what we can do for ourselves. Time has come for us to admit that we are facing death and to settle our accounts. God is more omniscient than the black box. He knows every thought you've ever entertained, every itch you've ever scratched, every word you've ever uttered, every fear and need you've ever felt." Forbes looked around the little room, into the eyes of the other survivors, each in turn.

No one spoke.

"Each of us has a black box," the churchman went on, tapping his chest with his good hand. "Here, inside us. Call it conscience, morals, whatever you like. I call it the knowledge of sin. Our secrets devour us from within, and we suffer in our hearts the private hell of our sins."

"You're saying we should pray for deliverance," Reese chimed in, "for a miracle?"

"If you wish, Mr. Reese. Nothing is beyond the power of God." Forbes winced and struggled to draw a breath as if his inner wounds were sapping his strength. "But first we should seek forgiveness and make our peace with God. I thank Him for permitting me to live this long, to offer you this chance to reach out for the peace that passes understanding."

"Dorothy," Reese said, "didn't I see some whiskey in that stuff the captain brought back from the plane last night?"

"I don't think so," she said with a frown. She had used the whiskey to sterilize the senator's leg, and though there was some left, she didn't think they should waste it by drinking it. Reese looked sullen, and Dorothy reconsidered..

Dorothy had done all she could for Senator Meyer. She had to admit that a drink wouldn't hurt Reese in his condition. It wouldn't do him any real good, but neither would anything else, short of rescue, so she tossed him the bottle.

Reese caught the bottle, nodded, and then groaned, "My feet are starting to hurt."

"Mine could use a little help, too," Jack admitted.

Helen ignored the side discussion and turned toward Forbes with a puzzled look on her face. "Bishop Forbes, what exactly were you just trying to say?" she asked.

"That we are all fallen sinners, Ms. Bridwell. We are lost and are desperately in need of God's grace."

"I'm not sure that I understand what it means when you say we're all sinners," Helen said.

Forbes pushed himself up slightly. "When Christians speak of sin, they're talking about missing the mark, like shooting at a bull's-eye and not even hitting the target. We all know there's a right and a wrong, but that's not really the issue. The problem is not just something we didn't do right in the past but that no matter how hard we tried, we still can't reach the righteousness of God. Here's the bottom line: We've come short of what God intended us to be."

"I understand." Helen ran her hands nervously through her hair.

"We need God's forgiveness." Forbes raised his eyebrows. "Make sense?"

"And we should ask for it?" Helen asked softly. "Is that all there is to it?"

"That is a beginning, Ms. Bridwell."

"And then what?"

"And then God is able to come into your life, to be your loving Father. He grants you peace..."

"And then you die," Reese put in before taking a sip of whiskey.

"But you go to heaven, right?" Helen asked.

"To be with God," Forbes assured her.

"And to be with people you've lost?" Helen persisted.

"You've lost people, Helen?" Dorothy asked, concerned.

Helen nodded her head slightly. "He knows," the woman said quietly.

The bishop nodded. "Indeed." He thought about what Helen had told him when they had talked quietly earlier in the day. "Yes, God gives us the opportunity to be restored to the people we've lost from our lives."

"Most of us don't want to admit it," Dorothy said, "but we know that we don't have much of a chance of coming out of this place alive. If rescuers don't get here in a few hours, we will obviously freeze to death."

Helen ran her hands through her hair again and patted her chest nervously. "You shouldn't talk like that."

"The bishop's right," Dorothy insisted. "We need to make peace with this terrible situation we're in, and that means getting things right with God. No one knows how much time he has left. We could have died in the crash. Or even in a car accident at home. This roof could collapse and we'd quickly freeze even now. I urge every one of you to realize that God has graciously extended our lives to give us a chance to make things right with Him. We can't let this moment slip by. Each of us must act."

"Dorothy's right," Forbes added. "I don't believe we have much time left on the clock. The days have been reduced to hours. The minutes are running out on us."

No one spoke. A heavy silence settled over the room. Reese turned away from the group and looked at the wall. Jack lowered his face into his hands and covered his eyes.

"Maybe no one will find us," Dorothy continued, "but then again, maybe they will. I believe that one of the ways we make our peace with God is by being honest and facing ourselves truthfully. I, for one, want to leave something behind that might help a family member, a friend, or even someone who I didn't know, make sense out of my life. I think such an act would help us get right with our heavenly Father."

"What are you suggesting?" Jack looked up. His eyes looked red and watery.

"What if we wrote out our final messages on a piece of paper? Our will? Whatever we wanted those closest to us to know that we were thinking just before we died?

Mary Lee nodded her head mechanically. "Yes," she said factually. "A sort of final listing of the data we wanted to leave behind."

"Bad stuff about me!" Reese protested.

"Don't flatter yourself," Mary Lee shot back. "You've already missed the cut to make it into my final thoughts."

Forbes spoke up. "I think Dorothy has an excellent suggestion." He looked around the room at the bewildered survivors. "We could agree that no one would look at what has been written. If they rescue us, we'll destroy the letters. If not, they're here for posterity."

Mary Lee reached into a bag she'd taken off the airplane and pulled out a pad of paper. "I'm going to do what Dorothy has just described," she said, ripping out several sheets of paper. "Anybody else want in?"

28

Dorothy walked around the room handing out the pieces of paper from Mary Lee's notebook. The reporter watched her unemotionally. Bishop Forbes took his sheets with a smile. Jack reluctantly accepted the paper. Reese and Meyer seemed more confused, but at least they didn't resist. Helen appeared to be the most nervous.

"You don't have to do this," Dorothy said but still offered her the paper.

Helen shook her head. "I don't know," she muttered. "The whole thing seems too final, so ultimate."

"I'm afraid that's what we're facing." Dorothy kept holding the sheets of paper in front of her. "I know it's hard to reduce your life down to the size of a piece of paper." She looked around the room. "I don't mean a legal size. Simply one of those of eight and a half by eleven stationery sizes. We're all terrified to face death, but that's where we are. We have to push all that stuff we used to live for aside and become extremely simple right now. What matters in life? I've found that I regret not spending more time with my family more than not being able to buy that new car I just had to have. Are you ready?"

"You're right." Helen finally took the paper into her hands. She sighed deeply and looked down at the blank white sheets. "I'm ready." She looked around the room. Each of the other survivors appeared to be lost in their own thoughts and fears.

"Think about the most important issues in your life." Dorothy squatted down in front of Helen. "Just let whatever you need to make peace with come to the surface. That's what I think we're all trying to do."

"It's so painful." Helen began to cry gently. "I know that I've done so many silly and wrong things," she sobbed. "So many times...but I was only trying to push away the pain."

"That's okay." Dorothy put her hand on Helen's shoulder. "Everyone has areas that hurt deeply. I know what it's like to want to shove the pain so far down that it won't ever come up again...but you can't avoid it."

"No," Helen sobbed, "some things simply won't stay down."

Jack looked at them for a moment. He took a deep breath, bit his lip, and then looked away.

"Don't be afraid to get in touch with what truly hurts, Helen," Dorothy encouraged her. "Just let it come out."

Helen rubbed her forehead until the skin was crimson. "I'll try," she said softly. "I don't want to live in the shadows anymore."

"Good!" Dorothy gripped her shoulders tightly. "You don't have to."

"His name was Eddie," Helen began. "Edward Lee, really, but I only called him that when he was in trouble. 'Edward Lee,' I'd say. I'd yell it out like my mom used to yell my whole name when I did something wrong. He'd know he was in trouble then."

Helen looked around her for her purse. Finding it, she dug through it and came up with a photograph in a lidded frame. She popped the catch and the lid opened, revealing three faces, a man, a woman, and a young boy. The child looked pale and drawn, with dark circles under his eyes. She held it up, turning it so that all of the survivors could see Eddie.

"This was taken on our last trip together, to the Rockies. See how he's waving and smiling? On a great adventure." She put her hand to her mouth and sighed, a tear trickling down her chin. "That's me. That's my husband, John. And that's Eddie. He had cystic fibrosis...he died."

"There is no greater loss than for a parent to lose a child," Forbes said softly.

"John and I...got lost after that," Helen muttered, looking at the photograph. "I don't know how else to say it. John got transferred to Hong Kong, of all places. And...our marriage wasn't strong enough."

"Helen, you have already told me these things," Forbes reminded her gently. "You've confessed your sins. Why speak of them again?"

"I want them to know," she answered, gesturing with her hands at the others in the room.

Helen lowered her head into her hands. "I've been very irresponsible," she confessed. "Sort of crazy. I'm afraid that I'm going to be left alone. Thinking about death, about Eddie's death, makes me do things that I normally wouldn't. Do you understand?" She looked around the room.

"Sure." Dorothy patted her on the shoulder. "We understand."

"I've done things that I shouldn't. Actions that were wrong. I knew they were wrong, and I did them anyway." Helen took a deep breath. "That's what happened to me in Hong Kong.

I guess everything in my world collapsed." Helen shook her head. "John had the same experience. Hong Kong is so different. So foreign. It's easy to pretend it's a dream. That nothing is really real. And I embraced the dream—the nightmare—it swallowed us whole.

"You see," Helen continued. "Our problem was in how we dealt with losing Eddie. Because we didn't have any kind of relationship with God, we were simply lost. The unbearable silence of being completely alone in this vast world stripped my husband and me of everything that we believed in and held dear." Helen's eyes filled with tears. "If I had known then what I've learned through this airplane crash, I'd have known how to handle my son's death."

Dorothy hugged Helen. For a few moments the room became as silent as a mausoleum. Helen's sniffs broke the silence. "Don't worry," Dorothy comforted her. "It's okay now."

"The emptiness," Helen sighed. "Oh, the emptiness!" she sobbed. "My husband got in the habit of telling me, 'We aren't in Kansas anymore.' He called Hong Kong 'the fast lane.' Sex, drugs, whatever it took to ease his pain. I guess we thought that somewhere along the way we'd erase the hurt. Instead, we turned into different people. We did things that I once wouldn't have thought possible for us. We ended up living in two very separate worlds."

Jack nodded. "I understand. With each new thrill you need more to fill the hole, to kill the pain. And nothing you do is ever enough. You feel like your senses are slowly dying. You don't feel anything anymore."

Reese shrugged. "Sure. Anybody who's been around the big boys understands how that works. You go looking for the bigger thrill, thinking it will take your mind off the horror your life has become. Get as much as you can. You keep running to prevent the pain from catching up with you. But the fallout of emptiness settles everywhere you step. Keeps you moving faster and farther from the person you used to be."

"Remember," the bishop cleared his throat and added, "God has forgiven you, Helen."

"I guess I haven't forgiven myself." Helen wiped her eyes. "I've done too much wrong in my life." She took a deep breath. "I was on this flight because I was going to meet a man in New Delhi, a business associate of my husband's. Can you believe it? We were flying to India to do nothing more than fool around."

"Do you think God's punishing you for that attempt?" Forbes asked.

"No. It wasn't my first time. I've had dozens of affairs. I don't know how many anymore. You lose count, you know? If He were going to punish me, He would have done it already. Without killing all those other people." Helen looked around the little room at the other survivors, listening, thinking. None of them looked at her.

"I didn't want to be alone," Helen said. "Eddie was gone. John was gone as far as I was concerned. I was lost. I wanted... I don't know, a connection. I wanted to belong to someone, to be something to somebody. I latched on to Meyer on the plane because I couldn't stand being alone. I was nothing by myself. My life was...desolate. Is that a good word?"

"A very telling word," Forbes acknowledged. "And you didn't reach out for God in your desolation."

"No." Helen shook her head. "God killed Eddie, at least that's the way I saw it," Helen said. "Do you know what I mean?"

"I certainly do," Forbes said, nodding. "Death is the most difficult challenge to faith any of us faces."

"What do you mean, Your Holiness?" Reese asked. He raised his palms toward Dorothy, to show her that he wasn't intending to make trouble. "I have a real question. I'm serious, what do you mean by 'challenge to faith'?"

"It's called *theodicy,*" Forbes explained. "The problem of evil. If we begin with the assumptions that God is all-powerful and beneficent, then why is there evil in the world? Moral evil, like the Nazi holocaust. Natural evil, disasters that claim thousands of innocent lives. The most difficult question is why an innocent child must die."

"What's your answer?" Reese asked seriously, his attention focused on the bishop. "I'd really like to know."

"Theologians have debated the question for centuries," Forbes began thoughtfully. "There are Augustinian and Irenaean schools of thought, but many of their arguments seems sterile and insufficient in the face of personal experience. A man named Irving Greenberg wrote that no statement should be made, theological or otherwise, that would not be credible in the presence of burning children. That's an incredible burden, isn't it?"

"What's your answer?" Reese insisted.

"Faith in Christ." Forbes' eyes locked on Reese. "Faith is all I have to offer. We must accept God's love and omniscience and take the step of faith. God's will and His plan for each of us are beyond our understanding, but He does have a plan and He gave His Son in redemption of our sins. When we accept the salvation He offers, the confession of our sins and profession of faith doesn't exempt us from the evils of the world. If anything, we have more persecution. God never promised that this life would be easy. But we see that there's more to it than the pain on this earth."

"Sounds familiar," Reese grumped before draining the last sip of whiskey from the bottle. "But there's one significant problem that you're overlooking. A big problem. *We're* the ones suffering, burning, freezing down here on this hard earth. The Big Guy gets to sit up there in that heaven he created like a king while we're the ones being held over the fire. Where's your God, Your Holiness, while we're the victims of this vast eternal cosmos that He created?" Reese flippantly smirked.

"Where is He?" Forbes' eyes widened. "I suppose God is in the very same place that He was the day this world crucified His Son, our Lord Jesus Christ." Forbes shook his head. "You are wrong, Mr. Reese. God doesn't passively watch us sweat and then look the other way, unmoved by our pain. If I've learned anything from the Scripture, it's that God hurts with us and suffers with our agony as much as if it were happening to Him. The stories in the Bible always show me Christ walking with us, talking with us, and entering into the circle of other people's suffering."

Reese blinked several times and then shook his head. "Strong words, Bishop. Strong words."

"I believe they are the absolute truth," Forbes answered.

"I'll have to think on that explanation," Reese looked away.

Forbes smiled, nodded, and turned back to Helen. "Anything else, Helen?"

"Yes." She straightened up. "I thought so little of myself that I thought I was nothing without a connection to a man. When I knew we were going to crash, I was less afraid of dying than of being alone. That's why I reached out for Meyer. I reached out for him again, after the crash."

"What else, Helen?" Forbes asked.

"And then I confessed my sins, Bishop Forbes, and I felt the peace of God in my heart. In a way that I can't completely explain, I knew that Jesus Christ had died for me. Deep in my heart I realized that when He was raised from the dead, He had not only died for me but had been resurrected so that I might also receive eternal life through Him." The woman shook her head. "I simply can't believe that such a wonderful thing has happened to me out here in this terrible place. I feel at peace now, whatever happens. I know I'm going to see my Eddie again, and I know that God knows my heart, and His Son Jesus is my Savior."

"God bless you, Helen." Forbes sighed and closed his eyes as if his strength were ebbing away.

"God bless us all," Reese sang out, holding his empty whiskey bottle high.

"Cool it, Reese," Jack snapped.

"What's the matter, Captain? Got something you feel like confessing."

"I figure Dorothy's probably already done it for me," Jack grumbled.

"What do you mean by that, Jack?" Forbes asked.

"You tell me, Reverend," Jack snapped. "Seems like you got her to tell you everything."

"I didn't tell him anything." Dorothy fixed her eyes on Jack with a heated glare. "I told you that he already knew without me saying a word."

"Knew what?" Reese demanded.

"I'm pregnant," Dorothy declared. "I'm going to have a baby, and it's Jack's."

"Do you want to tell them?" Forbes asked.

"Yes," Dorothy said, standing up again as if getting ready for an ordeal. "That's not all."

"You and I have spoken of these things," Forbes reminded her. "You have made your confession to Almighty God, and needn't share what you've confessed in the presence of God. The matter is only between you and Him."

"I want to," Dorothy said. "I want everyone here to know how lost I was. Listen to me, Reese."

Reese looked at her, bleary-eyed, the whiskey making him drunk but failing to deaden the pain in his feet and hands.

Dorothy looked around the room at the survivors. "Bishop Forbes is right. We all run from the truth, even lie to ourselves. We forget that God never sleeps, and He knows what's in our hearts and minds...like Senator Meyer's black box. He's there every second, recording all our desperate maneuvers. We can escape only so long, and then we find ourselves up against the final barrier—death. When it comes time to face death, we have to reckon with God. The lying has to stop."

Mary Lee edged closer to Dorothy, her tape recorder in her hands. Still nailing down the facts.

Jack bowed his head, his whiskey bottles empty.

"I've always known men found me attractive," Dorothy said softly. "Beauty gave me a sense of power, and I reveled in it, always forcing the thought of the consequences of my actions out of my mind. Putting off the day of reckoning. We were a religious family when I was growing up and went to church every Sunday, but I got ahead on my looks. That was what people saw in me, what they valued me for. I was smart enough to figure that out, and I decided to make the most of it. I thought I was too smart for the 'Thou Shalts' and 'Thou Shalt Nots.'"

"Living in Christ is much more than a puritanical set of rules, Dorothy," Forbes said softly. "It's a loving relationship with a personal Savior who will never forsake you." He reached for a pocket Bible and then realized it had been lost. "There's a passage that I've found to be most helpful. Jesus Christ promises that if we invite Him in, He'll come into our lives, our hearts, and live with us. The issue is that we must stop, ask Him to come into the center of our existence, and then believe that He's there."

"I'm beginning to understand that now. I thought living life to the fullest meant living for pleasure, living to party. Then, I fell in love."

Dorothy looked at Jack, who avoided her gaze as if he could not face her.

"And I lowered my guard. Now I have a baby inside me." Dorothy pressed her fingers against her belly. "This child wasn't a blessing or a wonderful surprise. It was a problem, a crisis. And Jack had the solution. I was going to have an abortion on the layover in New Delhi. Jack had it all arranged."

Dorothy put her hands to her face, and the tears flowed.

"You are doing fine," Forbes comforted Dorothy.

"And..." Dorothy struggled to gain control of herself. "And...I believe that was what Jack was thinking about when he changed course. Because of the airplane's delay at the gate in Hong Kong, he was trying to make up time for the layover in Delhi. So we could...kill our baby."

Jack looked up from his slouch and found all eyes turned to him.

"What do you want from me?" Jack demanded. "It wasn't my fault. My copilot was a sot. He put in the wrong coordinates. It wasn't my fault that we crashed. The MiG shot us down. Remember?" He ground his teeth.

Dorothy shook her head and turned away. "Forgive me. I don't think accusing each other helps any of us. Arguing takes us down the wrong road." She forced a smile. "We're trying to take care of what's inside of ourselves, not explore what's wrong in anybody else's life."

"Dorothy's right," the bishop added. "We don't do any good attacking each other."

"Anyway, I now know that each life is precious, and if we get out of here, I'll be the best mother I can. I'm so scared to face the future, but now I can because I found strength in God. I know He's forgiven me of my past. I just want all of you to have the opportunity to see yourselves as I do. I was slowly dying on the inside. My beauty was just a shell that masked the darkness of sin inside. But this baby—this innocent new life—showed me how terrible I was. Now, Jesus has made me innocent again—like the snow covering the ground outside. And He'll do the same for you."

Helen nodded, a tear dripping down her cheek. Jack and Reese looked away, silent. Mary Lee took it all in but showed no emotion on her face, as usual.

"I'd suggest that we settle into writing our last will and testament," the bishop finally said.

"Anyone need more paper? A pencil?" Dorothy asked.

No one said anything.

"Then let's begin," she suggested.

Each of the survivors looked at the empty sheet of paper in front of them. The senator and Reese sat across from each other but facing opposite directions. Bishop Forbes held his pencil gently and watched Jack struggle. The women had already started writing. Quietness settled over the room. Outside, the cold winter winds whistled around the small hut. Snow bounced off the windows and icicles grew longer on the windows. The temperature was dropping.

■ ■ ■

Aboard the Shark in the China Sea, Lieutenant Stiles looked up as Captain Maxwell entered the data reception center.

"How's the weather up there, Stiles?"

"Pretty rough, sir. Fleet was right about the storm front, high winds and snow. Looks like the temperature's dropping significantly."

"Where's the mission?"

"Working its way up range, Sir. Magic is zigzagging them around local cells."

Captain Maxwell studied the radar and satellite image screens then looked over the radio traffic intercepts. "They'll run low on fuel and have to turn back if they don't land on schedule," he said.

"Yes, sir."

"They'll only get one shot if the weather turns worse."

"Yes, sir," Lieutenant Stiles answered.

"Don't stop praying for them," Maxwell ordered and walked out.

29

As the day progressed, the wind blew harder. The old hut creaked, and the windows rattled. Snow swirled in piles, covering the survivors' trails in the snow and making it difficult to walk anywhere. The wrecked back end of the 757 continued to accumulate ice and snow, each inch of ice causing death to loom that much larger above them. The possibilities of rescue grew slimmer as the snow deepened.

The survivors silently wrote out their thoughts and feelings on the sheets of paper Dorothy had passed out. No one said much or seemed interested in talking. Their sense of doom increased as the pile of firewood steadily diminished. They added less wood, and the room took on a decided chill as the fire shrunk.

Dorothy finished writing first. She laid her pen down and folded the two pieces of paper. After a few minutes of quietly looking out the iced window, the stewardess started rummaging through her purse and then turned to the large bag lying next to her. She found a handful of envelopes in her carrying bag and quietly passed them out as she checked on the rest of the survivors.

"You're doing okay?" the stewardess asked Mary Lee.

"I'm making it," the black woman answered stoically. "Thanks for inquiring."

"This envelope will keep your thoughts confidential."

"Sure." Mary Lee took the envelope. "Where we going to put these things?" She looked around the room.

Dorothy glanced around, recognizing that even the few pieces of remaining furniture would soon go up in flames in the fireplace. "Maybe we could put them in a pile up there on the mantel. They'd be hard to miss there."

Mary Lee nodded her agreement and went back to work, writing on her sheets of paper.

Dorothy looked at Senator Meyer. His eyes were closed, and the pieces of paper lay beside him.

"You okay?" Dorothy asked quietly.

Meyer didn't move.

Dorothy scooted closer and bent down near the senator's head. "Are you resting?" she asked.

Meyer slowly opened his eyes but didn't seem to be focusing on her face. The man's face remained red and flushed.

Dorothy reached out and felt his forehead. "Oh, my! His fever's gone wild. The man's on fire!"

Reese looked up. "How bad is he?"

"Senator!" Dorothy yelled into his face. "Can you hear me?"

"Y...e...s," Meyer more groaned than answered.

"I know that you're not feeling well," Dorothy spoke into his ear. "Are you in pain?"

"Uh-huh," the senator barely answered.

"Is there anything I can do for you?"

Meyer shook his head.

"Can I make you more comfortable?"

He didn't answer.

"What more can I do for you?"

The senator shook his head again.

"He's in bad shape." Reese scooted over by his friend. "Meyer's fading on us."

Dorothy looked around at the group. Jack didn't seem much better than Meyer, and Helen appeared totally dejected.

Time is running out on all of them, Dorothy thought. *These people are falling apart. They're dying in front of my eyes.*

"The senator's written something." Reese started to lean over and reached across Meyer's body.

Dorothy instantly stooped down and picked up the two sheets of paper lying by Meyer's hand. She folded the sheets and stuck them in an envelope she licked and sealed shut. "I'm putting all our letters over here where they'll be confidential." She walked across the room, putting her envelope and Meyer's on the mantel.

Reese looked angry but said nothing.

"I'd suggest that each of you put your letter up here when you're done," Dorothy stated authoritatively. "Everyone will stay away from them." She watched Jack, but the pilot wouldn't look at her. Dorothy realized that Bishop Forbes had not said anything for awhile. He seemed to be resting with his head turned sideways at an odd angle.

"Bishop Forbes?"

The bishop didn't move.

Dorothy noticed that he seemed remarkably still. Suddenly she realized that his chest wasn't moving either. Dorothy hurried toward him. "Bishop Forbes!" she called again.

"Oh my goodness!" Helen Bridwell cried. "I don't think the bishop is breathing."

Dorothy dropped down by the man's side. She grabbed his wrist and put her head on his chest. She didn't feel or hear anything. A deep sense of despair immediately settled over her. Dorothy couldn't avoid or deny the truth. The man that she had come to admire so greatly in such a short time was gone.

"Is he all right?" Mary Lee asked with more emotion than she normally demonstrated.

"No," Dorothy muttered and put her hand over her eyes. "No, not at all."

"What's happened?" Jack grunted.

"The bishop is gone," Dorothy explained softly. "I don't know what else to say. Our friend has left us."

Helen started to cry, and Dorothy held Bishop Forbes' hand. His fingers dangled loosely. Across his chest the sheets of paper lay in an aimless juxtaposition. Apparently the bishop had finished writing his letter and then died.

"Gone?" Jack echoed. "Just *gone*?"

Reese looked pained and started running his hand nervously through his hair.

"He simply ran out of time...out of life," Dorothy said.

"Thank You, God," Helen prayed. "Thank You for Anthony Forbes."

"Yes," Dorothy added. "Thank You for sending us such a good friend. He was just what we needed."

■ ■ ■

"Linus, correct to heading three-four-eight and hold."

"Roger, Magic, three-four-eight."

The helicopter pilot listened on his headset as his aircrew took their directions from the AWACS high above, and he thanked the good Lord for American technology. Looking forward past the HU-53's pilot and copilot, all the colonel could see was a murky darkness and swirling, foggy clouds. He had it on good authority from the AWACS that there was a full moon, but where they were flying, it wouldn't help.

The call from the gunner back in the body of the chopper brought Colonel Hawkins to his feet. He hustled back to see what the problem was, suspecting from the get-go that it would be the Chinese colonel.

He was right.

"Colonel," the Chinese began, half-bowing as if in acknowledgment of Hawkin's preeminence. "I humbly suggest that weather dictates we return to base. It is senseless to risk the crew and ship in this hopeless adventure, however noble."

Colonel Hawkins shook his head. "There's nothing to be concerned about."

"The weather is very dangerous. We should turn back."

"I understand," Hawkins said respectfully. "Your concern will be radioed immediately to our leaders."

Once again the Chinese diplomat half-bowed. "Thank you for your concern. It is important that my reservations are reported to the authorities."

Hawkins bowed and hurried back to the front. *That's all we need right now!* he thought. *Having one of these observers freak out is a huge problem this mission doesn't need!*

■ ■ ■

The senior American U.N. delegate got a call in his office from his counterpart on the People's Republic's delegation. They were both working late, and given the difference in time zones between New York and China, the fact they were both at work wasn't surprising.

"Good to hear from you," the American lied.

"I am indeed flattered that you saw fit to take my call," his Chinese counterpart prevaricated in return.

"What can I do for you?" the American asked.

"It is regarding the international rescue mission to Pei Song."

"Oh? What about it?"

"As you know, I share your lack of understanding of technical matters, but I am informed that weather threatens the mission."

"Really?"

"Quite so. But it seems that the operation commander insists on flying into the mountains."

"Does he?"

"I am afraid so. I thought perhaps that you could authorize a message recalling them. We do not wish to risk more lives in the small hope that there are survivors still alive at Pei Song. Isn't this so?"

"I couldn't agree with you more," the American delegate lied again. "As a matter of fact, I brought up this very matter within the hour."

"How felicitous."

"Exactly." The American diplomat swiveled in his chair to take in the view of Manhattan from his office window. "Unfortunately, these things tend to take on a life of their own. Especially when they're entrusted to the Marines."

"Ah, the Marines."

"You know them?" the American diplomat asked.

"Indeed. From the Boxer Rebellion onward, I'm afraid."

"Then you understand what we're up against here," the American explained, full of false sympathy. "Once you turn the Marines loose, I'm afraid there's no calling them back. At least, that's how it's been explained to me."

"Ah," groaned his counterpart.

"However, I will personally pursue your concerns."

"Thank you." The Chinese hung up the phone, knowing the American would do nothing.

■ ■ ■

At Pei Song, silence fell over the hut again. Dorothy, Helen, and Mary Lee had dragged Bishop Forbes' body from its place beside the fire into the cold back room and covered it with a blanket. They stood over his still form and prayed silently. Dorothy knew the men were of no use at this point. The whiskey notwithstanding, Reese had surrendered to the misery of his condition and fallen asleep, exhausted from his exertions with the senator and then bringing in firewood. Jack was no better. Forbes' death made the frightening and final nature of their predicament extremely clear. The pilot sank into a troubled and disconsolate state beneath the meager comfort of his blankets.

Flushed with fever and long since out of touch with reality, Senator Meyer was lost in a series of delusional conferences in which he managed to satisfy the Justice Department's demands of him while still preserving his viability as his party's next vice-presidential candidate. Beyond that, he sounded like he had managed to formalize his financial commitments to his mistress, channeling enough of his slush fund to endow some of her expensive tastes as long as she should live.

The three exhausted women hugged, bonding in their shared loss, and returned to the little room in front of the fireplace. Dorothy and Helen treasured their memories of the bishop for the peace they had found at his direction in the final hours of his life. Mary Lee didn't say much and seemed to struggle to assimilate the whole thing.

The effect of Bishop Forbes' death slapped a painful awareness into every one of the survivors. Their own demise could come as quickly as the bishop's had. Each person knew that the span of his life might now well be measured in hours, not years. The survivors dissolved from a group back into singular individuals, and each sank forlornly onto their separate pallets. The survivors responded to imminent pain of death by choosing to block it the one way they could—the numbness of sleep.

Thoroughly exhausted in mind and body, they gave no thought to assigning watches as they had done the night before to make sure the fire in the fireplace continued to burn. One by one, they fell asleep.

■ ■ ■

While the group slept, Senator Meyer abruptly sat up on his pallet and cupped his right hand to his ear, straining to separate the sound of an airplane's engines from the ambient noise of the wind outside. *No. Not an airplane at all,* he told himself. *A helicopter.*

He could make out the whup-whup-whup of a helicopter's rotors, that distinctive sound that always reminded him of the President landing on the White House lawn and waving to the assembled press corps. Meyer struggled to get to his feet, but his mangled leg was useless.

His fever deadened his senses while offering him the delusion of lucidity. He felt very little pain in his leg, but he couldn't make it work. It wouldn't hold his weight. Oblivious to the others sleeping on the floor around him, he dragged himself to the firewood stacked against the wall and, taking a long board in hand, pulled himself up.

The senator could hear the helicopter coming closer now. He had to hurry, or they might fly over and never see them. He had to get outside and wave them in.

That would play, Meyer told himself. *Senator loses leg in crash, still effects rescue. Yes, that would print all right.*

With the board under his arm like a crutch, Meyer clunked back across the floor to the door. It was all he could do, balancing on his makeshift crutch and leaning against the doorframe, to tug the crooked door open and hobble through it into the snow outside.

Finally outside, with the whup-whup-whup of the helicopter louder than ever in his ears, he took a moment to pull the door closed behind him.

Let the others rest, he told himself. *They need their sleep. They're not strong like me.*

Meyer would have cut a curious figure if there had been anyone out there in the snowy darkness to see him. Bundled up in a woman's mink coat, leaning on a rafter board from an abandoned Chinese barracks, he hobbled through waist deep snow, looking for a helicopter, guiding himself by the whup-whup-whup sound that was only the wind buffeting the battered hut, on the plateau at the top of the world.

The senator saw the helicopter. *There it is,* he thought. *They've landed. Out on the runway, of course. That's where they'd set down, safest place.*

Meyer had forgotten about the burned wreckage of the 757. The senator couldn't recognize the mangled steel on the runway. His fevered brain told him it was a helicopter, one of those big troopship jobs, the kind they would send for survivors.

Meyer pushed on through the swirling snow and darkness on the runway toward his rescuers. With his last ounce of strength and spark of life driving him on, he leaned on the rafter board and dragged his useless leg, fighting on through the deep snow.

■ ■ ■

When Meyer went out to signal the imaginary helicopter, the opening and closing of the door of the hut let in a gust of arctic wind that rattled through the little room and stirred the dying fire in the fireplace.

The remaining five survivors were so sound asleep that the noise of the door and even the wind whipping through hardly stirred them. They only groaned and wriggled deeper into their blankets, oblivious to everything except their troubled dreams.

Without realizing what had disturbed her, Helen roused to semi-consciousness and pulled her blanket down from her face. Something was wrong. She blearily gazed across the room before her mind could grasp the particulars. She realized the fire was dying. Where there should have been flames, there were only glowing embers. Tempted as she was to stay bundled in her blankets, she knew that if the fire died out it would be the end of them, and so she finally forced herself to stir.

After Helen had added new boards to the fire and banked the embers enough to make the new boards catch, she sat huddled in front of the fireplace and watched the flickering light of the fire wash over them. Her effort would keep the fire going for a while, but they were almost out of wood.

Turning from the fire, she knelt beside Meyer's pallet and reached out her hand for him, expecting to feel the heat of his feverish brow. Instead, there was nothing. She ran her hands the length of his pallet, rummaging through his blankets until the truth finally sank in.

Meyer was gone.

30

Dorothy had forgotten about the alarm on her watch. She had set it the night before to go off when it was her turn to stand watch over the fire and hadn't thought to turn it off. Shaken by the death of Bishop Forbes, she had not been concerned with standing watch when she lay down.

When her alarm went off, Dorothy suddenly remembered the fire and what it would mean if they let it die. She was jarred back from her dream of a baby in her arms in some warm, dry place to the nightmarish reality of the hut in the mountains.

Although the fire was getting low, it had not died. Dorothy had to double-check her watch by the firelight to orient herself. They had been asleep for hours, but the fire was still going. Someone must have gotten up and tended to it during the night.

Wrapping a blanket around her, Dorothy pushed herself to her feet. When she took a step toward the fire, she tripped over something beside her pallet and very nearly fell. As she struggled for balance, Dorothy saw in the firelight that someone had stacked food beside her makeshift bed with something else, something small and metallic.

When she had added a board to the fire and satisfied herself that it would burn properly, Dorothy turned back to her pallet to see what she had tripped over. She found two of the individual rations of food she had so meticulously divided up for everyone. The other thing on the floor was Mary Lee's tape recorder.

Dorothy looked around the room at the others. Mary Lee was in her blankets, her shoulders rising and falling in the rhythm of sleep. She counted again and had to stifle a scream when she realized that two of the survivors were not in their beds. Meyer and Helen were gone! She quickly checked out the back room behind the fireplace, hoping that Helen and the senator had gone there to be alone together, but the back room was empty.

She went to the door and saw that it was closed but that the rags that should have been stuffed into the cracks in the door were lying on the floor. From one of the small windows, Dorothy could see nothing but darkness and swirling snow, snow that had drifted up almost to the windowsill.

"Oh good heavens," she muttered. "What have they done?"

■ ■ ■

Tucking the recorder under her arm, Dorothy hurried to the back room and closed the old dilapidated door behind her. She pushed the earpiece in her ear and rewound the tape for a short distance. Listening carefully, she suddenly realized what had happened. The woman's voice buzzed away in her ear, filling in the blank spaces.

"No, no," Dorothy groaned. "We didn't need this problem!"

She snapped the machine off and returned to the room. She could see no other alternative but to wake up the group and at least make them aware of what Helen had recorded on Mary Lee's machine.

"Everybody up!" Dorothy said loudly. "I'm sorry to wake everyone, but you need to know what's happened."

"What?" Reese rubbed his red eyes. "What's going on?"

Mary Lee shot straight up. "Everybody okay?" she blurted out.

"Huh?" Jack rolled over and tried to get his eyes open. His face looked red and puffy.

"I hate to tell you but we have another disaster," Dorothy explained. She held up Mary Lee's tape recorder. "Helen left us a message. I'm going to play it for you." She waited a moment to make sure each person had given his or her complete attention.

Jack didn't seem to be able to push himself up, but Reese was now fully awake. Mary Lee's dark eyes were locked on the flight attendant.

Dorothy pushed the "play" button and the machine started to roll. "Meyer's gone," the voice of Helen Bridwell rang through the room. "I don't know why he left this building except that he's probably delirious. I'm going after him. I didn't want to wake any of you because I knew you'd try to stop me. I want to do this for him."

Mary Lee looked around the little room, as if to confirm what she was hearing on the tape. She couldn't believe that Meyer and Helen were really gone. Jack hung his head and stared balefully at his swollen feet, then looked across the room at Reese, who shrugged and shook his head. There was nothing that anyone could do.

"Dorothy, I wanted you to have our food," Helen's recorded voice continued. "You have the most to live for. Your baby is the top priority in my book. It's just as well that things worked out this way. I'm not afraid to die, not anymore. I am at peace with God, and I know I'll see my Eddie soon. Tell John.... Tell him...it's not too late. Tell him I said I love him and I hope he finds the same peace I have now. I'm going now because I don't want Meyer to be alone at the last. He's lost when he's alone, and I know how that feels. Good-bye, and God bless you all."

Dorothy turned off the recorder and huddled in her blanket, staring at Mary Lee's little black box as if the voice was a cry from beyond the grave. She wiped tears from her eyes and looked around the room.

"I'll share the food with all of you," she said, "divide it up evenly and..."

"No," Jack said softly but firmly. "She's right. You have the most to live for."

"There's not enough there to fight over," Reese offered laconically. "Those three rations all together will barely last you through the day."

"You need to eat," Mary Lee added. "Think of your baby."

"I wonder how long they've been gone," Dorothy pondered. "Did anybody hear them leave?"

The other three shrugged and shook their heads.

"We were all sleeping like logs," Reese said. "It could be hours for all we know."

"She must have tended the fire before she left," Dorothy observed. "It would have died if she hadn't, and it was still going pretty good when my alarm woke me up. I'd say she left about an hour ago, maybe a little more. I can't say about Meyer, sometime before that."

"The senator?" Reese shook his head sadly. "No telling what he thought he was doing."

"How long until daylight, do you figure?" Jack asked.

Reese raised himself off his pallet far enough to see out the window nearest him, and groaned with the pain of the effort.

"Not long, I'd say," he offered. "Looks like it's lightening up in the east there. Why do you ask, Captain?"

"I was thinking maybe you and I would go out and have a look around."

"For Helen and the senator?" Dorothy asked skeptically.

"For firewood," Jack said. "And if we see any sign of those two, we'll see if there's anything we can do."

"Makes sense," Reese agreed.

"It does not," Dorothy said, looking from one of the men to the other. "Are you two crazy? You wouldn't last..."

"But before we do that," Jack interrupted, "there's something else I want to do."

"I don't think..." Dorothy began, but she didn't finish her thought. She looked at Jack and felt the first stirrings of her old love for him. She knew everything was coming to an end, and she couldn't help seeing that special something in him that had once drawn her to him so powerfully.

"Mary Lee," Jack said, smiling tenderly at her, "would you mind if I borrowed your tape recorder for a minute?"

"Help yourself," Mary Lee said.

Dorothy handed him the small black recorder, and he looked at it for a moment without saying anything, collecting his thoughts. Finally, he clicked it on.

"I'm not sure where to start," he began. "I was going to do this last night, when Bishop Forbes was talking." He suddenly stopped talking and looked out the window. His eyes became watery.

Dorothy watched him regain his composure.

"He was saying we have to have faith that God has a plan, and trust Him for our future.

"Faith," Jack sighed. "Faith doesn't come easy for me. I'm too technical. I like to know exactly how something works. But it's more than that.... It's pride. That's what devours me. That's about all that I am inside—is pride."

Dorothy looked at the plane's black box lying amid the jumble of blankets on Meyer's pallet. She swallowed hard.

"What that black box is going to tell everybody is that the crash was my fault, all my fault." Jack sighed again and wiped away tears. "I was arrogant. I thought I was the hero, I could do anything. Beckman tried to warn me, but I wouldn't listen. He screwed up the coordinates, but I knew he was a drunk and I should have booted him off the crew long ago. Maybe I liked having him up there with me because it made me feel...I don't know...like a big man. I had power over him and...Lord, I am sorry." He began sobbing. "I am so sorry."

Jack slumped forward on his pallet and bowed his head, his shoulders shaking with the racking sobs that echoed through the little room. Dorothy knelt beside him and put her arms around him.

"This all happened because I wanted to make up the delay," he went on, looking up at Dorothy, "so we'd have time in Delhi for your...operation. I wanted you to kill your baby." He stopped and looked at the floor. "I guess I should say *our* baby."

Dorothy nodded and held him close.

"Can you ever forgive me? How could I have been so blind? All that mattered to me was this notion I had of my freedom. I wanted to leave the world behind me every time I took off in an airplane with all that power at my fingertips. Pride. Stupid pride. And now all those people are dead because of me."

"It was an accident, Jack," Dorothy whispered. "The MiG shot us down."

"And even afterward, my one concern was to dodge the blame. I didn't want to be responsible, I told myself that. I was going to blame the whole thing on Dave Beckman."

"We'll face it together," Dorothy promised, "whatever comes."

"No. I have to face this one by myself. The bishop was right about that. There comes a time when the lying stops and you have to face God alone. I can only hope that He can forgive me."

"Of course, He forgives you," Dorothy said softly. "That's what the bishop was telling us, that God's waiting for each of us to turn to Him and reach out for the love He offers. Confess your sins and accept Christ and His forgiveness, Jack. Put it all in God's hands."

"I do, I do," Jack sobbed. "I've always thought I was a strong man, but in my heart I know I'm weak and that I need God."

Dorothy held him close and rocked him gently like a child. The room grew silent, and she felt the warmth of his body pressing next to her. She had always thought him to be an indomitable force, an unstoppable strong man who wouldn't bend even when the pressure was insurmountable. Yet he lay in her arms broken, sobbing, crumbling before the face of death. At this moment, Jack's fear of losing his life seemed overwhelming.

How strange, Dorothy thought. *I always considered myself to be the weak one...but now I discover strength in a Source greater than myself.*

For several moments, Dorothy rubbed the top of Jack's head and ran her hands affectionately through his hair. The pilot huddled next to her with his eyes closed and eventually fell asleep, more like a wounded little boy than a grown man. Dorothy continued cradling him in her arms while he slept.

"I remember an old hymn from when I was a kid," Reese mused. "I was in church a time or two. I think it was called 'Farther Along,' something like that. There was a line in it, 'We'll understand it better by and by.' Maybe that's what His Holiness meant. We're supposed to have faith so that we'll understand it all by and by."

Dorothy kept staring at the black box. "I think it must be something like what happens with embroidery. From the back side, the thread looks like a mess, but when you turn it over, there's a beautiful picture in front of your eyes. Only God knows fully how everything will work together for good in His eyes."

"This baby is part of a plan, Jack," Dorothy told him so quietly that the words never became sounds. "Whatever happens will be the gift of God or it won't occur. If we live or die, the final moments of our lives remain in His hands...not ours."

31

The room had grown quiet. Jack seemed to have found peace.

"I'd still like to hear why you think God took the bishop out like he did," Reese broke the quiet.

Mary Lee watched from her pallet, saying nothing but taking it all in as if she had become the tape recorder. She turned and gave Reese her attention to encourage him to keep talking.

Reese sat slouched against the wall beside the door of the hut and eyed Dorothy with a keen interest. "Just to test our newfound faith, you reckon?" he added.

Dorothy looked over at Reese. "Maybe to give us the chance to find Him on our own. Bishop Forbes had shown us the way. Perhaps God was letting us know the rest was up to us."

"There's one other thing I'd like to know," Reese said with his wry smile. "The bishop said he had heard your confession and you had heard his. That right?"

Dorothy nodded, still holding Jack in her arms.

"Well, what did he confess to? Or is that a secret?"

Dorothy shook her head. "Not now, I guess. When the bishop was young, he hit a boy on a bicycle, when he was drunk. He threw his whole heart and life into being a priest, trying to make amends." She looked around the room.

No one spoke.

"Bishop Forbes had always doubted his own faith," Dorothy said softly. "He chose the church for a lot of reasons, and he always believed in his heart that he was playing a part, not really acting from a deep and abiding faith."

"This is the faith he urged us to find," Reese scoffed, but his eyes held disappointment.

"No, he found the peace in faith that he'd been looking for during the crash. He said he felt a sense of renewed understanding, and he thanked God for this opportunity."

"He called this an opportunity?" Reese's voice elevated.

"Think about it, Mr. Reese. Think about all those other passengers on our plane. Death came to them suddenly and violently. How much time did they have to make things right before the end? We're the lucky ones who lived through that terrible moment. No matter what happens now, the bishop knew that truth, and he knew God had blessed him by preserving his life and giving him this opportunity to share the true faith he had found with us. There's no greater blessing than to offer your faith to someone else, Mr. Reese. No greater honor."

"Well, I don't know if I can go all the way down that road or not, Miss Dorothy. And I don't have any last words I want to say into that girl's little black box, in particular." Reese turned to Mary Lee. "But if you want to roll tape for the record, there are a couple of things I'd like to get off my chest."

Mary Lee took the recorder from Jack's side and moved closer to Reese.

"And I won't take long," Reese added, looking out the window over his shoulder. "It's gonna be daylight in a little bit, and Captain Jack and I have business outside there."

Dorothy looked at Jack's closed eyes and shook her head.

"I was born dirt poor into a family of sharecroppers. I guess that's redundant, poor and sharecropper." Reese laughed. "My daddy ran off when I was about the size of Helen's boy that died. The way I heard it, he just got fed up with being broke and having too many mouths to feed and lit out. My momma worked hard all week, honky-tonked Saturday nights, and went to church every Sunday. There's plenty of churches where I come from, every kind of tabernacle and lame-brained Holy Roller outfit you can imagine. That's where I heard that hymn I told you about."

Dorothy could see the first hint of light outside, brightening the dirty window behind Reese's head. It wouldn't be long now before the new day began.

"Well, imagine my surprise one Sunday evening when I came home and caught Momma in bed with one of them preachers. That didn't do much for my respect for religion. I still see them every time I turn on a TV or read a newspaper, 'Preacher so-and-so caught in a motel with a hooker.' 'Brother what's-his-face indicted for embezzling church funds!' It kinda turned me to hanging out with what I call honest crooks. People like me. We may not be much, but we don't claim to be. At least we're not hypocrites."

"It's your mortal soul," Dorothy said, shaking her head and looking at Reese like he was drowning. "Eternity is between you and God. You can't let what other people do cut you off from God, Mr. Reese."

"I'll go this far with you, Miss Dorothy. I'm truly sorry for any wrong I've done, and I know that covers a lot of territory." Reese hung his head and looked at the floor. "Our thing was making money. I lied, cheated, stole...did whatever was necessary to make the big bucks." He shook his head. "And look at what it got me. I'm nothing more than an empty shell. Unhappy, lost, worthless. I hope God can see in my heart and know that I'm truly sorry and that I regret not making more of my life." He looked Dorothy straight in the eye. "I've seen the change He's made in you, and in Helen, too. That's a powerful witness, Miss Dorothy. I thank you for it. You got through to me."

Reese winced as he pushed himself slowly up the wall and onto his feet. He let the blanket fall from his shoulders onto the floor and tugged his coat tightly around him.

"You get all that?" he asked Mary Lee with a smile.

She nodded.

"Good. Here you go, Miss Dorothy. You can have my rations too, I guess."

Dorothy felt Jack wake up and as she looked into his eyes. He smiled and kissed her on the forehead. The pilot struggled to his feet. He wrapped his blanket around his shoulders.

"You ready, Mr. Reese?" he asked.

"Ready as I'll ever be, Captain."

"You don't have to do this," Dorothy said, pleading with her eyes. "You don't have to go, either of you."

"Yes, we do," Jack said calmly.

"Sure," Reese added. "That firewood won't last forever. If there's any more to be found, we have to take a stab at finding it."

"If we don't," Jack explained, "then it's better for you to have all the rations. We can't all last for very long on what we have, but you can last a lot longer. Ration the firewood, too, and stay by the fire. One person can make it a long time that way."

"What about me?" Mary Lee asked. "I'm strong."

"Sure you are." Jack answered. "But the snow is deep outside."

"I'll come with you," she offered.

"No, I don't think so. You stay with Dorothy. Somebody has to make her eat."

"You said yourself she has the most reason to live," Mary Lee argued.

Reese laughed. "You've got a story to tell, kid. We've got to keep you warm, too."

"It doesn't seem like much now," Mary Lee sighed.

"Maybe it's not the story you started out with," Reese said, his face softening into a warm, genuine smile. "But you think about it. I think we've lived out a good story in this old building. An important one." Reese stood up and kicked his legs for a moment. "I guess it's time for ole Jack and me to get to work!"

■ ■ ■

Aboard the Shark, Lieutenant Stiles relayed the latest news to Captain Maxwell. Colonel Hawkins' HU-53 had turned back from the route to Pei Song and landed at the advance base in the foothills to refuel and wait out the weather.

"That's about all she wrote, then," Maxwell muttered when Lieutenant Stiles had finished.

"They'll call it off, you mean?"

"I don't know," Maxwell said dryly. "But there may not be any point in getting up there if they have to wait too long."

"Satellite imagery still shows chimney smoke, sir."

"I'm glad, Stiles. And I hope they're all inside roasting marshmallows around a toasty fire, but I wouldn't get my hopes up if I were you. I think this rescue is all over."

■ ■ ■

Harris and Reese had been gone less than an hour. Dorothy stood at the little window, praying for a sign of them, when Mary Lee brought her a warmed roll, a cup of soup, and two chocolate candies.

"Not now, Mary Lee. I can't eat."

"You have to. For the baby."

"But I'm not..."

"It doesn't matter if you're hungry or not. You have to eat. Sit down by the fire. I'll keep watch."

"I don't know," Dorothy fretted.

"Come on. It's for the baby."

"Oh, all right. You win."

Dorothy took the food and sat in front of the fire. It took effort to get down the first couple of bites, but there was no nausea. The soup was hot and nourishing, and she suddenly realized how famished she was. She even forgot for a moment the pitiful sight of the two men staggering through the door to flounder in the snow outside, both of them on crippled feet and half-starved.

She had watched them from the window until they finally moved beyond a drift in the direction of the old barracks. At least they were making an effort to locate firewood. They weren't just hiking out into the snow to end it all.

Mary Lee, standing at the window behind her, said something. But it was so low that Dorothy couldn't make it out.

"I'm sorry. What did you say?"

"I said I'm envy."

"I don't understand."

"I was thinking what Jack said about pride. The truth is that envy is what eats me alive."

Dorothy turned and looked at her for a moment. "Really?"

"I've been thinking about it, and I don't live much of a life myself," Mary Lee said slowly. "I don't seem to feel very much or care about people the way you do. The way most people do, I guess. I'm like a machine, a computer, or that black box. I just process data, nail down the facts, write a story. Nothing seems to mean very much to me."

"We all have our own ways of looking at things."

"I see it all so differently now," Mary Lee whispered. "We all have a black box inside us, don't we?"

Dorothy nodded.

"Conscience or memory or whatever," Mary Lee continued. "It's a shock to find that *something* that's been there all along. I guess I've been denying mine, hiding it away in my mind somehow. But now I can't hide it anymore."

"None of us can," Dorothy said. "I think we've all found that fact out."

"I write stories about people," Mary Lee said, staring out the window. "Usually negative stories about their mistakes, their weaknesses. I'd never thought much about it before, but I think I envy them. I'm drawn to them and hunt out their secrets because I'm jealous."

"Have you always felt that way?"

"Since I was a kid. I didn't have a very happy childhood." Mary Lee looked down at the floor.

"Would you like to tell me about it?"

"It's not very interesting, really. My parents were killed in an accident when I was small, and I was an only child. I lived with aunts and uncles, got shipped around a lot. One of my uncles mistreated me, if you know what I mean. I guess I just kind of withdrew."

"That's a natural reaction. Wasn't there anyone you could turn to?"

"No. I was pretty much on my own."

"Come here, Mary Lee. Sit by me."

"I'd better keep an eye out for the men."

"It's all right. Come here."

The black woman crossed the room and settled beside Dorothy on the floor in front of the fire.

"What the bishop was saying last night, about reaching out to God..." Mary Lee began and then stopped.

"Did he mean me, too, do you think?"

"Oh, Mary Lee. Of course he did."

Dorothy put her arm around Mary Lee and hugged her tightly. Even though she was a grown woman, there was still a little girl inside just wanting to be loved. The fire flickered in the fireplace, and the two women held each other. Outside the hut the snow fell and the wind roared.

■ ■ ■

Harris and Reese staggered through the piles of snow. The two men staggered across the ice on crippled feet and were quickly forced to make their way to the corner of the barracks. Looking back as he reached out to help Jack come alongside him, Reese realized that they were out of sight from the women. Looking out either of the windows in the front of the little hut, Dorothy and Mary Lee wouldn't be able to see them anymore.

"How about a little breather?" Reese suggested.

"We haven't come very far," Jack said.

"They can't see us." Reese gestured over his shoulder.

"Okay then," Jack agreed. "A little breather."

By leaning on each other, the two men managed to reach the corner of the barracks. They leaned against the stone portion of the wall, using the corner of the building to shield them from the worst of the wind. Neither of them said anything, but they both knew that if they sat down they'd never get up again.

"Did you see any trail in the snow?" Jack asked, gasping for breath and wincing at the pain in his tortured feet.

"Yeah," Reese nodded, exhausted already. "Meyer must have made the path, heading off toward the runway and the wreckage. Helen must have seen it too, because there was no other trail leading from the cabin."

Without saying so, both men knew what that meant. She had followed Meyer and almost certainly found him out there in the snow somewhere. They hoped she had found him before he died so she could be with him at the end, like she had wanted.

"I think I'll have a smoke," Reese said, digging into a pocket of his coat. "If I can still find one down in there somewhere."

Jack rubbed his hand over his forehead weakly. "I'm amazed at what's been running through my mind." He shook his head. "One thought just keeps coming back to me."

"What?" Reese puffed on his cigarette.

"I keep thinking...over and over again. I can't believe that I've lived this long and couldn't see that the hand of God was there all the time." His chest heaved up and down as he tried to get his breath. "Without me even knowing it, God was there. Just as close as the air I was breathing." He shook his head. "Now I wonder what my life would have been if I'd given it to Him thirty years ago."

Reese grimaced and looked away. The cold seemed to be cutting through the padding that he was wearing. His face looked tired and worn.

"My trouble was that I let the things that people did distract me." Jack shook his head. "Instead of looking for God, I got irritated. Annoyed. Just didn't make myself look for Him."

Reese tried to control his discolored, shaking hands enough to shake a cigarette out of the pack and get it to his mouth. He couldn't manage it, and Jack leaned over to help him but couldn't.

The two men looked at each other, shaking their heads. "I think we better try to push on," Jack said.

"Yeah," Reese agreed. "We've got to keep moving."

They made their trek as far as the door of the barracks and stumbled through into the ruined interior of the building. There was no wood in sight, and after a few minutes of weak and ineffectual effort, they gave up trying to dig in the snow to find any.

"Even if we found something," Jack muttered, "we'd never make in back to the terminal with a bundle."

"Sure." Reese looked around him and shook his head. "We're running out of energy."

On his knees in the snow, Jack turned around and sat down, leaning against the interior of the stone wall. Reese joined him, and they sat side by side, looking up at the lightening gray of the cloud cover through the gaping hole where the roof had been.

Reese felt the numbing deadness in his legs and hands working its way up to his body, his whole body slipping off toward a deep sleep. He didn't feel any panic in his heart, just a little regret. A peaceful sleep stole over him.

"I'm sorry," Jack said softly.

Reese heard Jack's voice as if it came from a distance, even though the two men sat shoulder to shoulder in the deep snow.

"Don't be."

"This is all my fault."

"Not any longer, Captain." Reese's own voice sounded foreign and far away. The white snow darkened around him as his eyes grew heavy and dim.

"What do you mean?"

"I've got a feeling this was...all part of a plan."

"A plan?"

"Maybe God does work in mysterious ways," Reese mumbled thickly, laboring to get the words out. "Isn't that what it says in the Bible?"

"Yeah, but..."

"Maybe it took...something like this for...God to get through to me."

"Yeah. Me too."

"Captain, God bless you."

"You too, Reese."

Sleep came quickly as peace fell them both.

32

The weather didn't break all that day or the night that followed. By the time dawn lightened the dirty windows of the little hut at Pei Song the next morning, the two women inside were beyond caring. The last of the firewood had burned down to embers, and cold was seeping into the hut like a dense, impenetrable fog.

Dorothy lay on the floor in front of the fireplace, wrapped in all the blankets the survivors had salvaged from the crash. Mary Lee had piled them on herself and Dorothy to keep her warm and had slept close beside her, holding her tightly to add her body warmth. Neither of the women stirred when the first light of day fell down the mountains around them from a clearing sky.

Mary Lee had not gone outside since Jack and Reese left. She had thought about an attempt, thought about making the sacrifice the way the two men had, the way Helen had done for Meyer. Yet she told herself that Dorothy needed her, that she would do her more good by staying inside with her, making sure she ate and keeping her mind off their situation.

Mary Lee had eaten nothing since the men left, and she felt weak. A dozen times, she had thought she heard helicopters and airplanes overhead, even voices at the door. She had staggered to the window and looked out once in the dark of night and imagined she saw them all out there in the snow—Meyer and Helen, Reese and Jack, all waving to her. It had taken all the mental strength she could muster to block out the delusions and keep herself in the real world. She had prayed to keep herself sane.

Dorothy had realized Mary Lee was not eating, and she tried to share food with her. Mary Lee put her off and tricked her a couple of times, but it didn't matter now. The food was all gone, as well as the firewood.

Mary Lee had done all she could, and so had Dorothy. It was just a matter of time now. A matter of letting worries go and drifting off to sleep one last time.

Mary Lee had been afraid of dying because her life was so empty and cold. She didn't fear death now but instead faced it with a deep regret. To have learned so much, to have reached out to God in what she had thought was a godforsaken place, and to have found such a deep and wonderful sense of peace, only to slip off into eternity now without ever having the chance to bring that gift to life seemed so purposeless.

And yet, as she felt herself slipping into unconsciousness, Mary Lee realized that, whether she lived or died, the last few days had been a precious, undeserved gift from the hand of God. She was grateful to have found meaning in her life. That discovery was a wonderful gift. A new sense of warmth worked up her body, and Mary Lee slipped into peaceful sleep.

■ ■ ■

The Marines barged through the door of the hut with a clattering uproar, sending the rags the survivors had used to plug the cracks flying. Their HU-53 helicopter waited on the runway with the blades still beating the air.

The five marines searched the little room in a matter of seconds and found the dead bishop in the back. They uncovered two women, wearing layers of clothes and huddled together under a pile of blankets. One woman, looking more like a girl, wore earphones around her neck and clutched a tape player in her arms. A marine touched the girl's throat to check for a pulse, while a second marine examined the other woman.

"Corpsman," he muttered. Then louder, "Corpsman! Get that corpsman in here!"

"They're alive," the officer standing behind the soldier pronounced. "Barely. They're half-frozen but still breathing."

The marine didn't show any reaction, but he was relieved that their mission had been in time to save someone. "Hurry. Let's get them to the chopper. Grab those papers, that tape recorder, everything that's laying around. Pick it all up and put it in that sack. We've got to gather as much evidence as we can and get on the road. That's an order."

The other marines yelled, "Aye, aye, sir," and quickly began grabbing the final letters.

■ ■ ■

While the Chinese colonel was busy prowling around the wreckage on the runway and slowly realizing that he was only looking at the back two-thirds of the 757, a second marine scouting party reported back from the end of the runway that they had spotted the rest of the wreckage, including the cockpit that had gone off over the berm and rolled at least a thousand feet down the side of the mountain.

Hearing the message relayed by radio, the Chinese colonel allowed himself a broad grin. He assumed that the report meant he could stop searching, that the black box was gone. However, in the hut, the first scouting party had already spotted the black box and scooped it up. To avoid upsetting their

Chinese observer, they slipped it into one of the corpsmen's bags and brought it out of the hut along with the two women borne on litters.

In less than an hour, Hawkins' marines had found four more bodies, dead of exposure. The rest were too badly mangled or burned to be readily identified. In case one of the bodies was the senator, they were all loaded on board the helicopter in body bags, along with the remains of Bishop Forbes.

Knowing the break in the weather was not due to last much longer and satisfied they had what they had come for, Colonel Hawkins ordered his men back aboard and gave his pilot the signal to lift off.

As the big helicopter rose, pirouetted, and then lumbered up the valley the way it had come, Colonel Hawkins put his arm around the shoulders of his communications man and quietly dictated a message to be sent at once.

■ ■ ■

Aboard the Shark, Lieutenant Stiles watched over the shoulder of the sailor on the communications console as the coded message from Hawkins morphed into plain English.

"What's the word, Stiles?" Captain Maxwell stepped through the hatch with a cigar in his hand.

"It's coming in now, Skipper. Four bodies outside in the snow, dead of exposure in the last twenty-four hours."

Maxwell cursed under his breath.

"One body in the hut, apparently dead of natural causes or internal injuries..."

"Foot-dragging diplomats," Maxwell muttered.

"And two survivors. Two survivors!"

"I can't believe it," Maxwell said. "Two people held on."

"They're weak, in serious condition. But the corpsman has them on IVs, and they're responding. That's all, sir."

"It's more than we had any reason to hope for, son."

"And they got the black box."

"How did they do that, with the Chinese riding herd on them?" Maxwell shook his head. "Leave it to the colonel and his boys. I don't suppose the senator's one of the survivors?"

"Negative. Two women."

"And the other bodies?"

"Four men and one woman."

"Really? And four of them outside in the snow?"

"What do you figure happened, Skipper?"

"God only knows, son," Captain Maxwell said, finally striking a match and lighting his thick black cigar. "God only knows."

■ ■ ■

The blankets and the muggy interior of the helicopter slowly warmed Dorothy and brought her back to consciousness. At first, she thought another strange dream had swallowed her. The sound of a terrible loud humming filled her ears and unsettled her. Dorothy could see forms, shapes, hovering and moving around her, but she thought they were part of her dream.

After ten minutes of flying, Dorothy was able to identify the noise of the helicopter blades, beating away above her and drowning out all sound within the chopper. What seemed like a dream evaporated and turned into the concrete shape of people that she realized were soldiers, marines, corpsmen working on and around her. The vibrating movement of the helicopter shook her gently into full awareness.

She didn't try to speak but only watched the blur of activity. The soldiers didn't seem to realize she was awake. Dorothy closed her eyes again and thought about the extraordinary experience she had lived through.

I'm still alive, Dorothy thought. *How did I survive that horrible crash? There must be a reason.*

Dorothy bit her lip. A few days before, she never would have believed she had the strength to make it through such an ordeal. How could she, Dorothy Chandler, simple flight attendant, absolutely nobody in this world, have survived what had killed everyone else? The idea seemed too big to fit in Dorothy's head, and she kept pushing it aside, but the thought returned again and again.

Could I be the only survivor? I wonder what happened to Mary Lee. She had fallen asleep, and Dorothy hadn't been able to wake her, no matter what she did.

For a few moments, Dorothy thought about the other survivors. Poor Senator Meyer. The man had been more like a puppet than a person. She hoped he had found peace in the end.

And tragic Helen. She had died without having a chance to let the best in her come into full bloom.

Jack's face drifted before her closed eyes.

"Goodbye, Jack," Dorothy said under her breath. "God hold and care for you." She bit her lip. "I love you." She turned her face to hide the tears running down her cheeks.

Dorothy knew that God's hand had been on them all. Bishop Forbes had been His tool, and the bishop's words had surely allowed the Almighty to speak to each of the survivors a message that they needed to hear. The warmth of God's goodness had turned aside the cold deadness that had crept into their souls. The bishop gave her the courage to carry on when Dorothy thought everything had turned purposeless, meaningless. She was grateful.

Maybe *that* was why she was still alive. Could it be that Dorothy's decision to save the life growing in her had been honored through her own life being spared? Could she have inadvertently saved herself by deciding to give this little child the opportunity to live? Strange as it seemed, Dorothy knew that she had truly been snatched from what should have been her death for reasons that seemed beyond her grasp, too far away to completely understand. She recognized that the life within her was far more important than she could have ever guessed before. Dorothy knew that wherever this strange journey took her forward from the frozen mountain, the most important thing ahead would be caring for this unborn child. Her commitment was fixed, her purpose set. Dorothy would give the rest of her life to raising this little one growing inside her.

"Dorothy?" She turned her head when she heard her name. Mary Lee was lying beside her. Overcome, she held out her hand and Mary Lee grasped it.

"Don't worry, Dorothy," Mary Lee said, seeming to read Dorothy's thoughts—thoughts that were similar to her own. "I'll tell their story."

Epilogue

Facing Death and Finding Life: The True Story of Flight 027
Mary Lee McMurray

As a reporter, I've searched for truth and faithfully recorded it for you, my reader. But I've never looked for it in my own life or exposed myself in my writing. That's why this article is different than all the others I've written.

The truth is that life is unpredictable. I never thought I would die in a plane crash. Alone. But that's almost what happened.

And yet, I wasn't alone. I don't just mean the company of my fellow survivors. You may say that I had a "foxhole" conversion. Faced with death, I hedged my bets and accepted Christ. But I'm a fact girl, and the fact is, it took a situation like that—being stranded on a mountain in Asia with little hope of rescue—for me to face the evidence of God.

I grew up poor, passed from uncle to aunt to uncle after my parents died. I started to grow a shell around my heart. Then one of my uncles mistreated me. And the shell thickened. Eventually, I lost all care for my fellowmen, which made it easy for me to report breaking news, even when it might hurt people.

I won't be doing that any more.

On February 18th, I boarded a plane in Hong Kong. I had followed Senator George Meyer (R-Iowa, deceased) to China to expose the nature of his negotiations. The plane crashed. That's another story, one you read on the front page of many papers soon after.

I want to tell you the real story—a story of heroes.

First is Jack Harris. The pilot of Flight 027, he did everything he could to save us, both in the air and on the ground. His piloting skills would have saved us all, if there had been a better runway available. He scouted a place for us to stay and risked frostbite gathering wood and supplies. As did Albert Reese. Though we had our differences, Reese was a gentleman, who slept farthest from the fire to give more warmth to the rest of us.

Helen Bridwell gave up her own life to be with Senator Meyer at the end of his life. Her heart was larger than life. She gave up her food ration for others, and I learned from her how to give my heart and loyalty.

Dorothy Chandler was one of our flight attendants on Flight 027. Without Dorothy, I don't know if we would have survived at all. She'll deny all of this, but it's true. Dorothy organized us, fed us, cared for us, tended our wounds, mothered us. Dorothy has the spirit of a mother. She will always care for those around her.

Dorothy was the only other survivor. After we ran out of firewood, we talked a lot as we waited for the end. Dorothy is the first friend I've had in a long time. She taught me to trust again. I know that she will always be there for me.

This story is mostly a tribute. A tribute to friendship, love, sacrifice, and hope. And now I will introduce you to the man who gave us all hope.

His name was Anthony Coleridge Forbes. He was an Anglican bishop. And in our hour of need, he pointed us to a

Savior and showed us that life on this earth is not all we have to live for.

Tony, as he liked to be called, was one of those rare Christians who lived his faith. In every situation, he was helping, sharing, teaching. He taught me that there is a love greater than any other—the love that will give of itself for a brother. I've witnessed that love firsthand.

Anthony Forbes used his dying words to tell us that Jesus came to earth and died on a cross for us. He left behind a letter that I'd like to share with you now:

> My brothers and sisters in Christ,
>
> I don't have any family left, so I am leaving this letter to my church family. I pray that the message will touch you and that you will share it with the world.
>
> Soon I will go to be with the Lord. I can see the Father waiting for me with open arms. And I know that He has forgiven this Prodigal Son. As in the Bible story, He forgave me a long time ago, but I thought my place was with the swine.
>
> I have shared my testimony many times in the years since I became a Christian. I say with Paul that, of all the sinners, I am worst. But God has shown me grace as an example to those who would believe on Him and receive eternal life.
>
> If I can leave you with one thing, my inheritance, your heritage, it would be this thought:
>
> "I can do all things through Christ who strengthens me" (Philippians 4:13).
>
> I can survive a plane crash. I can bring hope to the hopeless. I can bring life to the dead. I can bring salvation to the lost. But only through Christ.

> I have tried to be all things to all men, so that I might save some. I hope I have succeeded. But it was all for the glory of the One who will judge me when my time on this earth is passed. To Him be all glory and power and honor, forever. Amen.
>
> God bless whoever reads this letter, my final words. Remember, always, that God loves you. Loves you so much that He sent His Son to die for you. Will you go to Him now?

I don't know why Dorothy and I survived. I can only say that I think God had a plan for us. Sharing my story is part of that plan.

About the Author
Larry Jones

Larry Jones is the founder and president of Feed The Children, an interdenominational nonprofit organization providing aid and assistance to children and families in need. Larry and his wife Frances started the organization twenty-five years ago. Today, Feed The Children is the tenth largest charity in the country.

Larry Jones was born in 1940 in Scottsville, Kentucky, and grew up in Bowling Green. He attended Oklahoma City University for his bachelor of arts degree and Phillips Seminary in Enid, Oklahoma, for his bachelor of divinity degree. Larry has received Honorary Doctorates from Southern Nazarene University in Oklahoma City, OK and Western Kentucky University in Bowling Green, KY. Larry and Frances have two children: Allen and Larri Sue

Over the years Larry Jones has received national and international recognition for his service to others, including the H.J. Heimlich Humanitarian Award for relief efforts throughout the world in 2000, the Humanitarian Award from the National Conference of Christians and Jews in 1995, Oklahoman of the Year in 1994, the National Caring Award in 1993, ABC News "Person of the Week" in 1991, plus Humanitarian Commendations from Armenia, El Salvador, Guatemala, Iran, and Lebanon. Additional, Larry Jones is the author of numerous books, including *How to Bend without Breaking, How to Make It to Friday, The 15-Second Secret,* and *Life's Interruptions, God's Opportunities.*

Feed The Children

Founded in 1979 by Larry and Frances Jones, Feed The Children is a non-profit, Christian charitable organization with a mission to provide food, medicine, clothing and other aid to needy children and their families in all 50 states and in more than 100 countries around the world. Feed The Children's U.S. programs focus on providing food and disaster relief, while international programs provide food, education, childcare, medical care and community development.

For more information and to find out how you can help children and families in need, you can write to:

Feed The Children
P.O. Box 36
Oklahoma City, OK 73101

or

Call 1-800-627-4556

or

Visit Feed The Children's website at www.feedthechildren.org